DARKENED DAWN

OTHER TITLES BY E. J. MELLOW

Way of Wings

Scorched Skies

The Mousai Series

Song of the Forever Rains

Dance of a Burning Sea

Symphony for a Deadly Throne

Praise for E. J. Mellow

"Lyrical, vibrant, imaginative. E. J. Mellow's striking, original voice will draw you into a mesmerizing world."

—Emma Raveling, author of the Ondine Quartet

"E. J. is one of those authors who deserve to be immortal just to continue writing mind-blowing novels for their readers."

—Book Vogue

"It's so easy to lose yourself in Mellow's evocative and engaging prose."

—Charlie Holmberg, author of *The Paper Magician*

DARKENED DAWN

WAY OF WINGS

BOOK TWO

E · J · MELLOW

Montlake

This is a work of fiction. Names, characters, organizations, places, events, and incidents are either products of the author's imagination or are used fictitiously. Otherwise, any resemblance to actual persons, living or dead, is purely coincidental.

Published by Montlake, Seattle

www.apub.com

EU Product Safety contact:
Amazon Media EU S. à r.l.
38, avenue John F. Kennedy, L-1855 Luxembourg
amazonpublishing-gpsr@amazon.com

ISBN-13: 9781662540790 (hardcover)
ISBN-13: 9781662515453 (paperback)
ISBN-13: 9781662515460 (digital)

Cover design by Logan Matthews and Caroline Teagle Johnson
Cover image: © wanlmd, © mkvolkova, © Roxiller13, © CHREMOS, © Avgust Avgustus / Shutterstock
Map design by Emil Mellow

Printed in the United States of America

First edition

For all those who look to the sky,
your wings are strong.
Fly.

NOTE FROM THE AUTHOR

As with all art, there is subject matter I have explored that may be of a sensitive nature to some. I have worked to handle it with great care, but you, the reader, know best what may be triggering. This book contains the following content and dark elements: mature language, violence, sexual assault, self-harm mentions, substance use, death, racism, classism, explicit romance scenes, and grief. It is intended for readers eighteen-plus years of age.

MAP OF CĀDRA

CĀDRA
ESTÉ OCEAN
PELK FOREST
CITY of DURDEL
NORTHERN CLAN TERRITORY
QUEEN HABELLE'S ISLE
ASPERO SEA
GALIA
HIGH GODS TEMPLE
DRYGUL
Low Gods' Territory
HARVEST FIELD
BEDRYG CLIFFS
WESTERN CLAN TERRITORY
TOWN of UNIG
CITY of ORDYN
ZOMYAD FOREST
ONIS OCEAN
TOWN of FUEL
BANDON LANDS
Both Island
EASTERN CLAN TERRITORY
CITY of WREN
GARW FOREST
GALIA

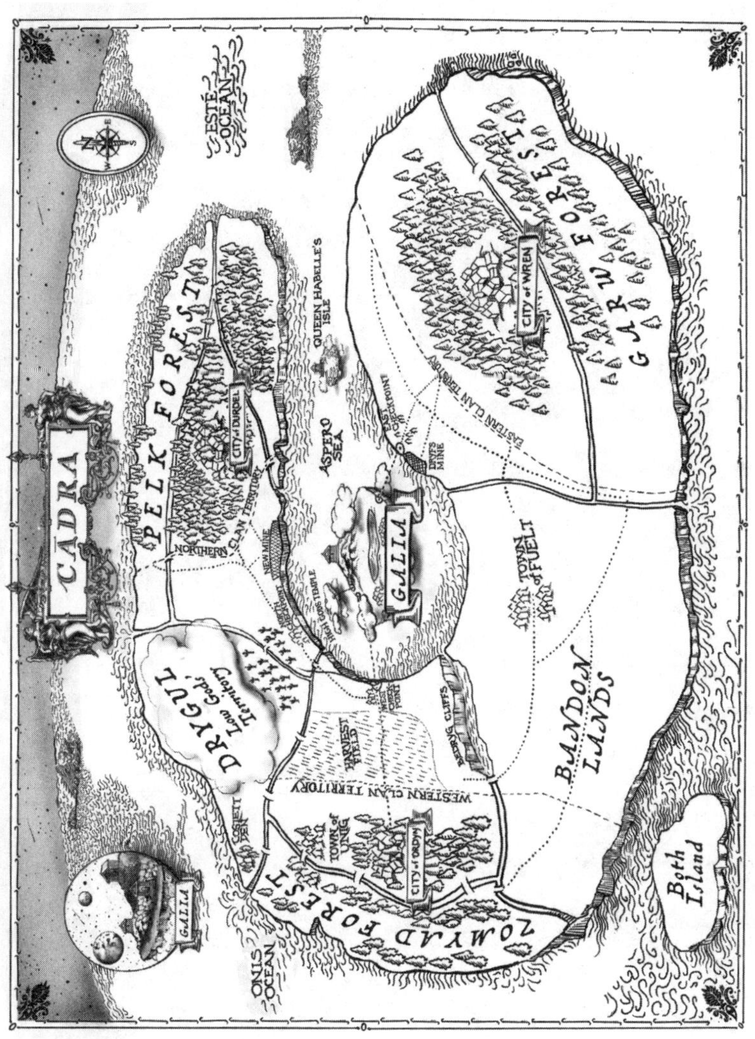

Prince Zolya

GLOSSARY

Süra Horns by Clan

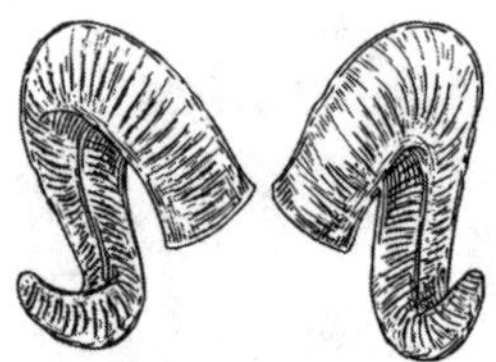

Northern Clan

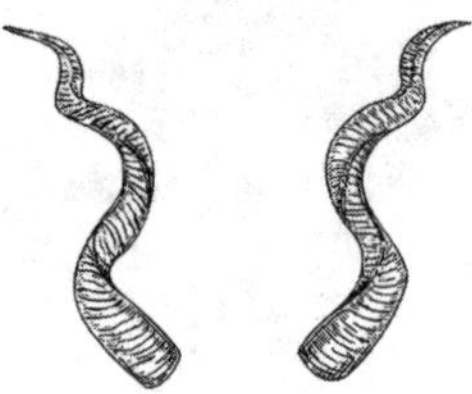

Western Clan

Eastern Clan

Volari Sky Magic Symbols

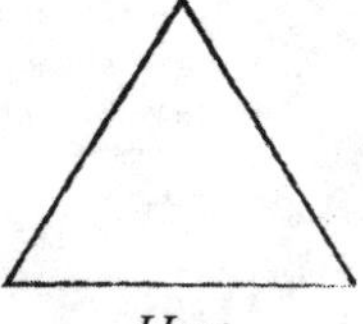

Heat

Wind

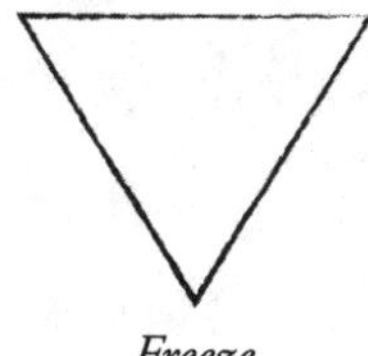

Freeze

Rain

PANTHEON OF GODS

The Twelve High Gods

- **Ré**—God of the heavens, sun, and sky. Father of the High Gods. Brother of Maryth.
- **Nocémi**—Goddess of night. Wife of Ré.
- **Maja & Parvi**—Twin moon goddesses.
- **Orzel**—God of the sea.
- **Hyfel**—God of war and justice.
- **Leza**—Goddess of beauty.
- **Ilustra**—God of love and lust.
- **Udasha**—Goddess of fortune and luck.
- **Naru**—Goddess of artistry.
- **Izato**—God of revelry.
- **Zenca**—Goddess of destiny.

The Twelve Low Gods

- **Maryth**—Goddess of death and time. Mother of the Low Gods. Sister to Ré.
- **Ridi**—God of mischief and chaos.
- **Bosyg**—Goddess of the forest.

- **Nen**—Goddess of rivers and water.
- **Eya**—Goddess of fertility.
- **Tyrith**—God of land, soil, and mountains.
- **Poti**—God of cleverness and wit.
- **Thryn**—Goddess of nurture and healing.
- **Hylio**—God of summer.
- **Mog**—Goddess of winter.
- **Fohl**—God of autumn.
- **Wynya**—Goddess of spring.

PROLOGUE

On a jagged cliffside, a woman faced the raging sea.

Waves lashed against her island, freezing wind tearing at her skirts and leaving icy sprays of salt on her cheeks.

The cold did not seep beneath her skin, however.

Fire burned in her veins, chasing away the chill.

At her back, her amber wings—limp and clipped—hung like her regrets: useless, heavy, inescapable.

But it was not the past that darkened her gaze this day.

Her eyes remained locked on the frothing waters below—a muted gray mixture, the same lifeless shade that cursed every moment in this godsforsaken place.

Though, the longer she stared, colors awoke in her mind. A vision of what a sunlit sea *should* be. Bright and beautiful, a saturation of blues and greens and indigos.

"Governess," a gravelly voice called from behind, snapping dullness back into her vision. "Are you ready?"

She didn't answer, her gaze remaining fixed on the tumultuous waves. Orzel, the High God of the sea, was fuming—more than usual.

Her eyes narrowed, thoughts clashing like the water below.

"Ma'am?" inquired her guard once more.

She clenched her teeth in quiet annoyance, gave a curt nod, and placed the stone circlet back atop her head.

She had needed a reprieve from its weight.

The crown was a crude, sharp carving that bit into her forehead. A ragged symbol of those who came to survive here.

With one last glance at Orzel's seething abyss, she turned away.

But she carried forward a flicker of hope she hadn't dared to feel in over sixty years.

Change was brewing—she was as confident of this as she was of her strides forward—and it stirred the vow she had made the day she had been left here to die. A promise born from every woman scorned and from every mother robbed of motherhood.

Revenge.

PART I

Fracture

1

The peace meeting was going to end in bloodshed.

Not a historical first, certainly.

Still, as Tanwen stood at the back of the tent, annoyance flared in her gut that she had trudged this distance only to die.

This was what happened when men handled what women understood better—compromise.

"You are fools," declared a Volari councilman, one of the countless insults hurled at the Rebellion party in the past half hour.

"And you are all pompous parrots," rebutted a northern-clan delegate.

"You will suffer lashings for such insolence!" growled the councilman, his pale face growing as red as his wings.

"Which is still better than enduring the stench of your cologne!"

From beneath the shadow of her hood, Tanwen exhaled sharply, frustration curling through her as the tent descended into chaos. The kidets at the seam of the opposing parties struggled to calm the two groups.

If blades had been allowed inside, they would have been drawn. By some miracle the Volari were keeping their sky magic in check, while Süra held clenched fists to their sides.

But for how much longer? wondered Tanwen as she angled her head around the audience of Rebellion supporters clogging her view.

The Volari Royal Council sat on a raised platform at the front of the room, antagonizing in their painted plumage and lavish robes, the torchlight catching the gold embroidery and bringing the intricate patterns to life.

Tanwen and her peers, on the other hand, stood on a muddy floor in muted browns and worn leather, their boots caked with dirt from their long journey to this neutral gathering place.

It was a discomforting contrast only heightened by the encroaching winter's chill, which slunk into the tent uninvited.

"These men are idiots," grumbled Huw beside Tanwen.

"No argument there," she replied as she glanced at her friend.

Huw's arms were tightly crossed, his hood similarly hiding his features. Only a sliver of his blond hair and his curling northern horns poked free.

Despite each of them passing as Süra, they felt safer keeping to the shadows.

For only Süra had officially been invited here today.

The peace meeting may have been aimed at discussing the liberation of Mütra, along with changes to the trade agreements and the Recruitment, but the persecution of their mixed-blood race persisted.

It would not be advantageous to be recognized.

At least, not yet.

"I stand by this being a waste of our time," muttered Huw.

Tanwen resisted an eye roll. His petulance during this trip was growing as tiring as the speaking delegates in the room. "You *know* why we needed to come," she whispered. "It's taken six months for this meeting to happen and for all our planning to align. If the Rebellion is heading up this movement, we needed someone from Drygul's council to be present."

"Yes, but why did *we* have to be these someones from Drygul? Brynn was more than eager to come, as well as Zephyr. We're both fugitives—"

"*Hush*," hissed Tanwen as she eyed those nearby, but they remained preoccupied with the commotion in front of them rather than beside them. "They clearly could not pass as Süra," she explained. "But we are not in this alone. Do not forget who else stands here with us."

Despite her reminder, or perhaps because of it, Huw regarded the crowd with displeasure.

Since the king's poisoning and the flooding of the new mine—claiming countless Süra lives—the past months had been more than tense. The citizens on Cādra had finally been awoken like yellow jackets whose hive had been kicked one too many times. Frenzied and desperate, they unleashed decades of repressed anger.

Quiet revolts across the continent had erupted into roaring chaos: Volari outposts burned, Recruitment strikes paralyzed operations, and some clans even cut off trade with Galia, defying century-old agreements.

With the king in a coma—and his usual swift, brutal repression absent—those on Cādra had found their boldness. Not that there was a lack of Volari retaliation.

Casualties were mounting, and the brink of a war loomed.

Hence the call for this peace meeting between the nascent Rebellion organization and the king's Royal Council.

The Rebellion's demands: fairer trade agreements, revised Recruitment contracts to end lifelong servitude, and the emancipation of Mütra.

But Tanwen knew these demands were anything but simple to achieve.

"I don't think you should go through with what you have planned." Huw's worried tone brought Tanwen back to the tent—to the crowd pressing against them and the guards loitering at the seams.

"Which part of the plan?" she asked.

"*Both* parts," he insisted. "But if I had to choose, I'd say your rogue one."

Guilt settled under Tanwen's ribs—not for herself, but for the risk she had placed on her friend. Before their journey, she had told Huw the *real* reason she had insisted on coming, unwilling to put him in more danger without his consent.

I should have pushed harder for him to stay behind, she thought, her brows drawing tight with her regret.

But between convincing her parents to let her attend this meeting and preparing for the journey, she'd had little energy left to argue with Huw. Though it felt like he was leaving her no choice now.

"I have to do this," she murmured, tone hard. "For my parents and for . . . Thol." Her brother's name caught in her throat, but she forced it out. Months might have passed, but his death still haunted her and her family. His ghost was an invisible wedge between her parents—a couple once inseparable now moved cautiously around each other. Tanwen hated it. "They deserve peace after everything," she finished.

"And you don't?"

Tanwen clenched her teeth as a weight settled in her chest. "I need to finish what's been started."

"I beg to differ."

"Then let us agree to disagree and leave it at that."

"It might not even work," Huw reasoned, repeating the same argument he had voiced throughout their journey. "And what peace will it bring your parents if you end up dead today? Leaving them to mourn both their children."

Though Tanwen understood he didn't intend his words to be cruel, she still held back a wince of pain. "I am *not* going to die," she assured, or hopefully she sounded reassuring. "This congregation promised immunity to all present. They must uphold that, even to us."

Though, the longer the air in the tent rose with confrontation, a tangling of angry voices, the more she began to doubt her convictions.

Her only assurance of safety was in the hands of another, which Huw knew nothing about.

Another prick of guilt dug between Tanwen's ribs.

"I sometimes don't know whether to admire you or pity you," said Huw. "But I do know you're all insane to attempt this."

She let out a tired sigh. "*Again*, you can leave. You can slip out now before—"

"*We argue in circles*," boomed a deep voice, cutting off her words as well as the tent's uproar like a blade.

Tanwen stiffened, pulse stuttering as silence fell.

She braced herself before following everyone's gaze.

The prince regent sat, a spectacle of beauty and power, in the center of his council.

Even in a simple gray coat, black trousers, and boots, he outshone his lavishly adorned lords. His broad chest stretched the width of his bench, his sharp jaw set, and his light-brown skin glowed smooth under the candlelight. Only a golden laurel threaded through his shoulder-length alabaster hair marked his rank.

Beauty and power coiled around Zolya, an invisible force like the charged air before a storm—cool, metallic.

Thump. Thump. Thump.

Tanwen's heart raced.

Ached.

Stopped and restarted whenever she looked at him.

Which was exactly why she had been doing her darndest *not* to look at him.

The agony was too great.

Especially as he regarded the crowd with his cold indifference. As if they were ants in his path as he silently decided whether to step over them or crush them with his heel.

Until now, he had remained quiet, an unmoving mountain at the heart of the tent.

"Unless we wish to spend another day within each other's presence," he said in a low rumble, "which it is clear none of us do, I suggest we find a conclusion to this discussion."

Tanwen swallowed down her unease as a now-thicker tension wove through the crowd.

"Your Highness." A Süra elder bowed at the front. "Our desires have not changed since yesterday. We are open to . . . *constructive* amendments from you and your council," he carefully clarified while shooting a glare at the offending party. "The Unified Labor Law Compensation Act and the Mütra Integration Act are newly born, ready to be molded by *all* our hands. I beg of you, sire, let us make a new history today."

While the Rebellion's demands were clear, the path to meeting them was not.

Raising wages and adjusting trade percentages across the nation would require a substantial influx of funds—and only a select few in this room knew the truth: The royal treasury was nearly empty, drained by King Réol, who had spent far more during his reign than he had ever earned.

As for freeing Mütra, that power lay solely with the ruling monarch—the very one who had signed their banishment into law—and he was currently lying unconscious.

Not to mention the stigma surrounding the Rebellion's demands—the Volari were not accustomed to yielding, only to fighting back, even when it hurt them more.

Tanwen watched as Zolya pensively strummed his fingers on his armrest, seeming to size up the Süra delegate. "How exactly are we to make a new history," he began, "when your clans are still not unified in your causes?"

"I . . . beg your pardon, sire?" stuttered the delegate.

"The eastern clan is absent here." Zolya's gaze ran over the crowd.

"That's because you've bought their obedience," hissed Huw a bit too loudly beside Tanwen.

She nearly expired on the spot as the prince regent's stare speared to the back of the room. "You have something to add . . .?" He seemed to dare whoever had spoken.

Like a peplos unraveling, the crowd fell away in front of them.

Tanwen and Huw stood exposed as her friend shot her a panicked look. *Oh gods,* he seemed to say. *I'm so sorry!*

This was not how it was meant to happen.

It was not meant to be Huw.

Tanwen's pulse was a stampede through her veins; her nerves were frenzied as she watched Huw flounder to respond.

Tanwen stepped in front of him, shoving back her hood. "Tanwen, sire," she announced to the room.

The prince's blue gaze met hers.

And

her

entire

soul

froze.

For a breath it was only the two of them.

A heartbeat of connection that spread wildfire across her skin.

A flash of emotion passed over Zolya's features before it was gone. Shuttered. The prince regent regarded her now through narrowed eyes. "I know you," he rumbled.

Tanwen resisted a shiver as she remained silent, desperately attempting to keep her expression even.

This is it, she thought. *This is happening.*

"You were Princess Azla's atenté," he went on to declare.

The tent stirred at that, a wave of confusion and dismay.

The princess, who was convicted of conspiring to kill the king with her lover, Lady Esme.

Here stood her servant, rumored to have fled Galia alongside her.

Who had helped poison the king—though none here knew that, *thank the gods*, not even Zolya.

But such worries were quickly dashed as guards rushed her.

"I gave no orders to apprehend." Zolya's tone was the deadly tip of a blade, stopping them. "*Yet*," he added as his attention held to her. "Tanwen Coster, was it?"

She took a deep inhale, summoning her courage.

"Tanwen . . . *Heiro*," she corrected. "Daughter of Gabreel Heiro."

The significance of her reveal—of her horns and no wings—slithered through the tent like a startled viper, hissing in shocked whispers before erupting into outraged cries from the Volari councilmen. *"Mütra!"*

"Seize her!" demanded the head of the guards, who stood nearest the Royal Council.

It was Kidar Osko Terz—the man who had captured her brother and father. Who had held a knife to Thol's throat. Tanwen had recognized him immediately on her first day here, and judging by his scowl as he glared her down, their hatred was mutual.

Tanwen braced herself as strong hands finally fell upon her. She frantically looked for Huw, but he was gone.

Good, she thought with a slip of relief, grunting past the pain in her shoulders from her arms being tugged back.

Huw's ability to blend in and disappear would be his savior today.

"Stand down!" thundered Zolya as a loud crack vibrated overhead.

A fearful hush stilled the tent, a sting of ancient power dusting across Tanwen's cheeks.

Her heartbeat thudded quick as she met Zolya's gaze once more.

He remained seated, but his eyes blazed azure, his features a dark brewing storm. "Everyone will stand down, *now*," he ordered, his voice dangerously calm. "Let go of Ms. Heiro."

"But, sire," countered Kidar Terz. "She's Gabreel Heiro's daughter. He *lied* to us. He had another spawn."

"I said, *let her go*." The prince regent's stare clashed with the head of his guard's, a silent battle of wills.

Kidar Terz's clenched jaw and furrowed brow betrayed his displeasure, but he stepped back, nodding for the kidets to do the same.

Tanwen's pulse raced as she was released.

The room held its breath, waiting as the prince voiced what they all were surely thinking. "Do not mistake my command for your safety, Ms. Heiro," he began. "It was risky for you to come here today. Riskier still to announce your heritage. Which might be what saves you. My curiosity is piqued. *Why* are you here?"

Tanwen straightened with her resolve. This was her rogue plan sliding into place.

They deserve peace, she repeated silently. *Thol deserves peace.*

"After the death of my brother and father," she replied, "I can afford risks, sire. For I have nothing else to lose without family."

Zolya studied her as if discerning the truth of her words. "Their deaths, you say? Are you telling us that Gabreel Heiro and your brother didn't survive their escape from Galia?"

"Do *you* believe they could have survived jumping from such a height, sire?" she countered.

"It was reported they had gliders," answered one of his councilmen.

Tanwen met the man's stare head-on. "So you are saying that a man-made invention can match the power of your wings, my lord?" She raised an inquisitive brow. "Can echo the precision of your flight through storm winds and rain? That Volari may no longer exclusively own Cādra's skies?"

"Well . . . no. That is . . ." The councilman floundered. "How *dare* you speak to me thus, you petulant—"

"If they didn't survive," interrupted Zolya, "you are then here to avenge their deaths."

If possible, the crowd grew stiller as the guards swayed toward her—awaiting his command.

"I am not here for vengeance, sire."

"No?" His head tilted. "Then pray tell, Ms. Heiro—I ask again—why are you here? Is it to tell us where we can find the princess?"

Tanwen blinked, momentarily caught off guard. "I . . . do not know what you mean, sire."

His gaze narrowed. "You should also not mistake my patience for foolishness. You disappeared the same night she did."

Tanwen resisted shifting under his scrutiny. "Princess Azla is safe."

Gasps filled the tent.

"Sire, we *must* apprehend this woman," demanded Kidar Terz. "Hiding a traitor's location is an act of treason."

"The princess is in Drygul," Tanwen added quickly, cutting his accusation off at the knees. "But you'll need Udasha's luck to get in there."

Kidar Terz's gaze flashed, his ire clearly rising with Tanwen's admission and taunting grin.

It was known that the Low Gods' territory had become a haven for Galia deserters and refugees, but even the Volari understood that attempting to breach it would mean waging war against the Low Gods—one battle they had no power to win.

"Well, well, Ms. Heiro," breathed the prince as he leaned elbows on armrests to steeple his fingers. "You have created quite the stir here today, haven't you? Though despite sharing the princess's location, you still have broken Cādra law."

"And what law is that, sire?"

"You are Mütra."

Guards shifted at her back, the room hanging in a tense silence, a dangerous precipice.

"I am also Mütra," said Huw.

Tanwen swung her gaze to find her friend appearing at her side, chin tilted in defiant pride.

He hadn't left.

Tanwen's chest swelled as she resisted reaching out to clasp his hand.

"And I am also Mütra," declared a woman near the front, before—

"And I," echoed a man.

Mütra after Mütra revealed themselves, in the end making up half the present Rebellion delegates—each one easily passing as a Süra.

So many hiding in plain sight.

The Rebellion's planned performance.

Show a hint of their numbers, how easily they had gotten in—been *let* in.

Tanwen stood with her head held high, her confidence surging as she met Zolya's hard stare. "You asked why I was here, sire," she began. "This is why." She gestured to those around her. "Because we are not so few and we are not so forsaken. My father was stripped of his wings, all because of who he fell in love with. My parents and I were forced into hiding for decades because of me and my brother's mixed blood. My brother was then tortured by your father, the king, because he was found. But my story is no more tragic than that of any other surviving Mütra in this tent. And we only make up a fraction of our kind living on Cādra. We are here, Your Royal Highness, because we refuse to let history repeat itself. If we can set aside the wrongs done to us in pursuit of peace and a place in this world, surely you and your council can summon the same compassion."

The responding silence was oppressive as Tanwen waited.

As they all waited.

What greeted them, however, chilled Tanwen to the core.

The prince regent laughed.

Not with humor, but with something darker, something laced with cruelty.

"Compassion," he repeated as if tasting the word and finding it sour. "Yes, I can find *compassion* in letting you all walk away from here alive." He sneered. "Which I will allow, of course, for what is a peace meeting if we start making arrests and cutting throats. Right, Kidar Terz?" he asked his second-in-command, not bothering to wait for a response. "Yes, I will show you compassion there, Ms. Heiro, for I promised a sanctuary with this gathering, and I, like my father, am a man of my word. I only wonder what compassion you will then show us, hmm? Where is the compassion when striking against century-old trade agreements? Where is the compassion when setting fire to our Cādra outposts? You speak of compassion, and yet"—he leaned forward, his features sharpening—"what of your compassion for your fellow recruits on Galia?" He gestured upward as if the floating island were visible through the tent's ceiling. "Those who are *still* bound by their lifelong contracts. Do you think your actions down here have helped them up there?"

Tanwen stiffened, his words settling like hot ash.

"You see"—he looked to the room now, expression as brutal as his father's—"you may have your demands as well as hold Cādra's goods hostage, but you've now made hostages of your own people."

The air compressed with his meaning.

"You won't sacrifice your servants," said Tanwen, ire feeding her boldness. "Your people barely know how to lace their own gowns, let alone cook or tend their gardens. Even here, sire"—she pointed to their surroundings—"you brought staff to pitch your tents and warm your beds. You may be the children of gods, but you are not without weaknesses."

Offended grumbles rippled through the Royal Council, expectant gazes swinging to the prince.

"Who said anything about sacrifice?" His laurel crown sparked in the candlelight. "Since you've cut off trade, we'll cut recruit compensation from leaving Galia. As you know, it's not usually those on our island who need the pay, but families on Cādra. No exports. No wages. No word from enlisted loved ones reaching the continent. Let's see how loyal your people remain when survival outweighs rebellion." He paused, then added, "And if things escalate, we have no qualms with sacrifice. It is, after all, how we honor *our* gods."

Tanwen couldn't speak. Shock and fury warred inside her. She had not planned on this, planned on *him*, this monster sitting in front of her.

"What do you need to ensure our recruits' safety?" an elder in the crowd finally asked.

"An end to this uprising," replied Zolya plainly. "The rescinding of your demands."

Tanwen's breath caught, as did others' in the room.

It was an impossible request.

A call for surrender before anything had begun, before any progress had been made.

"If we do that," Tanwen found herself saying, "there will never be peace."

"Perhaps there was never meant to be peace between us," replied Zolya as he flicked a speck of dirt from his sleeve. "Perhaps Zenca has bound our fates to merely repeat, over and over. And in case you need reminding, Ms. Heiro"—his gaze lifted to find hers, a chilled blue—"history has never favored your kind."

Your kind.

Mütra.

Smug smiles spread across the councilmen's faces on either side of him—victory.

The air in Tanwen's lungs was replaced with a suffocating weight.

Zolya's declarations coiled like shackles around her chest, tugging down any hope she might have had when first arriving here.

Zolya would not help them.

No, not Zolya, thought Tanwen, her despair thick, her outrage sprouting thorns as she held his gaze.

The prince regent.

Her enemy.

2

That night, neither camp slept.

Wary eyes scanned the darkness. Unease heated breaths. Distrustful hands gripped weapons as restless souls lay on cots, feigning slumber.

Zolya soared above, eyeing where the Volari's lavish traveling abodes dotted the top of a hillside, tiny fires glowing like stars.

Even here on Cādra, his people would always look down on those who lived below.

They had positioned themselves strategically above the Rebellion's camp, which was a humble cluster of tightly packed tents. The only glimmer of light in their hovel was the twins' moonlight sparking across a rushing river that wove between their encampments.

Zolya pushed higher into the night sky, desperate for the winter wind to clear away his sullen thoughts.

Today had gone as planned in the sense that it had left his Royal Council pleased, particularly with him.

But Zolya only felt disappointment.

Disgust.

"We should apprehend the Mütra tonight," said Osko, who flew beside him.

Zolya let out an incredulous huff. "Which Mütra?"

"You know which," ground out Osko. "He *lied* to us, Zol. Gabreel had another child hiding in those woods that day. I bet his Mütra daughter is lying to us still and her mother lives! She didn't die in childbirth."

Zolya clenched his teeth in frustration before forcing his tone even. "No one is being arrested."

"Why not? You said it yourself, she's Mütra; they *all* are. Laws have been broken. Laws your father—"

"Do you not get tired?" Zolya drew up short, forcing them to hover in midair.

"Excuse me?" Osko frowned.

"You are like a hound chasing a hare that's already bleeding out in a ditch. We have put Gabreel and his family through enough, don't you think? We took his wings, banished him from Galia, and now he is dead. His son is dead. His wife is dead. Only his daughter is left. *Alone.* You must put your obsession with Gabreel Heiro to bed."

"I am not obsessed—"

"*You are,*" countered Zolya, his patience gone. "Just as my father was obsessed, and look where that got him. Gabreel is the one who suggested the treaty with Orzel, which ultimately led to the king being poisoned. I am not here to carry out old revenge plots any longer. We have bigger issues than Ms. Heiro being alive. More to fix than eradicating Mütra. We have an uprising that we can't afford to fight."

"What do you mean?"

"Our treasury," said Zolya. "We have no funds for a war, Osko. That is why I was so adamant about having this peace meeting and why I wish there had been another outcome."

His friend stared at him, shock clear in his expression. "I didn't know it was that dire."

"Yes, well, wars are expensive," he explained. "And my father certainly loved his wars. He's nearly drained us with his vengeance."

"Zolya," chastened Osko with a frown, clearly not liking when the king was spoken ill of, not even by his own son.

"I apologize," said Zolya, exhaustion tugging at his wings as he glanced to the distant sky. "Today was long."

"We should head back, then," said Osko. "You should rest before our flight home tomorrow."

"I'm not tired."

"Yes, clearly your good mood is due to your excessive amount of energy."

Zolya shot his friend a glare before he gave a great push of his wings and flew away.

Osko's annoyed grunt caught in the wind before he followed.

"I'm serious, Zol," he said once he was beside him again. "You'll be plenty tired in the morning if we don't turn in now."

"I'm restless and need to move," explained Zolya. "We've been cooped up for two days in those meetings."

"Yes," agreed Osko, "but it's nearly freezing up here, and I can think of a much warmer, much more relaxing way to cure restlessness. The council brought a few of their mistresses. I'm *sure* there are one or two ladies who would gladly—"

"I do not wish for company," Zolya bit out, his magic hissing through his veins along with his annoyance. "In fact, yours has grown tiresome. You may return to camp, and I will rejoin shortly."

Osko zipped in front of Zolya, pulling them both up short. They once again hovered in the night sky, glaring at one another.

"You are well aware that I cannot leave the prince regent unaccompanied," said Osko sternly.

Zolya rolled his eyes.

"It's nothing to scoff at," ground out Osko. "With your father still in his coma, you are the acting king, for gods' sake. The prince regent and *my* charge. I will not shirk my duties when it comes to you and your safety."

Since King Réol's poisoning, Osko had become even more dutiful, if that were possible.

Despite the whipping chill surrounding them, Zolya's frustration thawed as he witnessed his friend's loyalty.

"Osko, I am not asking as prince regent," he explained, a bit softer now. "I am asking as a friend. Please, there is much on my mind from today. I wish only to have a moment *alone* to clear it. If I am not back within one dip of the stars, you can send our entire unit after me."

Osko studied him like a stubborn boulder within a river, unmoved.

"When I return, I promise to come kiss you on the forehead while you're curled in bed, so you know that I'm back," explained Zolya extra sweetly.

Osko breathed out his annoyance. Given their history, he knew when an argument was at a close. "*One* dip of the stars, or I *will* raise the alarm," he warned.

Zolya saluted. "Kidar's honor."

His friend's furrowed brow only deepened. "You will be the end of me," he muttered, though he still turned and made his way back toward camp.

Zolya watched until his friend disappeared, swallowed by the night.

Then he shot forward, heading straight for her.

3

Zolya saw Tanwen before she saw him.

But he could always find her, even in the dark.

As he descended toward the quiet logging site, every worker now long gone and in bed, a faint glow caught his eye beside a stack of felled trees. And just beyond, in the shadow, was Tanwen.

She leaned against the wood, her brow pinched in thought as her gaze was fixed on some distant, unseen point ahead. An oil lamp rested by her boots, the flickering warmth fanning up over her long legs encased in sturdy trousers, her triad of medicinal pouches hooked to her belt, along with a sheathed blade. Her leather coat was fur lined and buttoned up to her chin.

The days were growing colder, but the nights on Cādra seemed to have already embraced winter. A light frost covered the ground as small puffs of breath escaped from Tanwen's mouth, her pale skin like the impending snow.

As Zolya soared closer, he took a moment to enjoy the sight of her undisturbed. A view he hadn't been given in a very long while. Despite the chill, his skin warmed, his magic sliding with longing through his veins.

Mine, it crooned.

Tanwen must have sensed someone nearing, for she grew alert, hand instinctually going to her blade's hilt.

Zolya landed in the clearing.

Despite his arrival, Tanwen remained tense, cautious. Her horns caught the moons' light as her eyes narrowed.

It had been agonizingly long—over a fortnight, at least—since they'd last been alone together. Since he'd last held her, kissed her, breathed in her familiar scent.

His torment had only been amplified since seeing her yesterday and neither of them able to even share a smile.

He was growing mad for their reunion.

Yet, still, Zolya kept his distance.

The weight of earlier that morning in the peace negotiations—and of the long, weary weeks before it—pressed thick between them. Their mounting duties and the relentless strife of their two factions bore heavy on their backs, wishing to pull them apart. The longer he was forced to be without her, it seemed to stretch their future further out of his reach, until Zolya found himself waking in the night, gasping, afraid he could no longer see the path that led to it.

To a future where a Volari king could stand beside his love, a Mütra rebel.

These hidden meetings, these stolen moments, had become more than a salve for his longing—they were his cure. A vital, necessary reminder of what they were fighting for, and of how empty the fight would be without her.

So when he saw the hesitation in her gaze now, the doubt, it nearly brought him to his knees.

"Tanwen—" he started, but his words faltered as another presence appeared.

Glowing green eyes emerged from the shadows behind the stack of logs nearest Tanwen.

One might describe the beast as an enormous wolf, though its size was close to a bear's and its fur had a peculiar way of blending into its surroundings, drinking in colors like a rag sopping up liquid.

Currently, it was as dark as the night, with only its piercing eyes and its needlessly massive, razor-sharp teeth visible as it bared them at Zolya. A low growl rumbled from its chest, and he felt it reverberate down his spine.

"Oh, good," said Zolya, unable to keep the dryness from his tone. "You brought *her*."

Tanwen's gaze further narrowed. "Loji insists on accompanying me anytime I travel at night," she explained, running a gentle hand through the mongrel's fur as it came to her side. Its shoulders rose slightly above her own.

Loji was a lunagwar, an otherworldly creature Zolya hadn't previously known to roam the mortal realm. And perhaps it still didn't, seeing as it was a companion Tanwen had acquired in the Low Gods' territory of Drygul.

"She's protection, I'd assume you'd appreciate," explained Tanwen. "I also couldn't have made it here tonight as quickly as I did without her. This meeting place is a good deal farther for those who must *walk*," she pointed out frostily.

While Zolya had braced himself for Tanwen's anger, he hadn't anticipated that her gargantuan wolf would also be here, sharing in her fury and glaring at him as if he were a plump turkey ready to be plucked.

"Tanwen," he carefully began again. "I—"

"You went too far today." She cut him off.

Zolya's calm veneer disintegrated as he huffed his incredulousness. "The same could be said of yourself. You know I was against you revealing your identity."

Tanwen frowned. "Then why did you help in revealing it?"

"Because you forced my hand. When you stepped out like that . . . for all to see"—claws of panic squeezed his throat at the memory—"I needed to control as much of your madness as I could."

"It was not madness," she argued. "You knew I was to participate in the Mütra reveal."

"Yes, but to stand within a group was one thing. There is safety in numbers. To stand apart and reveal who your father is, plus your connection with Azla . . ." He swallowed down his rising fury. "You were almost apprehended, Tanwen. Could have been *killed*."

"But I wasn't," she reminded him. "And you very well know that the risk wasn't as great as it seemed. I had the protective sanctuary required of any peace meeting, and I had you. *We* had you."

"Me?" he nearly laughed. "I still am not king. You must remember that. My jurisdiction of power is limited to the will of my *father's* Royal Council. I am still under their thumb." He raked a frustrated hand through his hair. "I nearly leveled the entire tent when the guards seized you," he admitted, his magic a storm of distress through his veins with the memory. "And what would have happened to all our careful planning then?"

She chewed her lip, her frustration clearly mirroring his. "I'm sorry," she admitted after a pause. "But I had to do it—for my family. After losing Thol . . ." She inhaled sharply, as if holding back a sob. Zolya's chest tightened witnessing her pain, but she pressed on. "My parents need a chance to start over," she explained. "As different people. Having me confirm their deaths gives them that freedom. Without the palace hunting them, they can try to begin again."

Loji whined at her side, nuzzling her shoulder, clearly sensing her agony, her desperation.

Zolya frowned, despising the jealousy he felt toward the wolf.

I should be nuzzling Tanwen, he thought mulishly.

Instead, he remained stoically apart from her, loathing every second of it.

He knew Tanwen's parents would always grieve their son; the reports she shared of the growing rift in their marriage proved it. This was Tanwen's desperate attempt to mend what she saw breaking. A meddyg frantic to heal a festering wound.

But some breaks couldn't be healed.

Some left those who bore them limping for the rest of their lives.

But he could never tell her that. Could never further the crack he already knew sliced through her heart regarding her family and losing Thol.

"And I'm done hiding, Zolya," Tanwen went on, her green eyes now fierce. "I'm done pretending to be someone I'm not, some*thing* I'm not. Our world needs to change, and I'll either die fighting for it or live to see it happen."

The night seemed to still then, only the puffs of their breaths disturbing the quiet, along with the shifting of Loji's paws.

"*Gods*," breathed Zolya, his annoyance flaring. "You make it impossible to stay mad at you when you say things like that. Must you *always* be so magnificent?"

Tanwen's expression cleared, as if she hadn't anticipated such a response.

The air between them grew taut, heavy with heat, until—

"That's not going to work." She shuttered the moment as she folded her arms over her chest, brows slamming down. "My anger over today won't be charmed away so easily. I knew you were to be cold, Zolya, but to threaten the recruits on Galia—?"

"Is *exactly* what the son of King Réol would do," he explained. "You said you understood the parts we'd be playing."

"I do," she snapped. "It's just that . . ."

For a moment she appeared lost, tumbling down a cliff, frantically searching for purchase.

"What?" he implored.

"I wish you had warned me that you'd be holding the recruits hostage."

Zolya hated hearing the betrayal in her voice, seeing the hurt in her gaze, but these were the storms they'd need to weather. Otherwise, neither of them would make it out whole, least of all still together.

His heart felt split at the thought of losing her, his jaw tightening to swallow the pain. But today's actions were only a glimpse of the cruelty he might need to show to satisfy his father's council—and his people. To be king meant sometimes he'd need to put his kingdom above the interests of those he loved.

Would Tanwen understand this? Forgive it? Or grow to resent him, as his mother had resented his father—as he himself had?

Zolya wanted nothing more than to be with Tanwen, yet in quiet moments he wondered—no, feared—that wanting her was selfish. Selfish to tether her to a man who at times might need to put his people first, ahead of her.

Was that fair to her?

But, as always when his mind drifted to such dark places, he drew a deep breath and forced the thoughts down, burying them.

"I couldn't warn you about holding the recruits hostage because I didn't know I would be," he replied, forcing his tone even. "It was a move born from the necessity of the moment."

"What do you mean?" she asked, frowning.

"I had no way of knowing how the room was to react to your plans. I had certain contingencies in place for all number of outcomes; this was one of them. To save you, and the other Mütra tonight, I had to threaten something else. Plus, with the crumbled trade agreements and continued attacks, my hand was rather forced. What would you expect the prince regent to do in such a position? Cower to those who threaten his people? Or fight back, proving he *does* have the capability to rule like his father."

Tanwen remained quiet, pensive, her displeasure clear on her face.

"I could never concede to your demands at first blush," he went on. "It would give me no room for what we wish to eventually create together when I'm king. I must have my people—mainly my father's council—trusting and compliant while he still lives. Eventually they will stop wishing to be tied to my every move or witness to my every decree if they think I'm acting with his desires in mind. This is a long game. You must remember that. Until I claim the throne, I must behave accordingly. And while I may have threatened the recruits tonight, it could have been much worse."

She shot him a wide-eyed, disbelieving look. "How?"

"King Réol could be awake, and he would *never* have offered a peace meeting," Zolya explained. "Even if he couldn't afford it, he would have rained down his wrath the very moment the first attack on a Volari outpost took place. He would be burning Süra forests despite the repercussions. I ask you to remember that difference. This is hopefully the first of many negotiations our two parties will have. Let us agree that tonight was a victory, as there was no bloodshed."

Tanwen's features were pinched, as if she had swallowed something foul. "I hate this," she admitted. "What is the Rebellion to do now?"

"Regroup," he advised. "Work on the eastern clan's support. Despite your added Mütra numbers, the Rebellion will need more power if it wishes to be a threat to the children of gods. Galia may be suffering from the lack of trade and imports, but we have built our island to be self-sustaining if necessary. We have closed ourselves off before; we can do so again. But winter is coming to Cādra, and I'm afraid the people here will suffer more soon."

Tanwen eyed him skeptically. "And who am I to believe is offering this counsel? You or the prince regent."

"*I* am offering it," he said, unable to hide the flare of hurt in his voice. "The man who would give up his wings to ensure your safety."

Tanwen's gaze softened at that, her wall visibly lowering.

"Now," he exhaled, tiredness clinging to him. "Are we done fighting?"

She shifted her weight, hesitant. "I . . . suppose."

"Thank gods," he murmured, stepping forward, arms ready to pull her close—

A warning growl from Loji froze him in place.

"Do you mind?" Zolya gave the wolf a withering glare.

Loji responded by baring her teeth.

"Loji," said Tanwen soothingly, turning to rub behind the beast's ear.

Impatiently, Zolya watched as a silent conversation passed between the pair.

The wolf's green gaze bored into Zolya as she seemed to grunt with displeasure from something Tanwen said, but eventually she huffed her consent and trotted away.

Zolya watched with barely contained glee as Loji melted into a dark road behind them.

"She'll wait for me at the entrance," explained Tanwen.

"How about she waits for you back in Drygul," offered Zolya. "I can return you to your camp tonight."

"You really must work on getting along with her," she said, attention sliding to where the wolf had gone.

"And your beast really must work on her manners," he said. "Now, where were we?" He reached for Tanwen, and with an easy tug, pressed her to his chest.

Mine, his magic sang once more through his veins as heat feathered out from where they touched.

"She's not a beast," Tanwen replied, looking up at him. "And she's just protective."

"Well, so am I," reasoned Zolya, wrapping his arms tighter around her waist. "And I was born a prince, so I'm also terrible at sharing."

A small smile played on Tanwen's lips as she slipped her hands around his neck. "There's no one to share me with presently."

A strange pang settled between Zolya's ribs as he gazed down at her.

He had grown up in a world dripping with beauty and opulence, but nothing compared to Tanwen.

She was fire and ice and light and darkness. She was fierce and compassionate, cunning and courageous. Her unique Mütra power seemed to burn bright within her vivid moss green eyes. She was intoxicating and breathtaking, and she, by some miracle, had chosen him.

He may have been born into royalty, but this was his privilege—being honored with her love.

Gently, he cupped her jaw, brushing his thumb over her cheek.

Tanwen's lips parted, the space where they touched turning to fire.

He savored the coolness of her skin against the warmth of his.

And then Zolya dipped his head, claiming her mouth.

Soft.

Delicious.

His.

Tanwen's moan traveled like sweet wine down his throat.

Zolya lost all reasoning.

Gods, he had needed this. He needed *her*.

As he pressed her up against the pile of logs, he hooked one of her legs around his waist as they continued to kiss and grope and grind into one another.

It was a desperation that went beyond mere pleasure, like finally breaking the surface when drowning—a panicked relief to breathe air.

"Too long," he rumbled. "We cannot continue to suffer such long partings."

"No," Tanwen agreed with a pant, before trailing her lips up his neck to nip his earlobe. Heat swelled low in his groin. "It's been torture only living by your letters."

"I've missed you so much, my wildflower." He caught her wrists, pinning them above her head. She let out a startled but pleased gasp as he rolled his hips farther into her.

"*Zolya*," she nearly begged. "I need you. *Now.*"

Now.

The word seared through him, fire and a choke hold all at once—*Now.*

Because who knew when they'd be together like this again.

All they ever had were *now*s, suffering fleeting moments together before long separations filled with uncertainties.

A flare of dark determination erupted in Zolya. "Oh, Tanwen," he nearly growled as he tugged the hair at the nape of her neck so she was forced to meet his gaze. Her eyes were dark pools of lust. "I will give you such an undoing that the tremors will last until our next meeting."

Tanwen grew liquid in his arms, before demanding their mouths to collide, her hands rough, eager, pleading.

Zolya had never been so hard in his life.

He ran his hand over her breast as she arched her back, but her coat was thick, her buttons stubborn. They had too many blasted layers between them!

He needed them gone.

He needed skin to skin.

He needed—

A prickle sensation cascaded down his plumage.

An awareness that somehow managed to break through his lust.

Zolya spun, placing Tanwen on the ground behind him. He spread his wings wide to block her from whoever approached.

Zolya's magic rose to his skin, armor and sword as he scanned the dark clearing.

It remained quiet, a landscape of felled trees and discarded tools.

"Zol—?" questioned Tanwen, her breathing still uneven as she tried to glance around him.

"We have company," he warned, tone steely as he kept her at his back.

After another moment he began to wonder if perhaps what he felt was Loji, but then he saw them.

A figure slid into a pool of moonlight in the center of the clearing.

A woman encased in black—trousers, boots, thick jacket with the hood pulled up—but there was no darkness that could snuff out the pure white of her wings or her alabaster hair peeking from beneath her hood.

Zolya's breath caught in disbelief, brows furrowing with confusion. "Azla?"

The woman pushed back her hood, revealing beauty that unmistakably came from a mix of godly and royal blood—smooth light-brown skin, high cheekbones, full lips, and blue eyes that matched his own.

"Hello, Brother," she said.

Her greeting lacked any joy, however, especially when she summoned her wind, punching him in the side and sending him soaring across the yard.

4

For a moment Tanwen did nothing.

Too shocked was she, witnessing Zolya splayed out on the ground, sent there by Azla. A woman who had once struggled to lift a spoon on her own, let alone attack a man she had idolized since birth.

But then Loji was amid the fray.

"Loji, no!" shouted Tanwen, trying and failing to hold back the wolf from charging at the prince and princess. Tanwen dug in her heels as she was dragged forward, arms draped around the wolf's neck. "It's all right, girl, it's all right!" At least, Tanwen hoped it was. "It's Azla!" she added. "Only Azla."

Loji skidded to a stop, shaking her hide before sniffing the air. She gave a large harrumph as she sat.

"Good girl," placated Tanwen in relief, patting her friend's back. "I thank you for your protection, but it's not needed." *Actually,* Tanwen continued silently to her friend, *perhaps Zolya could use your help.*

They watched as Azla stalked toward him, glaring daggers.

I won't be rescuing him, argued Loji in Tanwen's mind. *He reeks of high blood. Too sweet.*

Azla is also of high blood, Tanwen reminded her.

She no longer stinks of it, though, Loji countered. *Her time in Drygul has bathed her well.*

Tanwen found the statement fascinating, but she'd have to save her questions for later.

Currently she needed to intercept Azla from charging once again at her brother.

"What have you done?" Azla demanded as she unleashed another blast of wind.

Zolya rolled away before she could land him a second blow.

He then shot forward faster than Tanwen could track. In the next breath he had Azla in a vise grip from behind, pinning down both her wings and her arms.

"Calm yourself," he demanded.

"Hasn't anyone ever told you," Azla hissed, "never tell a woman to *calm down*!" She stomped on one of his boots, eliciting a pained grunt from Zolya, but he impressively kept his hold.

"Both of you, please," implored Tanwen, rushing forward. "We need to keep quiet. We can't draw a crowd."

At her declaration, two pairs of blazing blue eyes snapped to her, as if only now remembering her presence—and not at all pleased by it.

Tanwen second-guessed intruding on their fight.

Thankfully, Azla seemed to find lucidity, for she took in a steadying breath. "I am calm," she stated.

"I don't believe you," said Zolya, still holding her tight. "Your temper lasts on average a full day."

"Oh, I never said I am no longer mad," she countered. "But I can be calm in my rage. I'm a woman, after all."

"Zol, let her go," pleaded Tanwen.

"No offense, my wildflower," he replied. "But you did not grow up with her tantrums like I did."

Tanwen shot Zolya a pointed glare.

He sighed, finally releasing his sister.

Azla spun away. "*Zol?*" she said, questioning Tanwen's use of her brother's nickname. "*Wildflower?*" she accused, voice rising as her understanding seemed to dawn. "*No.*" She shook her head. "No, no, no. This cannot be happening. Is this really happening? Are you two . . .? But no, that's impossible. You're *you.*" She waved toward Zolya. "You're the perfect prince. You'd never . . . not with a servant—and especially not with a—" She cut herself off, eyes wide in terror and atonement at what she'd been about to share.

"He knows," said Tanwen. "That I'm Mütra. He knows everything. He's on our side, actually. He's been holding off a war as best he can."

Azla's mouth popped open, but nothing came out.

"I understand this is all rather shocking," Tanwen continued slowly. "It was a shock to us as well when it first happened, but—"

"*First* happened?" breathed Azla. "I thought he was attacking you, Tanwen!"

"Attacking her?" Zolya frowned. "When have I *ever* attacked a woman."

"You attacked me tonight."

"I *restrained* you."

Azla scoffed. "A clearly guilty defense of an attacker."

"*You* are the one who shot your wind at *me*," he argued. "Twice."

"I was protecting my friend."

"You were?" asked Tanwen, strangely moved by the thought. "Thank you."

"You're welcome." Azla stood a little taller. "It's the least I could do after everything you've done for me."

"Are you both quite finished?" Zolya crossed his arms.

"Not in the least," replied Azla, mimicking his stance. "I'm just getting started. You need to explain yourselves, *immediately*. What exactly did I fly in on?"

Silence fell, an awkward stretch as Tanwen locked eyes with Zolya.

"Well, you see . . ." he began slowly. "When two consenting adults find each other attractive—"

"*By the gods*," Azla bit out. "Don't be droll. I'm asking how the two of you"—she gestured between them—"became the two of you?"

"Wait," said Tanwen with narrowed gaze. "Why are *you* here, Azla? You are meant to be in Drygul."

"Don't deflect," she countered.

"*Azla*," warned Tanwen. "What did you do?"

"*Nothing*," she snapped, defensively. "Everyone was anxious for news of how the meetings were going, your parents most of all. I decided to do some quick scouting."

"You could have been seen," said Tanwen.

"Or captured," added Zolya, darkly. "There is a bounty for your return to Galia."

"You realize the irony of your accusations, right?" Azla arched a brow at the two of them. "I came to ensure the Rebellion wasn't in bloody pieces after the Mütra performance. I was on my way back to Drygul when I saw *you* flying here, alone." She pointed to Zolya. "I wanted to see you. We haven't been together since . . ." She seemed unable to finish her thought, her expression growing sorrow filled, but then she blinked, as if shaking herself awake. "So, there's my answer. Now it's your turn. When did this happen? More importantly, *how* did this happen?"

Tanwen shifted, feeling a blush to her cheeks. "That's a rather . . . complicated answer."

"Luckily for you, I'm extremely smart," said Azla.

"It doesn't matter when *or* how it happened," snapped Zolya. "All that matters is that it *is* happening."

"Well, it must stop!" Azla threw up her hands.

"Excuse me?" said Zolya.

"If this ever went public, you'd both be executed."

"You think we don't know this?" said Tanwen with a frown.

"Then why let it continue?" implored Azla. "You're going to be king, Zolya. *King.* And you—" She spun toward Tanwen. "You're helping in the Rebellion. I mean, *by the twin moons*, you helped *me* poison the king. This cannot—"

"What did you say?" Zolya demanded, tone tight with disbelief.

Tanwen turned to ice.

Oh no. Oh gods.

Loji slunk closer to her side, no doubt sensing her panic.

She stopped breathing as Zolya's hard stare slid to her.

"Zolya," she began before faltering, panic seizing her. She hadn't wanted him to find out like this, if at all.

"You helped poison the king?" He appeared unnervingly calm, his expression a terrifying blank mask.

"It was before you and I were . . . you and I," she reasoned, guilt spilling across her heart. "It was an agreement made with a Low God to help save my family. I was going to tell you eventually, but—"

"You didn't," he finished for her, his voice low, a deep rumble that finally revealed his rage.

"Oh," declared Azla, remorseful eyes landing on Tanwen. "You said he knew everything."

Tanwen ignored her as she took a step toward Zolya, frantic to fix this.

His retreat hit her like a punch to the gut.

He eyed her as if a stranger.

A stranger that he couldn't stand the sight of.

Tanwen was flooded with terror and anguish.

"Zolya," she pleaded once more. "I'm sorry, but I was desperate. My brother was being tortured. You must understand."

"I *do* understand," he said, his brows knitting together. "After all, I am not such a hypocrite as to be shocked that you plotted to kill my father—when I've done the same myself. What offends, however," he continued, his tone sharp, "is that it has been *months* since the incident. Months of me confiding in you, of sharing what I knew of that night my father was poisoned, my compliance in it, opening up about how I've wrestled with that guilt, and yet here you have stood, holding the same confession and not feeling you could trust me with it. As *I* trusted you."

The tense silence that followed was heavy and brittle.

The coldness of the quiet logging site pressed in around Tanwen as she found herself too lost to respond.

But then Zolya spoke again, his eyes narrowing. "It makes me wonder . . . what else you're keeping from me."

"*Nothing*," she quickly assured. "This was it. And I regret every second I didn't tell you. I'm so sorry, Zolya. We both have just been carrying so much, dealing with so much that I never wanted to disrupt our moments together. They already are so few. I was scared that if I admitted to this, they'd cease altogether."

Zolya drew back, as if she had hit him. "Do you really think my love for you is so fragile? That *our* love is? After all that we've been through and are working toward."

Gods, how was she messing this up so badly?

"No, of course I don't think that," she argued.

"We need to be able to trust each other."

"I *do* trust you. I trusted you with my life today, for the gods' sake. I trusted you with it the night you learned I was Mütra. You can't possibly doubt that."

He regarded her a long moment, but whatever he was thinking, he hid it behind a cold mask. "I will be expected back soon" was all he replied.

"Zolya—" She and Azla spoke in unison, their shock clear, but he cut them off.

"We will talk of this later."

Tanwen's pulse rushed in fear. She felt as if she was falling, being pulled beneath the soil—lost to him. "Please, Zolya, don't leave like this." She snagged his arm, her grip tight. "We don't know when we'll be together again." She could hear the desperation in her tone, but she didn't care.

She *was* desperate.

Desperate to fix this.

Not just because she knew she'd been wrong to keep this from him but also because she couldn't stand being apart from him for the gods knew how long, without reconciling. For him to think she harbored doubts regarding the strength of their relationship or that she was not as honest with him as he was with her.

Her chest felt cleaved open, raw.

Especially when he gently pried her fingers loose, dropping them from his arm.

"I need time with this," he murmured, his gaze unable to meet hers.

She couldn't breathe, the air squeezed from her lungs as he stepped back.

"It was good to see you, Sister." He turned to Azla, his hand resting briefly on her shoulder. "Stay safe."

Tanwen stood cold and alone as he withdrew farther into the clearing and watched as he spread his wings.

But before taking flight, he finally met her gaze.

The look pierced through her, lodging deep in her chest.

"I'm sorry," she called to him one final time, her voice breaking from her rising emotion.

His expression remained steely, but he gave the slightest hint of a nod.

Then he was gone—launched into the night with a burst of wind.

Tanwen watched, her heart vanishing along with him into the dark.

"Well . . ." breathed Azla as she came to her side. "I messed that up. I'm sorry, Tanwen. I wouldn't have said anything—"

"He needed to know." She shook her head. "This is not your fault. It's mine for not finding the courage earlier."

Azla didn't reply, merely threaded her fingers through Tanwen's. A supportive squeeze.

It did little to steady Tanwen's spinning thoughts. She recalled the deal she had made with Bosyg, a bargain still unfinished. The king was not dead. Though he'd lain unconscious for six months, his condition hadn't changed.

And the Low Goddess never missed a chance to remind Tanwen of that whenever near.

Yet right now, the consequences of what might happen if the king awoke hardly mattered to her.

All that mattered was Zolya—and finding a way to fix what she'd broken.

"He's very angry with me," she said.

"He's always angry with someone," Azla reasoned.

Tanwen rubbed at the pain spreading through her sternum. "I need him to forgive me."

"If he cares for you like it's clear he does, he will," she assured. "But in the meantime, I'd be more concerned about what happens once your relationship gets out."

Tanwen looked at Azla. "It won't."

Azla huffed her incredulousness. "You are *not* that naive. Of course it will. He's going to be king, Tanwen. There's no one on Cādra who has less autonomy than a Volari king. It's not a matter of *if* you'll be found out, but a matter of *when.* I merely want you both to be prepared," she added, her features growing dark. "Because I wasn't. Life is crueler than any of us like to believe."

It was as if the ghost of Lady Esme pressed into the space between them. A chill of heartache clawing the air.

"I'm sorry." Tanwen was the one to squeeze Azla's hand now, wishing there was more she could do, more she could say to remove her friend's pain.

Azla shook her head, as if that could so easily rid her haunting. "Just promise me you and my brother will think of a plan."

"If he ever decides to talk to me again," murmured Tanwen.

Azla shot her a sharp look as her tone hardened. "*Promise* me."

"Yes, of course," said Tanwen. "We will."

"Good." She nodded, her brows growing pinched with determination. "Because if these past months have taught me anything, it's that in our world, something is always sacrificed for love."

5

Zolya rather preferred not having his wings singed.

So, in hindsight, insisting on a sparring match with Osko had been a mistake. But with his irritability only compounding since returning to Galia, he had seen no other option.

Spinning to the far side of the room, Zolya nearly dodged another lethal blast of heat.

He cursed as a searing pain fell across his bare shoulders and plumage.

"You're distracted," said Osko, though the accusation didn't stop him from advancing with his sword.

Zolya deflected the hit, his own blade vibrating against his friend's. "Or perhaps I'm bored," he countered.

Osko scoffed, fading a step. "Boredom would have you end this, not become an easy mark."

Zolya pursed his lips, annoyance flaring.

His friend was right, and he loathed when his friend was right.

Zolya *was* distracted.

But how could he not be?

His time with Tanwen had been frustratingly brief and then ended on even more frustrating terms. Despite a week passing since their meeting, he was still working through the hurt from her dishonesty.

How could she have kept this from him for so long?

She'd helped in the poisoning of his father . . . had played an instrumental part in the king's current state, had plotted with his *sister*, and there he had been, naive to it all.

Osko's blade crashed with his again, but he barely registered the weight as he shrugged Osko off.

His thoughts continued to spin.

He hadn't lied when he'd said he understood her motives. Of course she'd want his father dead—Tanwen had more reason than most to wish it. And if striking a bargain with a Low God was what it took to keep her family safe, he couldn't blame her for taking it or for needing to see it through.

What angered him was how she'd handled it afterward. They weren't just surviving on their own anymore; they were supposed to be surviving *together*.

Both of them were already risking everything to fight for what they wanted, what they desired in their hearts. Keeping secrets—especially one this big—was a risk they couldn't afford.

How could he trust she wouldn't hide something like this again?

But then again . . . hiding had always been how she survived.

His ire twisted with a new rise of guilt.

Should he have done more to help her believe he was a safe space?

Could he do more now?

Exasperation and irritation sparked through his veins as he spun away from a fireball shot from Osko's free hand.

Zolya was merely defending at this point as his thoughts, unbidden, turned to Azla next.

Her finding them.

Despite her interruption, he had been glad to see his sister after months apart.

Zolya had barely recognized her—clad like a midnight assassin, wielding lethal magic. But her dry candor revealed she was still the same woman, if a bit more frayed, a bit colder.

Though, weren't they all?

You're going to be king, Zolya. King.

The echo of her words tightened around him, a suffocating reminder of his daily burdens: council demands, court complaints, endless news of the uprising, his father's uncertain fate, and his own uncertain path to the throne.

Stolen moments with Tanwen were the *only* rays of light in his burdened life. When he could let down his guard, grow satiated, and—dare he admit—feel hopeful. But that reprieve had been soured, tainted, leaving him unsure if he was annoyed with Azla, Tanwen, or Udasha—the High Goddess of luck—for so thoroughly abandoning him in that moment.

So, *yes*, Zolya may have been bloody distracted for today's sparring.

"Well?" called Osko, redrawing his attention. "Shall I ring for tea? If I had known this was to be so civil, I'd have made sure we had refreshments nearby."

Zolya blinked, his annoyance now turning full force on his friend. A growl tore from his throat as he charged.

His power clung to him like dewdrops, ready to obey. A thrilling chill ran the length of him as he summoned a rain cloud to form behind Osko, all while aiming his blade at his friend's chest—two points of attack.

But Osko was the leader of the Royal Army for a reason.

Seeming to sense the threats, he summoned a wall of fire behind him and spun away from Zolya's deadly slash.

"That's better," said Osko, his grin sharp.

"Let's see if you're still pleased when I have my sword pressed to your neck," countered Zolya.

Osko laughed. "I so love it when you dream."

Their clashing powers filled the small domed rotunda with fog, steam hissing as Zolya's rain met Osko's heat. The echoes of their weapons striking reverberated against the stone walls.

For a glorious moment Zolya's mind was finally filled with nothing else but his next hit, quick evasion. As he breathed heavily, his shirtless torso slick and gleaming, he traded his grip on the hilt of his sword and lunged with his left hand.

Osko was momentarily caught off guard, unprepared to adjust his stance.

Zolya smiled, triumph sparking alive in his chest.

As he pressed his opponent, he unleashed a more powerful burst of his magic.

It filled the entirety of the room. A crack of lightning flashed across the coiling dark ceiling as rain pelted the ground in thick sheets.

Osko became drenched, blinking vigorously to see through the onslaught. His magic was no longer a match for Zolya's. He could not rely on it to shield himself.

This was when Zolya unleashed his final attack.

With a side step, twist, and lunge, he had Osko pinned to the wall, his blade's tip pressed to his neck.

All around them, his power surged—a storm swelling with fierce lightning and thunderous cracks.

"What were you saying about dreams?" asked Zolya.

Osko dropped his weapon in defeat. "You rainmakers are always so dramatic in your magic." Osko squinted through the downpour with displeasure.

Grinning, Zolya stepped back.

He waved his hand, evaporating the pouring fury.

A deafening silence filled the training rotunda.

It now stood bone dry, sunlight streaming back in through the open archway. The only one who remained drenched was Osko.

"Jealousy looks good on you, my friend," said Zolya. He walked to hang his sword among others on a far rack.

"Pfft, I knew you needed the win," replied Osko as he toweled himself off.

"Nice try," huffed Zolya. "Allowing defeat is not in your nature."

"Perhaps, but neither are lightning and thunder something you usually bring to spar." Osko shook out his dark wings, sending water flying. "You really did need this session."

Zolya's silence must have drawn his friend's curiosity, for Osko paused, wet rag in hand, to give him a once-over.

"What?" Zolya frowned, not enjoying the scrutiny.

"You know that I am always here for you," he said, tone earnest. "For more than a fight. I hope you can also trust me for whatever weighs on your mind."

Trust.

The very thing weighing on him now—though with Osko, at least he knew where he stood.

Zolya clenched his jaw, an ache of disappointment filling his lungs as he wished what his friend said was true.

Osko might be like a brother to him, but above all else he loyally served the crown, believed in the segregation of the races and the condemnation of Mütra.

Still, Zolya couldn't help wondering, wishing that perhaps one day that might change when he was king. That Osko's allegiance to the crown would have him reassessing his beliefs, or at the very least accepting who Zolya chose to love.

But you're not king. An unwelcome whisper slithered into his mind.

No, thought Zolya morosely, his brief reprieve consumed by one of his many dark truths—such power still lay with his father, a man who controlled him even in unconsciousness.

Zolya's aggravation flooded his veins once more, sharp pricks across his skin.

He was tired of being controlled. Of needing to be in control.

And he was certainly exhausted from every relationship in his life being fraught with complications.

"I hardly trust what weighs on my mind these days," Zolya found himself admitting. "How could I possibly expect anyone else to untangle it?"

"I may not understand what it is to have an entire realm on my shoulders," said Osko, "or the worry of a sick parent, but know that I am here to lessen your burdens however I can. As you have always done for me."

Zolya's chest constricted, both appreciating and resenting his friend's words. They gave him false hope. "Thank you," he began. "I appreciate—"

The arrival of Queen Habelle interrupted whatever jumble of a response Zolya was about to form.

She swept into the rotunda, a horde of guards on her heels.

Zolya and Osko dropped to one knee, bowing as she halted in the center of the room.

"My queen," said Zolya. "What brings us the unexpected honor of your presence?"

Per usual, his mother was a vision of impeccable dress in her royal blue stola draped dramatically over one shoulder. Beneath she wore an intricately beaded dress, her smooth black skin and strong amber wings defying her centuries of age. Her hair was plaited and topped with an ambrü-encrusted gold crown.

"You may rise," she said, tone clipped.

They did as they were told.

"Your sparring session has stirred quite the crowd," she explained, one delicate brow raised. "I fear every lady at court has abandoned their post to be a witness."

Zolya glanced to the archway, where a throng of women huddled close to the entrance. Upon his attention, a fit of giggles erupted, and the group quickly cleared, taking to the sky.

"Your son does have a way of drawing attention, Your Majesty," said Osko.

"Indeed," she mused, chin lifting, "but how is it that *you*, Kidar Terz, are also always close at hand when he does?"

"Someone must carry the burden of cleaning up his messes, ma'am." Osko respectfully inclined his head.

Though barely noticeable, the corner of the queen's lips tilted up. "I'm sure someone does. Especially when they are such pretty messes." She waved in the general direction of where the ladies once stood.

"The tribulations of serving the crown." Osko grinned, oozing charm.

By the High Gods, Zolya was going to be sick.

"How can we be of service to you, Mother?" he asked rather desperately.

Queen Habelle turned her full attention on him. "We have a visitor."

Zolya frowned. "A visitor?"

"From Kaiwi," she explained, tone deceptively even.

Ice froze Zolya's blood. He didn't dare to draw another breath.

"It appears," continued his mother, features unreadable, "our benevolent creators have sent someone to wake the king."

6

Tanwen had always taken pride in her adaptability.

After all, she had moved countless times, had concealed her magic for years, and had been posing as a Süra since birth.

But never would she grow accustomed to living among immortals or the plethora of strange creatures slinking about Drygul.

Tanwen scooted around a large globular form rolling along the forest floor, careful not to step on the mushrooms sprouting within its residual sludge before she found herself needing to duck as a swooping animal—bird or bat, she couldn't tell—nearly grazed her horns before vanishing into the colorful tangle of trees.

"Must they always do that?" she grumbled, gingerly checking her head to ensure no droppings were left behind—as had happened many times prior.

"It appears they must, at least to you," said Huw, who walked beside her. "They rather like me."

As if to emphasize his point, one of the flying rodents briefly landed on his outstretched hand, unfurled its long tonguelike appendage to lick his skin, then leaped back into the air.

Tanwen resisted a shiver. "Disgusting."

"Aren't you supposed to befriend all animals?" he asked while pointedly looking at Loji, who sauntered on the other side of Tanwen.

Not if they are unworthy of Tanwen's friendship, answered Loji in Tanwen's mind.

"I fear your flattery will soon go to my head, my friend." Tanwen grinned as she stroked the wolf's thick hide. Loji's fur danced between brown, green, and yellow—the colors that made up their surroundings.

The village in Drygul, like many Süra villages, was composed of a mix of tree dens and root burrows, linked by wooden bridges and rope ladders.

Sunlight filtered through the bright, multicolor canopy as townsfolk strolled, bartered, or wove baskets in front of stoops. Soft conversation and laughter filled the cool air, blending seamlessly with the forest's quiet rustle. But what set it apart from any other place in Cādra—besides the odd creatures and appearance of a Low God—was the people.

It never ceased to fill Tanwen's chest with hope, seeing the diverse array of Süra and Mütra and even a handful of Volari refugees, all mingling together, peacefully.

A painting of what the future *could* be.

Should be.

"You know how I loathe when you engage in one of your one-sided conversations," huffed Huw. "It's terribly rude."

"Some things are not for your ears," explained Tanwen.

"I'd like to be the judge of that. What did she say?"

"You'd only ruin the compliment if I told you. Just know it was lovely and completely true."

"Yes, well, one's truth is subjective."

Tanwen gave Huw a long look. "That is the very opposite definition of the word *truth*."

"For *you* perhaps."

"Well, here is a truth we can both agree on," she said, brows raised. "You're extremely exhausting."

"Exhausting in bed, perhaps." His responding grin caused Tanwen to laugh, despite herself.

"You really have me regretting helping you off Galia," she said.

A mistake I can fix, replied Loji, eyeing Huw with a glint of hunger.

If Huw sensed the threat, he ignored it, as he often did around the wolf. He seemed to find antagonizing Loji a sport, especially when he could disappear at will, dodging her attacks. Though his invisibility wasn't endless; he could only hold it for short bursts—just long enough to gain the upper hand.

"Now *that* is a lie," Huw said, his blond hair and curling horns catching the sunlight as he waved to a passing woman and her daughter. "You'd be dreadfully bored here without me and not nearly as well liked. It is because of *my* delightful constitution that this misfit bunch has warmed to you."

Tanwen scoffed. "And here I thought it was due to my meddyg skills and the work I've done on the Rebellion Council. Or should I say *our* council, now that you're a part of the Rebellion."

"Who's exhausting now?" he countered.

"Come on, Huw." She tugged at his elbow, bringing them to a halt. "You must admit that you got a thrill standing up to the Royal Council like we did?"

"Thrill? No. Irritable bowels, yes."

"Be *serious*."

"I am. We could have been killed. It's actually rather odd that we weren't." His gaze lingered on her, sharp with skepticism, as if she alone held the answers to his unease.

Huw had been watching her like this more often—studying her, waiting, as though he knew she was keeping something from him.

Guilt gnawed at Tanwen's stomach. But she couldn't afford anyone else to know about her and Zolya—especially with Azla now aware. It was too dangerous.

Not to mention she was still raw from how things had ended with Zolya—his anger, and worse, his disappointment, clawed at her chest.

She didn't have the strength to clash with someone else she loved, to have Huw upset at her for keeping such a secret. But unlike her part in the king's poisoning, this wasn't hers alone to confess. Zolya's safety was at stake too.

And she couldn't risk breaking his trust more than she already had.

"Clearly our demonstration worked," she explained. "We opened their eyes regarding the existence of Mütra. Don't you want to be a part of freeing our kind?"

"I want to live a long life," he replied. "And I don't see that happening while being a part of a rebellion. I've survived as long as I have by minding my own business."

"So you're not angry with how Mütra are treated in Cādra? How we're hunted?"

"Of course I'm angry," he said sharply. "But I also understand what my mother sacrificed to keep me alive—her unwanted child, I might add. She gave up everything to raise me, to keep me safe. I can't dishonor her by being reckless with my life."

Tanwen had countless responses at the ready, but she swallowed them. She had learned much about Huw over the past months, yet very little about his past or his family. She didn't want to shatter this rare moment of openness with a rebuttal. Instead, she asked, "Where is your mother now?"

"Where most of our loved ones are," he answered. "In the Eternal River."

A pang of sorrow tightened in Tanwen's chest. "I'm sorry."

He shrugged, but his clenched jaw betrayed the weight of his emotions.

"She didn't have an easy life," he admitted after a pause. "She was born with a rare illness that left her weak, but she was a survivor. She endured the Volari who attacked her, survived my birth, and fled to raise me among the priestesses of Eya's temple in the depths of the Pelk Forest. She used to joke that my magic was a gift from her. *You have your mother's ability to disappear,* she'd say. And yet, despite everything, despite being so young, so alone—she was always smiling, always laughing. Even the day Maryth took her, she was grinning. I can still hear her soft voice as she gripped my hand. *My sunlight,* she said. *Keep surviving.*"

Huw's story slid between Tanwen's ribs, a grip of sorrow to her chest that stirred awake her own buried grief.

In so many ways, his past mirrored hers—a parent who fled their family to raise an illegal child, hiding in the woods, fighting to survive.

Yet, despite these similarities, she and Huw clearly moved through their trauma differently.

"So that's what I've been doing ever since," he said, meeting her gaze. "I keep surviving. For her."

"And if anyone understands that, it's me," she said. "But if you had the chance to live, not just survive—don't you think your mother would want you to take it?"

"I am living," he countered. "Here, in Drygul. This is the first time our kind hasn't had to look over our shoulders, think about where we'll be tomorrow. We've found sanctuary. Why should we risk losing it?"

"Because Drygul won't last forever," she explained. "You know it as well as I do. This is temporary. The Low Gods haven't promised us permanence. They're sheltering us now so we can grow, so we can be their weapons against the children of the High Gods. We are a means to their end, Huw. Which is why we need to make plans for our future. A future out there." She gestured in the general direction of the border, where their forest gave way to rolling fields before mist.

Huw fell silent then, his expression dark, no doubt knowing she was right.

"This is our chance to change everything," she pressed on. "I understand the need to survive—we all do—but I refuse to live in fear any longer. We may not need to look over our shoulders here, but we still do every time we step beyond the Low Gods' territory. We owe it to those still out there, terrified and alone. I owe it to the Thols of the world."

And here was her truth, her purpose—just as Huw's mother was his. She swallowed down the rising ache in her throat. Aberthol's death had frozen a piece of her heart, fueling her resolve. No other Mütra should suffer as he had. She had made that promise to him the day he fell from the sky: No more children or parents would suffer for who they were or who they loved.

If Mütra, Süra, and Volari could live together in Drygul, then so could the rest of the world. So could she and Zolya be together freely. No more tearing of wings and slitting of throats. If she could not heal what had been done to her parents because of their love, what had been done to Thol, and what Huw's mother had endured, what hope did any future generation have?

She couldn't bear to imagine that reality—nor could she accept that Huw was content to simply exist, day by day, without striving for more.

"So, have I changed your mind yet?" she asked, forcing her tone to be light, along with her smile. "I'm headed to the Rebellion meeting now. You should join me."

Huw glanced around the village, his expression unreadable as he observed the children darting past and the elders watching from their stoops—a blend of wings, horns, and fragile peace.

"You make a rousing argument, little fawn," he murmured. "But perhaps we should accept our differences that are so clearly etched in our magic. Yours is one of connection and communication, and mine, well—"

His words never finished as he vanished.

Loji let out a low growl beside Tanwen as she stared at the space where her friend had once stood.

If she tried hard enough, she could just make out his translucent form slinking away.

Huw had left—but in his absence, something heavier remained.

Disappointment.

7

Tanwen was only half listening.

An easy feat when Drygul's Rebellion Council was engulfed in its usual heated debate—how to make the Volari Royal Council take their demands seriously. An issue that had only intensified after reviewing the reports on the peace meeting.

"We *know* the importance of gaining the eastern clan's support," said Brynn, her four brown wings held taut against her back as she faced off with another member of their party. She looked like a bull poised to charge, her small horns angled downward beneath the weight of her glare. "That's not the issue," she continued. "The problem is that the eastern clan won't back us unless we can guarantee a real chance at victory. They're too reliant on their earnings from the Dryfs Mine, meager as they are," she finished, her voice edged with frustration.

"Then we need to find a way to convince them," Zephyr replied, brows pinched. "The prince regent practically gave us that directive."

"He also threatened the Galia recruits," came a quiet voice at Zephyr's side—his sister. "We must pose some kind of threat for him to push back like that—even without support from Garw."

Zephyr turned to Lyra, his sharp expression softening. "Well said, darling."

The siblings were as inseparable as their shared resemblance—the same copper-tinged hair and wings, their pale skin smooth beneath the afternoon light.

Along with Azla, they were among the few Volari exiles who had found refuge in the Low Gods' domain—and fewer still granted a voice on this committee.

Nestled in a secluded clearing, shrouded by dense forest, their council was a small gathering of ten members—Tanwen, her parents, Azla, Brynn, Lyra, Zephyr, and three other Mütra. However, despite their size, their varied backgrounds proved to offer both invaluable insights *and* constant discord.

"A point we can make clear to the eastern clan," continued Zephyr. "We should reassemble with them. Invite the west and north—"

"I swear," ground out Brynn while pinching the bridge of her nose. "If you make me repeat myself *again*, Zephyr, I will cut out your tongue."

"No one is stopping you from doing that now," said a cheerfully cool voice within their circle.

Tanwen's muscles tensed as reluctant glances shifted toward a figure who sat—or rather floated—above a log.

Ridi, the Low God of mischief, was unsettling not just in his presence but also in his appearance, given that he looked deceptively mortal. His short-cropped black hair was stark against his pale skin, his curling horns reminiscent of the western clan's. Yet, the illusion of his humanity unraveled in the details: eyes ever shifting in color, and the dark smoke trailing behind his movements, as if he were woven from shadows rather than flesh. Oh, and of course there was the floating.

Unfortunately, Ridi was not their only divine visitor today.

Beside him, Bosyg stood firmly in her merging tree form. Her blossoms unfurling and twirling as her roots subtly shifted in the soil.

While Tanwen understood Bosyg's interest in attending these meetings—a pointed reminder of their unfinished bargain, of King Réol's death yet to be delivered—Ridi seemed to attend for no other reason than his own amusement, finding uprisings great fun.

"I think what Brynn is trying to say," said Tanwen calmly, attempting to ease the strained moment. "Is that we have already tried to convince the eastern clan with our current arsenal. We can't approach them again unless we have gained more strength in a different way."

"Yes," said Brynn, emphatically sweeping a hand toward her. "Exactly that."

"There is always more than one solution to a problem," added Gabreel. "We merely need to reexamine it from a different angle."

Her father sat across from where Tanwen, Azla, and her mother were grouped together on a bench. The distance put there by her mother when they had first arrived, Aisling choosing the seat farthest from him.

An act that had torn—and still tore—at Tanwen's chest.

"Do you see how that is a *helpful* comment?" Zephyr raised a brow at Brynn. "Rather than your constant pessimism."

Brynn's claws retracted at her side, her gaze igniting. "I can certainly be *helpful* by defeathering—"

"Divine ones," Aisling interjected swiftly, looking to the Low Gods. "What of your siblings? Can we convince more of your family to support our cause as you have?"

"Our siblings have been tangled in this fight for millennia," explained Bosyg, voice the scattering of insects. "Many are as the east. They do not wish to be on the losing side, again. Our mother's disappointment is not a wrath easily survived."

"Then how else will we gain strength big enough to threaten Galia?" asked Brynn, brow furrowed. "Besides the eastern clan, there's no one left on Cādra to collect."

"Maybe it's not about numbers," Tanwen suggested. "Maybe what we need is more of an idea of power."

"What does that mean?" asked Brynn.

"I'm not exactly sure," Tanwen admitted. "But I wish you could have seen the Royal Council's reaction when we revealed the Mütra at the peace meeting. It was as if the sky had collapsed around them. They were devastated—terrified, of *us*. And we were only a fraction of our true numbers. Plus, no two of our magics are the same—and that's a hard thing for any army to defend against. We need to remember why Mütra were banned in the first place. It's because King Réol and his constituents fear what our mixed blood can create—something beyond their control."

Her words hung heavy in the forest air, settling over the group.

"So what else poses an equally terrifying threat to the Royal Council?" she challenged.

"The High Gods," answered Azla from beside her. "And . . . my father."

"Well, that's of no use," said Brynn, her four wings shifting with her agitation. "The High Gods *certainly* won't come to our aid, and King Réol is on Maryth's door."

"One hopes," replied Bosyg.

From no will of her own, Tanwen's eyes were forced to meet the Low Goddess's dark glare.

A chill ran down her spine. Once again, a reminder of their bargain yet unfulfilled.

Tanwen wasn't sure what would happen if the king recovered from his coma—if she failed to uphold her end of the deal—but she preferred not to find out.

"You were born in Galia." Aisling's attention shifted to Zephyr and Lyra, across from them. "What was something that scared you?"

"Our mother," Zephyr answered easily, his tone cold.

Lyra placed a gentle hand over his, her expression pained.

"At least you knew your mother," Brynn muttered.

Zephyr's gaze darkened. "Trust me," he said, voice low. "It would have been better for everyone if we hadn't."

"She's gone now, though," Lyra added, her fingers tightening around her brother's. "She can't hurt us any longer. We made sure of that."

"What do you mean?" asked Tanwen.

Lyra met her stare, unflinching. "We killed her."

Tanwen held in a shocked breath, falling into a strained silence with the rest of the group.

Dear gods, she thought as she studied the pair again, her gaze lingering on Lyra. She had always found the woman timid, as delicate as a jadüri in bloom. Yet she was capable of matricide.

"They were going to send us to Both Island," Lyra went on, seeming not to notice the tension radiating in their clearing. "We escaped before they could."

"*Mm*, Both Island," Ridi purred. "Now there's an exciting thought, Sister." His grin was sharp as he looked at Bosyg.

"Yes," she mused, head tilting thoughtfully. "That is interesting."

Wariness was a cold hand to Tanwen's shoulders.

If the god of mischief and chaos looked this pleased by an idea, it surely was not to be trusted.

"Both?" Brynn frowned. "No offense, Almighty Ones, but what about an island where criminals get sent to die is interesting?"

Tanwen noticed Azla stiffen beside her, her lips pressing into a tight line. She knew she was thinking of her mother—Lady Callia—who had been dropped there.

Sadness stirred in Tanwen's chest, urging her to reach out, to offer comfort to her friend, but she held back. Azla had yet to confide in her about her mother, and Tanwen didn't want to overstep.

"It's not only for criminals," Ridi explained, amusement glinting in his ever-shifting eyes. "It's also home to those the old Volari kings deemed threats to their reign—creations that were not theirs to kill. Beings shaped by our mother and father, back when Maryth still had her wings and sat beside her brother Ré in Kaiwi."

"I've heard this child's tale," said Zephyr. "Creatures made from every kind of beast roaming our world. But I always thought it was myth."

"Myths are often rooted in truth," Bosyg explained.

"Yes," agreed Gabreel. "But they would have been banished centuries ago. How could such creatures survive this long on Both?"

"I'm sorry," Brynn interjected. "But what's the point of this, again? What does this have to do with us gaining leverage?"

"Do keep up, mortal," Ridi sighed, waving a tired hand. "You asked what would scare the Royal Council. What about unleashing an island of misfits and murderers?"

"Can we even do that?" asked Tanwen with a frown.

"You're called the *Rebellion*, are you not, child?" Ridi challenged. "What good is such a name if you do not live up to it."

Tanwen chewed her bottom lip, thoughts swirling. She'd be lying if the idea didn't excite her, though she knew it also came with a dozen more questions and doubts.

"Both Island is off the continent," Brynn pointed out. "Surrounded by Orzel's rough seas. It would take an age to get there. Nearly impossible by boat."

"Yes," agreed Zephyr. "And there's a reason Volari drop prisoners from the sky. It's said that the moment anyone sets foot on the island, they are as good as dead. No one has ever escaped, and no one has ever been rescued."

"That doesn't mean it's impossible," reasoned Tanwen. "No one believed anyone but those with wings could escape Galia, and my family disproved that. Also, like he said, there's always a solution to a problem; we just need to think outside the box. Because if these creatures *are* still alive—along with some of the prisoners sent there—they would have just as much reason, if not more, to want justice for what was done to them. To side with the Rebellion. If we could reach them, speak to them, we might strike a bargain. Offer them freedom in exchange for fighting with us."

"I hear a lot of *ifs* in that beautiful declaration," mumbled Zephyr.

"We could scout from the air," Tanwen pushed on, ideas now swirling. "You, Lyra, and Azla could—"

"Lyra will not be going anywhere near Both." Zephyr cut her off, his words striking like a hammer.

Tanwen blinked as the group grew tense. Lyra placed another calming hand to his shoulder.

"I apologize," she said. "My brother only worries over my safety."

"Of course," replied Tanwen. "I should never have assumed your involvement."

"It's all right." She offered a slight smile, easing the friction in the air.

"We need to back up a step," said Brynn. "You're plotting as if we are already at the southern cliffs of Cādra. But you forget it will take an age to get there from here. And that's if we don't get picked up by some swarming kidet vultures along the way. If we *do* reach the coast, how do the rest of us get onto Both? We can't only have Volari represent us. No offense." She nodded toward Azla and Zephyr.

"None taken," said Azla.

"Some taken," added Zephyr, arms crossed.

Brynn pursed her lips at him before looking back at Tanwen. "We still have no real way of reaching Both together. Let alone getting any prisoners off."

"By my mother's tears." Ridi huffed his exasperation. "Do all mortals lack such imagination? Children, observe who sits among you." He gestured to himself and Bosyg. "You may not have the full pantheon of our siblings, but you have us. Or perhaps, most importantly, you have *me*." His grin was the sharp tip of a blade. "I can get you to Both. And in a way that's not so laborious."

The silence in the clearing was deafening.

"You can?" Brynn's expression was uncertain—or perhaps it was distrusting.

For distrust was certainly what Tanwen felt. She knew all too well the danger of accepting help from an immortal.

"Of course I can," he replied rather mulishly. "I'm a *god*." As if to prove his point, he waved a hand, and a portal tore open behind him. In the middle of the sun-soaked forest now hung a window into a misty gray landscape—bleak and foreign. Only two indistinct steps beyond the threshold could be seen before the fog swallowed everything.

Gasps rippled through the group.

Tanwen's pulse quickened as she stared at what she knew was Both Island.

Then, in a blink, the portal snapped shut, the barren vista vanishing as though it had never been.

"*By the moons*," breathed Zephyr.

"Wow," murmured Brynn.

"I am, aren't I?" Ridi smiled smugly as he studied his nails.

"Divine One." Aisling spoke up beside Tanwen. "We are most grateful for such kindness, but I must ask—what do you require in return?"

Tanwen's chest tightened at the question, knowing exactly why her mother asked it. Aisling was one of the few here who understood the danger in accepting a god's help.

"Can I not grant my benevolence freely?" Ridi answered, a flicker of offense in his tone.

When no one spoke, only waited, he huffed a laugh.

"It seems you mortals are not so foolish, after all. I require little for my aid—only that you succeed. Release those held prisoner on Both." His wide grin flashed like sun reflecting on glass. "Nothing delights me more than freeing what others would contain."

Chaos, thought Tanwen. *Mischief.*

A gift to the god himself.

The council seemed to shift uneasily at his words.

But Tanwen seized the silence, unwilling to squander such a rare opportunity. Whether it was because she already owed one god—or in spite of it—she cast her caution to the wind and dared to risk a debt to another.

"With this portal access, we can get in and out quickly if needed," she said. "We can find whoever has survived there and talk to them. They may even believe we are prisoners at first, giving us time to plead our case."

"It's risky," replied her father.

"Isn't everything we are doing a risk?" she shot back. "Wasn't your love a risk?" She held his gaze, ire and determination rising in her chest. "Did that stop you and mother from loving? From starting a family? Having me and Thol and hiding us for over twenty years. All of us live with risk every single day we stay alive—and we endure it because we *deserve* to live. To *be* alive.

"Just like those banished to Both deserve their freedom," she continued. "Most of them were sent there for the same crimes as you and mother—for love, for sympathy, for daring to fight back against a tyrant. They were part of this Rebellion before it even had a name. They deserve to fight alongside us. This is our leverage," she declared, turning to the council. "An island of souls as discarded as we were—as angry, as ready to rise. Let us welcome them into our fold. Let us free them, as we ourselves wish to be free."

A beat of silence followed, broken only by the wind in the canopy and the faint call of birds—until the council erupted, rising to their feet with cheers. Several stepped forward to clasp her shoulders, offering their support and praise.

For a moment, elation swept through Tanwen, filling her chest—until her gaze caught on her parents, still seated across from each other, locked in a quiet stare. There was an ache in their expressions she couldn't quite decipher, but before she could dwell on it, Brynn wrapped her in a crushing hug.

"Who knew you had such a riveting speech in you?" Brynn set her back down with a wide grin. "Careful, or we might have you doing all the talking when we get to Both."

"So . . . we're going?" Tanwen asked, needing to hear it.

"Of course we're going," Brynn replied, her eyes bright with excitement. "Like you said—an island of souls with decades of vengeance built up against the Volari Crown. I doubt they'll need much convincing to join us."

The word *crown* snagged on her thoughts, and instantly they tumbled to Zolya.

Unease lashed through her chest.

When she pictured the enemy, it was always King Réol—the old guard, the suffocating traditions that held Cādra captive. The ones that had to be defeated. But she couldn't forget Zolya was tied to all of it, would feel the weight of this blow.

To everyone here, he stood a figure of the opposition.

But she knew the truth—that he wanted to help them. Believed in the Rebellion's cause.

And it broke her to wonder, to worry: When would the day come—if it ever would—when they could stand together in the open, fighting for the same cause?

"How marvelous this all is!" Ridi clapped from his floating perch, snapping Tanwen's attention back to the clearing, to where the council had begun to calm, reclaiming seats. "Your tiny minds finally see. Those on Both are no doubt filled with fury, overflowing with rage, boiling with the need for justice. Right, Sister?"

"Mm, yes, Brother," Bosyg replied evenly. "By now they are probably more than deserving of the name the old kings bestowed upon them."

Tanwen hesitated before asking, "What name is that?"

The goddess of the forest turned to her, unleashing a gaze so dark and depthless it felt like it reached through flesh and bone, straight to her marrow.

"Monsters."

8

Zolya was drowning in dread.

As he stood by the foot of his father's bed, he watched a meddyg—sent by the High Gods—hover over the king's unconscious form.

The healer's identity was hidden beneath a gold mask and white hooded cloak, gloved hands poking at seemingly random points on the king. Despite their disguise, their otherworldly power was palpable.

At any moment, Zolya imagined his father bursting upright, his ire-filled gaze hooking on him, and—finding the mess his kingdom was suffering under his son's rule—unleashing his full wrath.

Zolya clenched his hands behind his back, forcing composure as his magic kicked and scratched with his fluttering nerves, his wings ready for flight.

Across from the meddyg, Queen Habelle remained stoically silent by her husband's bedside, a painting of a loyal spouse.

She had kept quiet after announcing their visitor as they flew swiftly to the king's chambers. But Zolya sensed the tension in his mother's shoulders, knew the displeasure and deep-seated ire she must be feeling.

For a breath the queen had reclaimed her palace, her son, and her safety. But, once the king woke, it was to be torn from her grasp, again.

The meddyg stepped away from the king's bed, their emotionless mask turning to Zolya's mother.

"I ask you to dismiss your guards, Your Majesty," they rasped, a thousand layers of voices that sent chills down Zolya's spine.

Alongside the twelve High Gods, countless lesser immortals resided in the Kaiwi River, their numbers as uncountable as the stars. What mattered was knowing they were there to serve their deities, much like the Volari.

With the meddyg's request, Queen Habelle inclined her head to the soldiers patterned around the room.

Obediently, they left.

Only Osko remained, a step behind Zolya.

The meddyg angled their attention to the kidar.

"Pardon," said Osko, "I feel it prudent I remain with the royal family."

"Your loyalty is admirable, Kidar Terz," replied the healer, "and will be recounted to our almighty Ré, but you will leave and return to your barracks." A dizzying weight became laced in their words, a command robbing one of free will.

Osko turned on his heels and strode out the door.

Zolya momentarily met his mother's gaze, a new wariness seeping across his skin.

"Do you believe you can heal him?" she asked, her tone impassive, careful.

"The poison holds strong to his blood," said the meddyg. "Especially his heart. But whether I can heal him lies in whether you want him healed." In a sweeping flourish, they cast aside their golden mask and let their white hooded cloak fall.

Darkness poured into the room. Ancient magic surged in a terrifying wave of constellations, wind, and moonlight.

Zolya fell to his knees, his heartbeat a booming drum against his rib cage as a face sculpted from shadows and starlight revealed Nocémi, goddess of night.

She was a collection of midnights, dusks, and dawns. Her eyes glowed a soft silver, like the moons reflecting on still water. Her hair flowed in waves of inky black, streaked with shades of violet and indigo, as if the cosmos itself had woven its colors into her strands. Her wings were dark clouds of smoke as the air around her hummed with a quiet mix of slumber and dreams. The rest of her was swallowed in the ever-shifting expanse of night, a pooling skirt at her feet worshipping its queen.

Zolya's eyes stung with a punishing throb the longer he stared, but it was nearly impossible to look away. Nocémi was agonizing in her serene beauty.

"Our divine mistress," breathed Queen Habelle from where she knelt, head bowed in deep respect.

"You must wonder why it is I before you and not my husband," said Nocémi, her voice as gentle as a silk blanket, "given he hasn't yet visited his beloved king."

Zolya and his mother remained quiet, despite the topic being one that plagued both their minds.

Nearly every High God had arrived to pay their respects. Well, all except Orzel—for good reason. He continued to thrash within his seas, still outraged by his runaway bride.

"Know that it is I who has stopped him," continued Nocémi. "My husband has been naughty, as he has proclivities to be—more than once his rays have wandered to borders other than my night, and the strife he has set into motion among our children has gone on for too long. I warned him against allowing life to enter your sister's womb." Flashes of silver gazed at the queen, whose complexion paled at her words. "My husband has a disturbed sense of entertainment, but once his mind is set on a thing, it comes to be."

Zolya's knee dug into the plush carpet, a coil of ice and fire turning over in his gut as disbelief fed his rising volcano of anger.

The queen's sister, Lady Callia—mother to Azla, whose birth had torn his family apart. His mother had permanently secluded herself on her isle, his aunt had been sentenced to death on Both Island, and a young princess had been thrust into Zolya's lonely care—all because a god had sought a moment of amusement.

Zolya barely heard the goddess's next words, his magic roaring through his veins with his turmoil.

"Though I am well aware of his nature," Nocémi continued, "I have grown weary of his reckless whims, as I often do—and he knows this. As the father of light, Ré does not thrive long without reverent attention, especially from his wife. Every few centuries, he seeks atonement, and I have chosen now to entertain his plea. Which brings me to my purpose here today—I have expressed what I desire for him to earn my forgiveness."

The goddess let the silence in the room spread, as if enjoying her own spun drama.

"And what is the desire of our Ruler of Night?" asked Queen Habelle.

"King Réol's death."

With Nocémi's proclamation, Zolya watched his mother become granite.

In contrast, Zolya's shock rippled like cracks of lightning down his spine.

"And why would you desire this, blessed Nocémi?" His mother was a marvel for how steady she kept her voice.

Though Nocémi didn't smile, Zolya could sense the goddess's pleasure permeating the air. "Because he is my husband's favorite."

Games.

More games.

Zolya swallowed the outrage funneling up his throat.

They were nothing but playthings for the gods they worshipped, would continue to worship.

"A loss I know neither of you will mourn," added Nocémi, addressing them both. *Your secrets are not so secret,* her omniscient gaze accused, though without judgment. As if the goddess understood their own mortal strategies and accepted them.

A panic seized him with this realization—that the goddess of night knew what was in his heart regarding both his father and Tanwen.

Though his fear was mostly felt when thinking of Tanwen.

It was under Nocémi's night that they often met, cloaked in her darkness, hidden from the world.

The goddess knew of their relationship and yet had done nothing to stop them.

Yet.

His focus shifted when a sudden glint caught his eye.

Nocémi pulled forth a glimmering black blade. From where, he could not say.

It was merely suddenly there.

"You may stand," she instructed, holding the dagger in her grip.

Zolya's legs felt stiff and shaky as he drew himself up, attention remaining trained on the knife.

His pulse was a murderous flapping of wings.

Nocémi floated back to the king's bedside and reached out a gloveless finger. She barely grazed King Réol's forehead before he gasped awake.

Zolya took a defensive step back, burying his own shocked breath as his magic surged to cover his skin, becoming his armor.

But his father did not sit up. He remained lying, eyes open and clear as his chest rose and fell with labored breath, as if he had just finished a long flight.

His gaze wildly flitted about the room, snagging on his wife before Nocémi, terror a quick flash in his features. But then, too soon, he slipped into his familiar rage. He strained to move, yell, let out his power, but he could do none of it.

"Réol can feel," explained Nocémi as she apathetically watched the struggling king. "But he cannot hurt. He is quite contained."

Despite himself, Zolya felt a disturbing wash of pity for his father then.

Such a powerful, imposing man reduced to this.

But then he thought of the years of cruelty the king had inflicted—the abuse of power leveled at him from such a young age, at his mother and sister, the fear he instilled in anyone who dared step out of line, who dared threaten his perfect, polished reign. He thought of the countless lives crushed under that rule, the scars left behind.

And just like that, his pity curdled, vanishing.

All he felt now was cold.

"The blade will leave no trace," said Nocémi. "He will appear to have merely slipped into the Eternal River as he slept. I will ensure that is what is believed. He could not be saved, not even by a holy meddyg. His time was up." She held the knife out, an offering to either Zolya or the queen.

A decision to be made.

As he stared at the dagger, sudden nausea rolled through his gut, a cloying claustrophobia.

He knew what needed to be done, and yet . . . to do it like this . . . with his father unable to defend.

It felt wrong.

Dishonorable.

Yet the cruel taunts hurled at him since boyhood still hissed in his ear.

You are weak!

Soft hearted.

You do not have what it takes to be king.

Still, to take his life while he lay helpless felt like proving his father's words true.

Was this how a mighty monarch—tyrant or not—would be slain? How he, Zolya, would become king? How he would take the throne from his father?

It would have been with poison. A cold voice entered his mind. *And you accepted such an outcome then.*

Self-loathing dripped down Zolya's throat, sour and biting.

He now realized, perhaps part of his anger toward Tanwen's secret was that he felt ashamed. Ashamed that she had acted, Azla had acted, as well as Lady Esme, to get what they needed—what was necessary. And all Zolya had done was step aside. They had swallowed fear and pride and honor to do what so many could not. What he could not.

But he was no longer playing the same game he had been months ago, no longer trapped in that same uncertain role.

He now stood beside a god, who offered a blade.

Offered a path forward. A way out.

And Zolya understood how much better their world would be without Réol in it.

Time stilled as he studied his father from the foot of his bed, the room falling away.

Though the king had been trapped in unconsciousness for months, he still radiated power—his muscles remained strong, his appearance flawlessly maintained by his attendants' daily care.

He thought of his father surviving today, regaining his full faculties, and how he and his mother, and likely half of Galia, would suffer brutal punishment. Retribution for the uprisings would sweep across Cādra—a merciless purge of Süra and Mütra, leaving famine, despair, and scorched hope in its wake. Zolya would lose any chance of seeing Tanwen again. The dream of her safety and freedom in this world would be stricken.

That thought alone ignited a surge of resolve, propelling him forward. Propelling him to act.

His father had served his tenure, and this was where he had brought them. Their world needed a new generation to lead.

Zolya reached for the dark blade, but a hand gripped his forearm, stopping him.

He frowned at his mother, who now half knelt on the bed, leaning over to hold him back.

"I was unable to be there for much of your life," she said, her gaze a mix of remorse and burning determination. "I will be here for this."

Before Zolya could reply, she took the knife from Nocémi and moved to her husband's side. Her face was like stone, jaw clenched as she met King Réol's burning gaze.

He let out a furious gargle, eyes flitting between her and the blade, but she ignored him. "For me," she said, her voice rough with conviction. "And for our son. *Long live the king.*"

Zolya then watched his mother slit his father's throat.

PART II

Rise

9

The bells on Galia rang out in celebration, the day as bright as sun-struck gold.

Within the soaring marble throne room, a sea of observers filled the blinding-white hall. The scent of jasmine and honey wove through the crowd as a hum of anticipation reverberated through the air.

Though arguably, none of the guests were as eager as Queen Habelle.

Her husband was dead, and today was her son's coronation.

Yet from her position at the base of the towering throne's stairs, her expression beneath her mourning veil was as tranquil as a placid lake.

A portrait of patience.

Habelle could feel the scrutiny at her back, the curiosity hovering by her shoulder, and the unwavering attention of her ladies-in-waiting at her side.

All were watching.

Wondering.

Desperate to cast their judgment.

But Habelle had survived at court for more than two centuries for a reason.

Had outlived her tyrannical husband not because of luck.

Habelle was a woman born with a serpent's mind. She was clever.

And cleverer still by hiding it.

Or perhaps more accurately, knowing when to reveal it.

For her brilliance lay in timing.

She knew precisely when to laugh or cry, to be silent or speak, to be seen or to disappear. And when, most importantly, to take up a god-gifted blade and cut her husband's throat.

Habelle flexed her hands where she held them piously in front of her.

She could still feel the cool kiss of the obsidian handle, taste the metallic sting in the air from Nocémi's deathly magic seeping from the knife.

As she had watched Réol die, she had waited to feel guilt or remorse or a pinch of sorrow.

Instead, she had stood transfixed, awestruck as her husband's features morphed from fury to panic to slack-jawed, his gaze going glassy.

Blank.

Gone.

Dead.

Her husband was mortal after all.

And Maryth now claimed him as she would claim them all.

No longer did Habelle need to fear his touch.

Endure his twisted cruelty.

But most imperatively, never again would he torment *her* child.

Bring bruises to her son's flesh and cuts to both their hearts.

Habelle had nearly wept in her tidal wave of relief as she stared at Réol's lifeless body.

Their marriage had been far from a love match, merely a trade of power from her parents—one that had put Habelle in a position of weakness. And then further so when she became with child. For Réol may have once owned her flesh, but he now possessed a piece of her soul.

But despite the century of pent-up agony that was ready to be set free with her husband's death, she had not allowed herself to cry.

Not then.

That was saved for when she was in front of the Royal Council the following day as a grieving, inconsolable widow, imploring for a hasty coronation for her son. It would not do to wait, after all, given the unsteady state of their kingdom, their world.

It might have taken centuries for Habelle to get to where she stood that morning, to enact her vengeance against her husband and ensure her son's rise to power, but every step, every decision and sacrifice, had been deliberate, purposeful, planned. Nocémi was not the only one who held the patience to triumph.

As the murmurs in the hall silenced, Habelle refocused on her surroundings.

A choir began to sing from the rafters. Their ethereal harmonies wove through the stone pillars, lighting the air with a sense of hope and peace.

The crowd shifted, gazes drawn up to a skylight directly above the throne.

A figure descended within the beam of light.

Habelle's magic coursed through her veins with anticipation, darting and dancing like rain skittering off a marble roof. Her breath held as her pride swelled.

Zolya.

Her son.

Her heart.

Her whole life.

He touched down on the throne, his massive alabaster wings remaining unfurled, their gilded tips catching Ré's light.

Clad in white-and-gold armor, he gleamed of regal brilliance. His hair was polished perfection at his shoulders, his light-brown skin seeming to glow from within. His expression was severe, unreadable, but his azure eyes held confidence, determination as he looked out at the crowd.

Habelle's throat tightened, a tempest of emotion roaring within her—elation, awe, adoration, and unrestrained joy.

Yet, still, she kept her expression neutral.

Not yet. Not yet. Her heart thumped.

Habelle waited and watched as Zolya's crown was brought forth.

The gold circlet met her son's brow, and as it did, those in the throne room collapsed to their knees.

"Long live the king," came the chant, a thunderous wave of reverence. "Long live the king."

Above them, Ré's light ignited in a blinding burst, cascading through the dome in a celestial acknowledgment—a blessing, a declaration.

I approve, the gesture announced.

From beneath her mourning veil, Habelle allowed her lips to curve into a slow, triumphant smile. A single tear tracked down her cheek.

Happy.

She was deliriously happy.

At last, it was their time.

10

Tanwen realized—quite too late—that their plan had gaping flaws.

As she ran for her life, heart pounding and lungs burning, she nearly slipped on the wet, cold ground.

Both Island was, in a word, terrible.

"We should turn back!" she yelled to their fleeing group.

"The portal door won't be there," huffed her father, who kept pace at her side. "Ridi said it won't reopen until tomorrow when the sun dips to midday."

"What sun?" shouted Tanwen as they skirted a large boulder, pushing farther into the foggy landscape. Everything on this island was gray, layered in a cold dampness or frozen solid. A terrain of rocks and dead trees and charcoaled grass. The sky a solid white nothing.

Before they had arrived here, she had been grateful to the Low God, the ease with which Ridi had offered his help to bring them to Both. To this island, which sat in a barren scrape of violent sea, impossible to reach by boat and nearly impossible to see by sky.

But now she understood, his delight came not just from the chaos of freeing the prisoners but also from knowing he was dropping Tanwen and her group straight into a death trap.

Lesson learned: Never trust the god of mischief again.

"Duck!" yelled Brynn, who raced at Tanwen's heels.

An arrow whizzed between Tanwen and her father.

"Azla!" shouted Tanwen to where the princess flew above their group. "That was rather close!"

"Oh, I do apologize," Azla grunted while she pushed gale after gale at the onslaught of arrows soaring forward. She sent the recent barrage barreling in different directions. "Why don't we trade places and see if you can do better."

Tanwen ignored her friend's curt tone as she called to where Zephyr flew ahead of the group. "Zephyr, can you not help her?" He was doing his best to guide them through the misty terrain from an aerial view.

"I fear my rain will do little to help this already-drenched situation," he declared before he nearly collided with a low-hanging rock face that appeared in the fog. "We need to find somewhere to disappear and regroup!"

Tanwen sucked in air as they sped forward, her leg muscles screaming. Zephyr was right—if she was tiring, she couldn't imagine how her father was faring.

She furtively glanced to where Gabreel sprinted at her side, his complexion flushed, sweat covering his . . . everything.

The five of them had hardly set foot on Both when they had been attacked.

Their assailants had stayed hidden in the mist or behind blackened tree trunks, revealing themselves only through arrows and hurled axes.

Tanwen hadn't expected a warm welcome, but she certainly hadn't anticipated quite such an instant threat on their lives.

How naive.

"We need to . . . find . . . a cave," her father panted. "Or split . . . up. We are . . . easy marks as a . . . group."

Split up?

Not a chance.

Tanwen was about to voice such an opinion when a massive shadow suddenly loomed ahead. A boulder that was moving . . . no, running—*forward*?

"What in all of Cādra?" Zephyr cursed, angling to fly around it. But then a massive hand snapped out, closing around him in a tight grip.

"Dear Gods." Tanwen skidded to a halt, Brynn slamming into her back with a muffled grunt.

"What—?" Brynn's words died as her wide eyes traced the hulking figure up and up and up. The pounding of its heavy feet shook the ground, making Tanwen's teeth rattle.

Azla landed at their backs, ushering the group into a tight huddle as the creature came into focus.

"Giant," Brynn whispered, her voice trembling between awe and terror.

"No," Gabreel muttered grimly, staring up at the single glaring eye fixed on them. "Cyclops."

11

Tanwen had entered a storybook of nightmares.

Or perhaps it was wonder . . .?

Wonderful nightmares.

As she and her friends marched toward what was likely their doom, Tanwen could barely scrape her slack jaw from the floor.

As they traveled through the stale air of a dimly lit cavern, they were surrounded by hordes of fierce creatures only spoken of in myth or never spoken about at all.

Satyrs, half goat and half person, scowled with pinched brows, rugged daggers strapped to furry hips. Minotaurs loomed, massively foreboding, their glowing red eyes glaring as warm huffs billowed from their nostrils in the cold. Women and men with serpentine lower halves twisted forward, their beauty as sharp as a viper's strike. Hawk-headed beings craned their bloodstained beaks toward Tanwen and her group, their predatory stares chilling. The cyclops who had captured them had revealed three more of its kind, but these all had been forced to remain outside the cavern, too large for even these towering ceilings.

And then there were the centaurs—no one could forget the centaurs—who now drove Tanwen and her friends onward, marching at their backs. Half person, half horse, they had been their unseen attackers and who Tanwen presumed were Both Island's soldiers, from how well equipped they were with crudely constructed bows, axes, and blades.

In a fleeting glance, Tanwen took in those more familiar within the crowd—broken-winged Volari and Süra with chipped horns. Their faces were gaunt, expressionless, scarred. Survivors of their banishment much like the others here, but her gaze became consumed by the new marvel of creatures.

No one spoke, but a palpable hum filled the air, heavy with distrust, hunger, and a simmering fury.

Ridi and Bosyg had told the truth.

This island appeared teeming with souls overtaken by vengeance, their hearts growing frozen from the endless, unyielding chill of their banishment.

Tanwen should have been terrified.

Should have been shaking in fear.

At the very least, she should have been plotting their escape, but instead she was having the very ill-timed and inappropriate desire to share this Both Island discovery with Zolya.

What would he say? How would he react to such a revelation? Did he *know*, like the Low Gods knew, that these unique souls were trapped here?

Small movements within the crowd redrew her attention. At first, Tanwen wasn't quite sure what she was looking at, but when the reality seeped in, her stomach curdled.

Children.

Dozens, now poking curious heads from beyond protective caregivers' hips. Bundles strapped to others were now recognized as babes.

A cold rage filled Tanwen's chest.

A sour, bitter bite to her tongue to think of innocents birthed into this prison, raised to believe they were unworthy of anything beyond this cold, dead landscape. Those who had quite possibly never seen the sun, felt warmth, or smelled the sweet fragrance of a forest alive, flowers in bloom.

Tanwen swallowed her rising emotions. This all held echoes of her own upbringing. Raised to believe that what she was was not welcome on Cādra. But she at least had experienced the gift of seasons, witnessed the variety of beauty found on the continent.

Monsters, Bosyg had said.

But monsters were not born; they were created.

And here were King Réol's creations.

And just as with Mütra, Tanwen held a strong thirst to set them free.

Not merely because of what leverage it could bring to the Rebellion to have this group on their side but because no one, especially innocent children, should be so imprisoned.

Tanwen made a vow then: She *would* free them, no matter the cost.

That was, of course, unless she and her group were first killed here.

"Lord Heiro!" A man stumbled into their path, clutching at Tanwen's father. His copper hair glinted in the dim light, his pale face frantic. Behind him, a single black wing remained, its twin torn away. "You are here," he muttered, trembling. "I *tried.* I tried to be as you, but I failed, *failed.* How did you do it? *You must tell me.*"

Gabreel attempted to detangle himself, Tanwen coming to help, but the man's grip was like shackles—unyielding.

"Get back!" ordered a centaur as he galloped over, then he yanked the man away and shoved him back into the crowd. "Any more outbursts, and it's the pit for you," the soldier warned, before forcing Tanwen's group to keep moving.

"Who was that?" Tanwen whispered, her pulse still racing.

"My successor," Gabreel replied, his face ashen. "André Bardrex."

Tanwen glanced back, uneasy.

The man was gone, only faint sobs trailing behind. Her thoughts churned, unsettled by the revelation that so many exiles here were still alive—and not dead, as the world believed. She didn't know which was a worse fate, to survive one's torture only to live the rest of one's days in this purgatory or have the reprieve of entering Maryth's Eternal River.

"Stay close," said her father, his brow furrowed as an ominous orange glow seeped through a large doorway ahead.

Despite the looming danger, a welcome warmth brushed Tanwen's frostbitten cheeks, tempting her forward.

As she crossed the threshold, a wave of heat struck her along with a sudden flood of light, causing her to squint. On a shaky inhale, she breathed in the rich scent of cedar and spice as a cavernous throne room of jagged black rock stretched out.

And there could be no denying it was a throne room.

Its countless flaming orbs cast flickering shadows against towering pillars. Blazing bowls lined the polished pathway, all leading to the centerpiece: a colossal black stone throne. Seated upon it was a striking woman, her amber wings and dark hair a stark contrast to her pale skin. A deep scar ran from her cheek down her exposed neck, lending her beauty a battle-hardened edge. Her crudely carved crown matched her unyielding gaze, sharp and commanding.

But what truly was a marvel was what sat within her diadem—the largest uncut ambrü Tanwen had ever seen.

Despite its rawness, its red was as bright as freshly spilled blood.

Tanwen's thoughts spun. Where would this woman obtain such a precious stone in a place as barren and gray as Both?

But the answers would have to wait, as those who had watched their procession now crowded into the great hall, Tanwen and her group stopping at the base of the throne.

"Kneel before our Governess," ordered the rough voice of a centaur at their backs.

Obediently, they knelt.

And waited.

And waited.

And waited.

Until it felt as though Tanwen's kneecaps would split in two from the mercilessly hard floor.

"I have been told," began the Governess, her voice strong, clear, "that you have come to my island not by the usual way of a floating cage, but by a portal door."

My island.

Tanwen once again found herself in a mix of awe, curiosity, and terror. Here sat a woman, a *Volari* woman at that, who ruled over this prison.

Both Island was proving more and more astonishing by the star fall.

"Such magic is held exclusively by the gods," she continued. "Which is most peculiar, given no god, High or Low, has ever been interested in Both, let alone in dropping new banished souls in lieu of Réol's lackeys."

She said King Réol's name with a decisive sneer.

"Who are you, and why have you come here?" The hall echoed with her question, one whose answer clearly would decide their fate.

Tanwen bit her lower lip, nerves a tornado in her gut, not knowing who among them should speak.

But then her father shifted at her side. "Lady . . . Callia?" he asked with obvious astonishment. "Is that you?"

Lady Callia.

At the name, Tanwen's heartbeats froze, her gaze whipping to Azla, who knelt in front of her.

The princess's wings flinched, her eyes growing wide as they locked onto the woman.

Oh gods, thought Tanwen.

"Lady Callia died the day she was dropped here," said the Governess, stare narrowed as she studied Tanwen's father. "Who are you to think otherwise?"

"I am Gabreel Heiro," he explained. "Once the royal inventor for King Réol."

"Gabreel Heiro." The Governess repeated the name as if chewing on a candy long since enjoyed as a child, a nostalgic hum. "Yes . . . I remember you." Her eyes then slid to the empty air at Gabreel's back. Where his wings should have been. "Much appears to have happened since we last met, Heiro. You are like one of us now." She waved a hand to her mass of subjects. "Fallen from the favor of the almighty, blessed, king of Galia." Her lip curled with her obvious disdain for the man. "Not a difficult task, of course."

"Yes," Gabreel replied. "I no longer serve King Réol. Which is what has brought us here—"

"Are you truly Lady Callia?" Azla's abrupt question pierced through the throne room.

The Governess's stare fell to the princess, curiosity lighting her gaze. "And who may you be?"

Tanwen dared not breathe, think, move as Azla drew her chin up, a steel to her voice as she answered, "Your daughter."

12

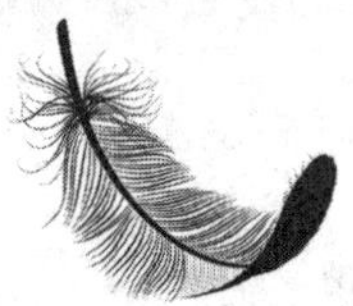

Zolya managed all of five blissful breaths alone in his study before his mother stormed in, shattering the tranquility like a rock smashing through glass.

"Well, you've had an eventful morning," said the queen dowager—her new designation now that he was king. "Perhaps unmatched in history, the number of century-old allies made foes by a new monarch in a single day."

Zolya glanced to his usher, who was stationed by the open door, clearly terror stricken to have let someone pass without Zolya's permission. The queen dowager's entourage hesitated beside him at the threshold.

"Leave us," Zolya commanded.

The group was gone in an instant, his usher emphatically shoving everyone back before shutting the door with a gentle click.

As king, Zolya was quickly growing accustomed to such unquestioned obedience.

Unless, of course, it involved the queen dowager.

"Hello, Mother," he said, shutting the ledger he had been studying. "You're looking lovely per usual."

"Do not change the subject," she curtly replied as she moved to stand on the other side of his desk. Sunlight streamed in through his office's open veranda, lighting her auburn wings. "Why did you not tell me what you were planning with the council?"

"I thought you'd be pleased to be one of the first women to ever occupy a Royal Council position?"

"*Pleased* is an immense oversimplification of what I am."

"So you wish to step down from the position?"

"Don't be daft, Zolya. Of course I want to sit on your council, but that does not eradicate the issue of myself, a lady, replacing a *lord's* seat. I applaud the progressiveness, but you really should have discussed this with me first."

"First, you are a queen, which title will forever be superior to a lord. Second, some actions have little time for shared planning." He eyed her pointedly. "Like when you neglected to seek my thoughts before going before father's Royal Council and pleading for my hasty coronation."

The queen dowager's lips thinned, as if the taste of her exposed hypocrisy was too bitter to swallow. "It was a necessity to have your coronation be in haste," she reasoned.

"But before Father's time of mourning had officially ended?" Zolya asked with raised brows. "Talk about creating foes at court, Mother."

She waved an unconcerned hand. "*I'm* the one who must wear these drab mourning clothes for half the year, not them. As for your coronation, given the escalations throughout Cādra, the Royal Council barely hesitated with my request. But then you went and immediately dismissed them!"

"It is no secret half of those men were no supporters of mine," Zolya replied darkly. "As you've stated, given the escalations throughout Cādra, it was necessary to make changes to those on my council. It is common practice for a new king to instate a fresh regime of councillors."

"Certainly, but to replace nearly *every* seat—and one with a woman. Coups have transpired from lesser transgressions."

"I have been king for no more than two days, and you've already brought up a coup? Even for you, Mother, that's impressive."

"Zolya," she huffed in irritation. "That's precisely *why* I am bringing it up. You have just acquired the throne. There are nuances and strategies that need to be considered when wishing for great change. Your father had been indisposed for months, which paved the way for your immediate coronation. Galia needed an *acting* king, and the council understood this. Half my ladies-in-waiting are daughters of the men you terminated today. Did you not think how this would affect me? How I now must decide what's to be done with them. It will only incite their families further if their daughters fall from my side, but to keep them will only make them spies. Every action has a reaction, Zolya."

He clenched his teeth, hating that he saw the validity of her argument.

It brought forth insecurities carved in him from his father's constant doubt of Zolya's abilities to be a ruler.

"I apologize for the troubles this may cause you," he said, wings tense at his back. "I merely have much I wish to do, have *waited* to do once king. With the treasury only growing weaker, Cādra a breath away from war, and our court's verbose unease, I cannot sit idly by for long. Father did not exactly leave a legacy of stability for me to inherit."

The queen dowager's gaze softened. "Yes," she said. "You have quite the mess to clean. But remember, you do not need to do it alone. Come—" She inclined her head toward the lounges on the other side of his study. "So much has happened, I forgot we haven't had a chance to properly talk. Sit with me."

Zolya unwillingly followed and sat, his wings feeling like a mountain of weight on his back. When was the last time he'd slept?

"How are you, my child?" his mother finally asked, hazel gaze assessing. "Truthfully."

Zolya let out a long exhale, alleviating some of the tension in his chest. "I am tired," he admitted. "But . . . also excited, and worried and . . . hopeful."

He braced himself—such a confession would have been met with a smack from his father, verbally or physically. *Hope is for dreamers and nitwits,* King Réol would say. *Not rulers. Not kings.*

But his father was no longer here. And his mother was nothing like him.

"That is why you will be a great king," she said.

Zolya blinked, momentarily speechless.

That is why you will be a great king.

His mother had never made such a declaration.

Zolya knew she believed in his abilities, of course—valued his mind—but never had she so clearly stated her thoughts on his future reign.

Perhaps she had feared, like he had, that the day might never come.

But here it was—Zolya king, sitting in his father's old study.

It still felt like a farce, for Ré to bless Zolya's ascension after Nocémi's visit. After he had been prepared to take a blade to his father before his mother had stepped in.

Though neither had spoken of that day, Zolya understood his mother's actions were her way of atoning—not just for herself, but for him. A mother finally banishing the monster that haunted her child's dreams.

Despite those transgressions, Zolya had felt Ré's kiss to his forehead during his coronation—a press of a flame before a potent thread of the sun god's power had seeped into his skin.

Zolya had been overtaken with euphoria, the chill of strength pumping into his veins to weave with his own magic.

The sensation still lingered, like a sleeping beast, and Zolya finally understood a piece of his father. The raw energy of a High God coursing through his veins was a dangerous temptation—a superiority that demanded constant control.

Fortunately—or unfortunately—Zolya's life had been a daily lesson in restraint.

"Thank you, Mother," he said. "Your belief in me means more than you know."

"I have always believed in you, my son." Her brows drew in with concern. "But I hope you also believe in yourself."

Zolya swallowed past his rising emotion. "I do. Though, it would help if my mother stopped questioning my decisions."

She surprised him by laughing, a light fluttering that eased the seriousness of their moment. "Well said, my king, well said. You are right. I shall do as you say and believe you have a plan."

"I do."

Her gaze turned pensive. "Even with your new council in place, and my position on it, I hope you know you can always rely on me—privately—for what is on your mind, as you have in the past. You'll find I'm still a safe place to confide in, Zolya. The Royal Council may advise you, but trusting them with your true thoughts, well . . . that's another matter entirely."

Zolya nodded. He understood her meaning.

Trust was a precarious business for a royal.

Which was perhaps why Tanwen's omission had hurt as badly as it had. She was one of the very few who he felt he *could* trust.

After all, he could hardly confide in his oldest friend about his radical beliefs, let alone what was in his heart. But neither could he share Tanwen with his mother.

The queen dowager might be a Süra sympathizer and disagree with the outlawing of Mütra, but there would always be certain standards her son—her king—must live up to. If he ever were to marry, it would be to a Volari.

Zolya shifted in his seat, his mood darkening at the thought.

Absently, his gaze slid to his veranda.

Tanwen and he hadn't been in communication since the night at the logging site.

Since he left in a rage.

Left her standing there, face pinched in anguish and remorse.

The memory brought further pain lashing against his chest.

He had hated to leave her like that but also had known he would not be able to work through all he felt in that moment.

He had needed time.

And time, it appeared, she was giving him.

He was used to her messenger birds arriving weekly, allowing for their constant correspondence.

But none had come.

And there was no way of reaching her without them.

A pulse of longing went through him, hot and cold at once.

Even when upset with her, he still missed her terribly.

Had she heard the news of his father's death? That he was now king? What must she be thinking, feeling? Had she made it back to Drygul safely?

His wings twitched, his magic jumping through his veins with his impatience to seek her out, to—

"I fear you have something weighing on you now, my child." His mother's voice had him blinking back to the room.

He refocused on the queen dowager, who now eyed the churning storm cloud overhead.

"My apologies," said Zolya, steadying his breath and dispelling his swirling thoughts along with what his magic had created.

That was something he'd need to work on. His amplified powers now slipped from his grasp with every surge of emotion.

"Is everything all right?" she asked.

"A complicated question to answer," he replied.

"You know my meaning." She arched a brow. "Is there anything *I* can help you with?"

He pressed his lips together in thought. "There is one particular subject."

She waited while Zolya hesitated.

"I am not King Réol," he said.

The queen dowager huffed a laugh. "And thank the High and *Low* Gods that you are not."

"An opinion not all of our people share," he replied darkly. "I know how Father would have dealt with the Rebellion. How our court and people expect me to deal with them: like we have dealt with every uprising over the centuries."

"But you do not wish to repeat history," she finished.

He shook his head. "With the state of our treasury, we can hardly afford a ball, let alone a war. But it's not merely that . . ." He stopped, hesitating once more.

"Yes?"

"I do not believe in the segregation of our races," he forced himself to admit. "I believe in the integration of them. And I believe in the Unified Labor Law Compensation Act and the Mütra Integration Act that were proposed during the recent peace meetings."

The queen dowager's expression grew unreadable in the following silence, a quiet that stretched for an awkwardly long beat.

"By the stars, Mother, do say something."

But she did not.

Instead, she drew him into a hug.

Zolya remained rigid, so unused to her physical affection.

But when she continued to hold him, he eventually found himself embracing her in return.

They sat like that for a long moment, until Zolya sensed something loosen in his heart. As if a rusty nail holding a door shut had wiggled out, allowing a painful part of his childhood to slip free. How many nights alone as a child had he called for his mother's arms yet only got a nursemaid. But here she now was, cradling him when he was most vulnerable.

"I am so very proud of you," she whispered, heavy emotion in her voice. "So very proud."

Zolya swallowed down the ache in his throat, tried his best to control his magic, lest the entire room become a monsoon. He needed to pull himself together.

The queen dowager sat back, eyes watery but cheeks dry. "Well," she breathed. "That is quite an admission, my son. One I am honored you felt you could share with me."

"You are not offended?" he asked.

"If I am anything, it is annoyed that I had spoken too soon earlier."

He frowned. "Regarding what?"

"Regarding your coup. It is not the reorganization of your Royal Council that will set one off, but this."

"Mother."

She laughed, a light sound that contradicted the weight of his admission.

"I'm glad you find this amusing," he grumbled.

"How else can we find joy in life, if not to be amused by it." She grinned as she patted his leg. "But in all seriousness, your plans may be ambitious, but they are not the first of their kind."

"What do you mean?"

"King Lexi," she answered.

Zolya gazed at her blankly.

"King Lexi of the third ruling," she repeated, brow furrowed. "His time was called the Blooming Years?"

"I know of King Lexi, but what specifically about him?"

"By the gods, did your tutors teach you nothing?" She shook her head with an offended huff. "The royal magister will certainly be hearing from—"

"Mother," interrupted Zolya. "While I draw joy from the imagined suffering you wish to dole out on my old tutors, it can wait. Tell me to what you are referring."

She pursed her lips in annoyance but conceded. "King Lexi was the third Volari king of Galia, and, as it is written, he ruled a world where all creatures roamed together. There were still the classes, of course. No society is without those, but who was richest and who was poorest was not determined by wings or horns or blood. His reign was said to have been the most peaceful four hundred years in all Cādra's existence."

Zolya's pulse fluttered as he sat straighter. "How did King Lexi achieve this reign?"

"It is said he had another council separate from his royal one. A gathering of all the races, brought together every few years to discuss grievances, trades, or ideas for improvements in their varied communities."

"Why is this history not more well known?"

"Certain histories have a way of being forgotten when those in power wish it so," she answered. "Your father certainly did his fair share of rewriting. Plus, peace is hardly a subject to gather crowds before heralds or town criers. Unrest, famines, droughts, and wars—these are the subjects which entertain dinner parties and strike fear in those a ruler wishes to suppress. Reason enough why history books are filled with times of war rather than times of peace."

Zolya frowned, his magic swirling restlessly. "A world council . . ." he mused. "It's quite revolutionary."

"For where we have fallen today, yes," she agreed.

"Gods, is this foolish of me?" He raked a tired hand down his face. "Wanting this? Thinking it's achievable. To wish to change decades of prejudice and beliefs. It will only further have my people thinking me incapable."

"You do not know what your people believe," said his mother. "If you and I wish for peace—a king and a queen—there are no doubt others of us who wish for it too."

Zolya's thoughts drifted to those at court, to Azla and Lady Esme—what they were willing to sacrifice for a better future for themselves, one King Réol certainly wasn't giving them. Visions of the other noble ladies came next. Those whom the princess had been teaching a wider use of their delicate magic. Their expressions of excitement and joy to finally be allowed to feel capable, powerful.

Then there was every Volari who had ever been ripped of their wings or sentenced to death because of loving a Süra, publicly supporting them, and the countless Mütra who existed and would continue to exist despite their banishment. None of it would stop, nor had it stopped under his father's rule or the rule of the kings who'd instilled similar laws before Réol.

The Rebellion hadn't emerged without cause. And wasn't the first in their history.

Change was being demanded, from both sides.

How to allow it to happen was the question.

"Perhaps," replied Zolya. "But a world council feels centuries away from what even *my* Royal Council would support."

"You know," began his mother as she flattened a wrinkle on her skirts. "A common mistake of our young is looking at the entire sky when learning to fly. It's no wonder so many are too frightened to jump. But what did I always tell you, Zolya, when you were learning?"

"To look at where I wished to land."

She placed a gentle hand atop his, which rested on his knee. "Your vision is great, my king, but to fly across the world in one leap *is* unachievable. Think only of where you wish to land first, before continuing."

He studied his mother, a swelling of wonderment filling his chest. "Did anyone ever tell you that you'd make a great king?"

"I tell myself that every day." She smiled. "But I am more than content to be the great queen who raised a great king."

"I hope I live up to that description."

"You already have, my child"—she squeezed his hand before sitting back—"with what you wish to do for our world."

Zolya took in a steadying breath, her advice settling along his shoulders like a cooling mist. "I shall think smaller," he declared. "The first minds to sway should be my new council's."

"And the Rebellion's," she added.

"We have already tried a peace meeting," he replied, frowning. "It did not end amicably."

"You had that meeting as the prince regent with your *father's* council," clarified his mother. "What would that meeting be like with you now as king? Without those old peacocks breathing down your neck, but supported by your new council. One that now has a very wise queen dowager occupying a position on it."

At his mother's words, Zolya's thoughts soared in every direction, a cascading of hope that kicked his pulse into a quick rhythm.

"Yes," he nodded as a plan began to slip into place. "Yes, you are right. Just as I was with my council, I will be more selective with which Rebellion and Süra delegates come to our next meeting. I will invite those who I think will better serve progress. Surely with a more progressive group, we will see a more favorable outcome than the last peace meeting."

"One would hope," said his mother. "But if you truly wish to sway minds, have the meeting take place here, in Galia."

His brows shot up. "Now you speak madness, Mother. There are Mütra on the Rebellion Council. They will never come here."

"They must if we are to have those on the continent believe the threat of the old guard is truly no more. We need to prove that compromise and reason exist with Galia's new king. That *you* are willing to negotiate."

"But the Mütra would be breaking a severe law by trespassing on our soil," he argued. "Punishable by death. I was hardly able to control Osko from slitting throats during the meeting."

"Then change the law. You are king now."

His mind went blank for a breath, her proclamation shocking in its simplicity.

You are king now.

"Osko and his men are governed by Volari law," his mother went on. "Give them a new one to obey."

"It's . . . not that simple," he replied.

"It was for your father."

Zolya was lost.

Lost in the truth of her words, in their radicalness.

It *had* been that simple for his father, hadn't it?

And yet, still . . . it was hard to imagine *he* possessed such power.

That something he had been born to obey, that their entire world had been demanded to uphold for centuries—and that had chased Tanwen her entire life—could be removed so swiftly by his hand.

You are king now.

Yes, he was.

Zolya's magic scattered through his veins, an impatient rush.

"How does one change a law?" he asked.

"Perhaps start by refreshing your history," she replied, pointedly. "You have one of the largest libraries in the world. Visit it. And may I suggest beginning your lesson in the Retired Collections. It'll be the section that needs a key to access. Your father's tendency to lock away knowledge was disappointingly literal."

After his mother's departure, the rest of Zolya's day was filled as a student, with him hidden behind stacks of dusty, barely held-together historic tomes and political ledgers.

Despite his rising fatigue and hunger, his burning eyes demanding sleep, he kept going.

There was too much risk involved in what he was planning for him to rest.

Would his Royal Council approve of his demands?

Would the Rebellion representatives accept his invitation?

Would the palace behave if they did?

Or would he prove his mother's earlier accusation right and inspire a coup.

One thing was for certain: When all was set into place, he'd need to have a meeting with Osko and set firm expectations with his friend and their soldiers.

You are king now.

His mother's words rose as a strong proclamation.

I am king, he silently repeated, his determination hot in his blood.

He had the power to make laws and to change them.

Realizing this, seeing the truth of it etched into the books scattered around him, nourished the hope he'd hungered for since the moment Tanwen had first kissed him.

Hope that there would come a time when they could stand together, openly, in love.

With a steadying breath, he closed the last book and pulled forward a piece of blank parchment.

The scratching of his quill was the only sound that echoed in the dark literary catacomb.

His strokes were sure and quick as he crafted the list of guests, candlelight flickering over the wet ink.

When finished, he leaned back, an exhausted sigh escaping his lips.

His gaze dragged slowly down the paper, before pausing on a name.

As he studied it, indecision swirled, knowing the risk it carried.

With a frown, he readied his quill to cross the name off.

But right before the sharp point made contact, he stopped. A pressure grew within his chest: a selfish, dangerous longing.

He let his pen fall from his fingers.

The name would stay.

For it was the only one that truly mattered.

13

The Governess's chambers carried the same sharp edges as their mistress.

Tanwen and her group had reached them through a series of tunnels branching from the throne room, narrow passages carved from jagged rock, to enter a singular cavern. The walls here were equally as hard, enough to scrape skin.

But the roughness was softened by the decor—sturdy wooden chairs and a table, a woven rug made from a variety of brown grasses laid across the floor, and endless bowls of fire casting golden light.

Though the warmth of the flames felt stolen by the yawning break in the far wall—an open edge that looked out over part of the island. Beyond it, fog rolled heavy through dead terrain, which whipped in the wind. Somewhere in the distance waves crashed against the island's cliffside, a rhythmic roar.

Tanwen took it all in with a quick sweep—most importantly noting that the only real exit was the entrance through which they'd come. Two centaurs now flanked it, their expressions austere, while her group huddled in the center of the room.

Zephyr and Brynn remained on their feet, tense, while she and her father sat across from Azla and—

Her mother.

The shock of it was still written plainly on Azla's face—her brown skin ashen, her blue eyes wide, fixed on Lady Callia.

Lady Callia, who seemed determined to look anywhere but at her daughter.

When the princess had declared who she was, the throne room had fallen into a deathly silence. Lady Callia had sat frozen, a stone statue, staring at Azla for what felt like an eternity—her expression unreadable—before abruptly ordering the group to be taken to her private chambers.

Not a single tear had been shed.

No joy.

No relief.

No emotion at all.

In fact, the matter was not brought up again.

Instead, Lady Callia listened as Gabreel explained the state of their world, the uprisings, the forming of the Rebellion, and why they had come to Both.

And if it hurt Tanwen to watch Lady Callia dismiss her daughter, she could only imagine what Azla must be feeling—her own mother, a woman she'd never truly known, sitting here now and ignoring her entirely.

"So," Lady Callia mused once Gabreel had finished, a twisted smile stretching. "Réol is bedridden. He who deemed himself immortal is mortal after all."

"It's left his kingdom weak," explained her father. "Enough to give us this time to plan. And to seek more strength—strength we hoped to find here."

"Now we've come to it, the subject of your stupidity," she accused, her voice hard. "You could have been killed coming here."

Though she addressed their group, her comment felt suspiciously aimed at the young woman at her side—Azla.

Look at your daughter! thought Tanwen, a prick of anger rising in her chest.

"We understood the risks in coming," Tanwen found herself replying, tone equally as chilled.

"No, you did not," Lady Callia shot back. "No one understands the threat of this island but those who inhabit it."

"The only way to reach anyone here was to come," explained Gabreel.

"A foolish risk." Lady Callia frowned. "And I do not deal with fools."

"All right," said Tanwen evenly. "Then let us leave." She made to stand. "Come, Azla."

"No—" Lady Callia's hand shot out, gripping the princess's arm, keeping her seated. For a moment, a flash of panic broke through her composed features.

Finally, thought Tanwen as she held back a smug grin, sinking again into her chair.

Lady Callia noticed, for her mask quickly returned, her eyes narrowing as they locked on Tanwen.

"M—mother." Azla's voice was barely a whisper. "We need your help."

It was as if she said "*I* need your help," a child's plea—*her* child's plea—for Lady Callia's eyes fluttered briefly closed, her brow creasing with pain. She drew in a shaky breath before finally turning to face her daughter.

She remained holding Azla's arm, yet neither made any move to break the contact. They seemed caught in a quiet trance—one steeped in longing, sorrow, and heartache, but also laced with curiosity, hope, and something else Tanwen couldn't decipher.

The moment was so intimate, so raw, that she felt like an intruder. Heat crept into her cheeks as she averted her gaze and met her father's instead.

He gave her a gentle smile, an encouraging nod.

And in that moment, she realized—despite the hardships of her upbringing, despite living most of her life in fear—she had been fortunate. Fortunate to know her parents, and to have their love.

"You look much like your father," Lady Callia eventually said, her tone revealing she wasn't exactly pleased by that fact. "I remember thinking this when you were born. Not a single red feather or dark strand anywhere to be found. But Réol always did know how to take up space."

Azla didn't reply, appeared not to know how to.

"But you have my hands." Her voice turned gentle as she lifted Azla's fingers, studying them. "And my cheekbones." She smiled, and the gesture seemed to soften the sharp angles of her face, melting some of the rigidity from her tightly wound posture.

Azla's own expression seemed to brighten at that, a grin forming—only to falter moments later. "I only ever saw one painting of you," she said. "As a child. In the queen's chambers."

"The queen's?" Lady Callia drew back, letting go of her hand. "Why would Habbie keep a painting of me?"

Azla's face seemed to warm, as if ashamed of the answer. "It was in her chambers on Galia," she clarified. "The ones she no longer occupied in the palace."

"Ah," she said. "That makes more sense. Her abandoned tomb."

Another beat of silence stretched between them—heavy, assessing—until, "You've grown magnificently, Azla."

Her mother's words seemed to light her up again, sunlight breaking through clouds.

"Thank you," she murmured, emotion thick in her voice.

"I wish I could say the same for myself." Lady Callia let out a huff of laughter that didn't reach her eyes. "I've only grown scarred." She gestured to the jagged mark carved down her cheek and neck—an old wound, yet its story was still raw in her gaze. "A keepsake from the last man who ruled Both," she said. "He was a formidable opponent, but his weakness was the same as many men's—underestimating the cleverness of a woman. In the end, his life was simple to claim. A mere satiating of lust before I set his bed aflame as he slept."

Shock rippled through Tanwen and the rest of her group, though Lady Callia seemed utterly unmoved by it.

"That's how you survive in a place like this," she went on, looking only at Azla. "You prove you're the strongest—and that you possess something no one else can offer." She turned her hand, and a flame bloomed alive in her palm. She let it dance idly as she spoke. "After that, I made sure I was the only heat wielder left. The only one who could give this forsaken island what it craved most—warmth."

A chill slipped down Tanwen's spine as Lady Callia clamped her hand shut, smothering the flame.

She didn't know if it was possible for the room to grow any more tense.

"Does my confession scare you?" Lady Callia asked her daughter, head tilting curiously.

Azla held her mother's stare for a long, thoughtful beat before answering. "No. We all do what we must to survive. I'm glad you did what you needed to. I'm glad you're alive."

Lady Callia's eyes flashed, pride glinting in their depths. She leaned over and clasped Azla's hand in a firm grip. "I'm glad too," she said, tone softer. "I'm glad I survived long enough to see you again."

Tanwen watched as Azla swallowed, her lower lip trembling for a breath. Her heart ached for her friend, but it was an ache that came with profound relief. Even if Lady Callia was the most terrifying woman she'd ever met, seeing the care she had toward her daughter—despite the decades of separation—made her forever grateful.

Azla deserved hope. Deserved happiness.

"We'll talk more later," Lady Callia promised Azla, her voice lowering, intimate. "Privately. There's much to be said and shared."

Her attention then shifted to the rest of the group. "As for the rest of you—" Her eyes narrowed as she regarded their watchful faces. "What makes you think my people or I have any desire to aid your little uprising?"

"We can offer you your freedom," said Zephyr, as though the answer should have been clear all along.

Lady Callia's gaze cut to where he stood behind Tanwen and Gabreel. "Freedom to fight in a war? To die just as we can already die here? Painfully. Where is the freedom in that?"

"But—" Zephyr floundered. "It's a way off this island!"

"This island is our home," she said simply. "It is a cold, barren home, yes, but it is *ours*."

Despite how tragic her declaration was, Tanwen understood it.

It was like her and her family hiding in the fringes of their forest. Or the dark corners of Cādra. It might have been a lonely existence, but it was a familiar existence, which—in a twisted way—made it feel safe.

These souls had been left here, forgotten, and in that forgetting came an emancipation.

"I understand your hesitation," said Tanwen. "This island is the enemy you know. Solitude was that for me and my family. It was safer for us to hide, disappear—certainly easier than to fight for what felt futile at the time. But *this* is no longer then. Cādra is demanding change, and it *will* get it. It's been building for centuries—centuries of failed attempts we can learn from to finally succeed. We have a king who is indisposed, his council scared, and Low Gods willing to help our cause. We must take advantage of that. For a time like this may never come again.

"Our enemy is the same," she continued, determination rising with every word. "They are the ones who dropped your kind here and took your wings"—she gestured to her father's bare back—"your flight." She saw Lady Callia's shoulders stiffen, though her plumage stayed limp. "They hunted your people down for being different—'abominations'—for having blood unlike theirs." Tanwen felt Brynn shift beside her, the faint rustle of her four wings. "They threw you into this abyss because your strength frightened them, because you threatened their power—or because they decided you no longer served their needs. They are the ones who dared to call empathy *tyranny*." She took a breath, her voice firm but imploring now. "Don't let them win, Governess. Don't let their crimes go unanswered. Give your people the chance at vengeance they've carried in their hearts all these years. Give them the life they were meant to live—on Cādra."

The chambers hung quiet, her words seeming to vibrate long after she had finished speaking.

"Who *are* you?" asked Lady Callia, her gaze fixed on Tanwen, a faint perplexity shadowing her features.

"I was an outcast like everyone on this island," she answered. "I am a sister who lost her brother because of King Réol. I am a meddyg and the daughter of Gabreel and Aisling Heiro. I am Mütra."

Lady Callia's eyes sparked, and though Tanwen couldn't be sure, she thought she caught a glimmer of respect there. Slowly, she gave a single, deliberate nod.

"She is also the one who helped me poison the king," said Azla.

"I beg your pardon?" Lady Callia's eyes widened as she swung her gaze to her daughter. "*You* poisoned the king."

Azla's jaw tightened. "In the end, it was my love, Lady Esme, who carried out the task—and lost her life for it." She paused, steadying herself. "But it couldn't have been done without Tanwen. She supplied the poison—a tear from Maryth."

"*A tear from Maryth*," she breathed, her gaze snapping back to Tanwen, now glinting with intrigue—a sharp mix of calculation and curiosity swirling in her eyes. "Well, well. It appears there's more to this little group than meets the eye. And more strength in my daughter than I ever could have dreamed. I know we have only just met, child"—she fixed the princess with a piercing stare—"but you have already made me proud."

Azla pressed her lips tight, as if to keep a tremor from breaking through.

Silence lingered, a heavy quiet that the princess seemed unable to fill.

So Tanwen did.

"Then will you join us?" she asked, forcing her voice to stay steady despite the impatience pulsing beneath it, the quiet desperation for this to go right—for their risk in coming here to pay off. "As I hope we've made clear, we are fully committed to this cause and what needs to be done to see change."

Lady Callia thrummed her fingers on her armrest, expression unreadable. "I understand what my people will suffer if we join you and this uprising fails," she began. "But what I want to have agreed upon, in writing, is what we will gain if we win."

"*Besides* your freedom?" asked Zephyr.

"Where will we live if not here?" she countered. "Where will prisoners and outcasts be allowed to call home on Cādra? Where will the races the old kings banished from the continent be welcome? They cannot all live in Süra forests, surely. I require land. A territory we can claim as our own."

"I'm sure that can be arranged," said Tanwen.

"It *could*," added her father quickly, brows pinched. "But it will cost more than helping the Rebellion. The land on Cādra is split between the different clans, it is not in our party's power to offer a plot of it."

"I am not looking for charity," explained Lady Callia. "I understand how our world works despite being separated from it for so long. Do you feel the clans will be swayed by an ample sum in exchange for land?"

"I'm sure it would help matters," said Gabreel. "But, if you don't mind my asking, what wealth could you possibly possess here?"

Lady Callia's grin turned serpentine at that. "Follow me."

She stood, prompting the group to stand with her. In silence, they worked their way out of her chambers, passing the two guards and returning into the dimly lit passage.

They had hardly walked ten paces before they were made to stop.

A burst of light awoke from Lady Callia's palm, flames. She lit two lanterns she had carried and handed them down the line. "Hold them toward the walls," she instructed.

Tanwen stood beside her father, who raised one of the lamps, and it painted the dark stone with a liquid glint. She squinted as he moved it closer until—

Gasps echoed through the passage. Her own breath caught, her heart pounding.

Ambrü.

Large pieces, small shards, half emerged from the stone wall, some nearly falling out—a glistening endless mosaic of red lit by their dancing flames.

"*By the gods*," breathed her father.

"It's everywhere," murmured Zephyr.

"It is," said Callia. "And as valuable to us here as the cold."

Still speechless, Tanwen reached out, feeling the cool gem in front of her. She'd never seen one this big in her entire life, let alone touched one.

It reminded her of—

Lady Callia's diadem.

"Of course," her father mumbled at her side, as if lost in his own thoughts now, eyes fixed on everywhere his lantern shone. "This island is perfect."

"Perfect for what?" she asked.

"A perfect home for this to be made. The harsh bashing of Orzel's seas on every side, the necessary pressure. We only find these conditions on our coastal cliffs, but an island—" He broke into laughter then, a sharp, unsettling sound, like a man whose mind has lost more than a few spokes from its wheel. "This island has been the king's most precious piece of property," he wheezed. "And he was using it as a *prison*!"

Tanwen watched him with concern as he doubled over.

Carefully she slid the lamp from his grip and was more than relieved when he finally worked to regain his composure.

He wiped at his eyes as Lady Callia stepped to their side. "So," she began, tone laced with triumph. "Do you think this is enough wealth to sway hands?"

"It's enough to sway more than that," huffed Gabreel.

Her grin widened. "Good. Then let's return to my chambers and discuss terms." She turned, moving down the tunnel toward the light at its end. "I'll have refreshments sent—we may be here awhile," she called back over her shoulder, "for there are quite a few stipulations of mine that are nonnegotiable."

14

Tanwen had barely taken five steps from the portal before she and her group were surrounded by a crowd of waiting Drygul refugees.

"You're alive!" Huw barreled into her, nearly knocking her over—until a greater force finished the job.

Tanwen hit the ground with a sharp *oof*, pinned beneath Huw and a mass of fur that immediately accosted her with a rough, smelly, slobbery tongue.

"Argh—*Loji!*" Huw grumbled as he squirmed out of the pile. "That's disgusting! I just laundered this outfit."

"I missed you too, Loji," Tanwen grunted with a smile. The wolf truly weighed a ton. "But can I stand up now?"

You were gone too long, said Loji, her worry clear as she backed up, giving Tanwen room to rise.

She honestly didn't know how long they had been away. Their time on the prisoner island had been a blur, marked only by shifting fog. The absence of sunlight erased any real sense of days. Discussions and crafting an agreement with the Governess had consumed their time.

"We had to stay on Both Island longer than planned," she explained, once on her feet. "I'm assuming Ridi didn't communicate that to any of you?"

"And keep us from going mad with worry?" scoffed Huw. "Why deprive himself of the joy of mayhem? When the portal didn't open when it was meant to, we thought the Low Gods had sent you all to your deaths."

Huw stepped aside to let Aisling pull Tanwen into a hug.

"We thought that, too, at first," admitted Tanwen, as she breathed in her mother's familiar scent. "But we're all okay," she reassured.

Her mother only held her tighter.

Guilt twisted low in her gut as she let her.

She understood what had haunted her parents since Aberthol's passing—that Tanwen would be next.

Despite their trust in her abilities and their effort to hold back their old overprotectiveness, she still felt their fear. It crept through their worried glances and relieved sighs each night when she returned to their den.

She appreciated how hard they tried to mask their worry, but it still stirred her constant grief—a sharp reminder that Aberthol was gone, no longer there to commiserate, to lighten the moment, or slip away with into the forest.

"*By the twin moons . . .*" Huw breathed, pulling Tanwen's attention back to the woods.

The forest's chatter faded into a stunned silence as every eye was trained on the glowing portal, their expressions frozen in shock.

Figures emerged, like spirits spilling out of the currents of Maryth's Eternal River. The island prisoners poured forth, their waxy skin and tattered clothing a stark contrast to the lush vibrance around them.

The Drygul citizens, slack jawed and rigid, took in the towering minotaurs, solemn centaurs, nimble satyrs, and other mythical beings now gathering in their sanctuary.

Wait until they see the cyclops, Tanwen thought.

Cyclopes are gentle creatures, Loji's voice interjected in her mind.

Tanwen turned to the large wolf, brows raised. "You knew they existed?"

Loji's glowing green eyes met hers. *They existed in a time when more of my own did,* she explained, a quiet sorrow lacing her words as she turned back to the unfolding scene.

The refugees continued to gape in awe, while the prisoners stared back, overwhelmed. Many broke into quiet sobs, their gazes lifting to the vivid canopy above. Children clung to their parents, their faces a mix of wonder and fear as they witnessed, for the first time, a world brimming with sunshine, color, and life.

Tanwen's chest tightened, a lump rising in her throat as she witnessed the scene.

"Do not be alarmed," came the commanding voice of Brynn, who stood near the portal door while Zephyr and her father were helping to shepherd in the group. "Our visitors come in peace, seeking this sanctuary as we all have. Here are more victims of King Réol's prejudice." She gestured to the amassing prisoners. "Condemned to be forgotten and perish. The only crime they have committed is existing. We will call a town meeting to discuss the integration of our new guests. In the meantime, our benevolent Low Gods have allowed them entry into Drygul, so we ask you to welcome them as we have been welcomed."

The forest lit up then, Drygul refugees crossing over invisible lines of tension to help prisoners carrying babes, shuffling others off to be fed. Her mother left her and stepped forward to care for those who seemed injured.

There were still in their group some who remained wary, eyeing the clomping centaurs and bulging minotaurs with unease. But Tanwen knew that if anyone could accept the unusual, it was the refugees of Drygul. Soon, the prisoners of Both would belong here too.

The thought filled her with hope—hope that Cādra would be next.

"Their numbers are endless," exclaimed Huw.

"Not all will be coming to Drygul right away," said Tanwen. "Ridi will keep the portal door open for our two clans to work together for what we have planned."

"Mm," Huw replied absently as his gaze shifted to a nearby satyr. He was shedding his heavy coat, exposing a lean, muscular chest as he basked in a shaft of sunlight piercing through the canopy. "It appears your mission was a success. You've certainly brought home some delightful surprises."

"You have no idea," she replied, as her attention slid to where Azla lingered, away from the crowd. The princess's expression was pensive, gaze unfocused amid the commotion.

Worry tightened Tanwen's throat.

It was clear Azla hadn't wanted to leave her mother, despite how bleak and cold Both remained. Tanwen suspected it was the fear—that after all these years, finding her alive had felt like a miracle, and leaving now might mean never seeing her again.

It had taken considerable convincing—from both Tanwen and Lady Callia—for her to return with their group. Lady Callia had entrusted only Azla with the copy of their agreement. The Governess would come to Drygul when it was necessary. For now, she needed to ensure her people's safe pilgrimage to this new land.

"We've had our own surprises," Huw said absently, still admiring the satyr. "King Réol is dead."

"What?" She whipped around, grabbing his arm. *"What did you just say?"*

"The king," he repeated, startled. "He's dead."

"How did you not tell me this *immediately*?" She shook him, her pulse a stampede.

"Sorry." He pried her hands off. "Clearly, we've all been a little preoccupied." He gestured toward the prisoners. "The news only arrived this morning. From the palace, in fact. Prince Zolya is now king."

Tanwen's hands fell to her sides as a dull ringing filled her ears.

The king is dead. The king is dead. The king is dead.

Prince Zolya is now king.

Her knees nearly buckled, her breaths uneven.

Zolya.

Now king.

He had done it.

He had done it!

Her chest swelled with pride, her mind racing with hope—and questions.

How was he feeling? What had this cost him? Her blood rushed as her longing to go to him, to see him, flamed hot along her skin—restless and demanding. A torture.

Around her, the animals began to stir, clearly agitated by her torrent of emotions.

Birds flitted and chirped and cawed along nearby branches. Furry tree dwellers squeaked in agitation.

"That's not all," continued Huw, glancing to the disturbed animals overhead. "King Zolya has called for another peace meeting between Volari, Süra, and Rebellion representatives."

King Zolya.

It was surreal to hear.

Incredible.

Perfect.

She wanted to sob.

"That's good." She nodded, forcing her tone as even as she could make it.

"Yes . . ." Huw hesitated.

"What?" she asked.

"He wants it held in Galia."

"Galia?" Her heart stopped.

"Yes. He's also been *very* specific about who he wishes to come from Cādra."

A tense silence stretched.

"*And?*" Tanwen demanded, impatience sharpening her tone.

"And"—Huw's calculating gaze bored into her—"your name is on the list."

15

Tanwen doubted their den could hold another person.

"You can't seriously be considering going," said her mother as Tanwen squeezed past Huw, then Azla—and her wings—to reach the seasoning shelf.

Travel had taught her one thing: Food on the road was not only cold and questionably chewy but also utterly bland. If she had to sleep on the ground for the next few days, she'd do it with a decently flavored meal.

"I can't be the only invited delegate who doesn't attend," she reasoned.

Her family's kitchen felt even smaller with Azla and Huw crowding the space while her parents hunkered around their table, watching her pack. Thankfully, Loji's hulking form remained outside, the wolf's head resting on the den's front threshold.

"I'm certain you won't be," said her father. His expression was equally as worried as her mother's. "The northern clan leader is on that list, and the Pelks would never send their nyddoth to Galia. One of his councillors will go in his stead."

"Well, the others from Drygul are all going," Tanwen pointed out.

The list included ten names from Cādra: three from their Rebellion outpost in the Low Gods' territory—Brynn, Tanwen, and Zephyr. The remaining seven were from the various clans.

"Zephyr is not going," her father corrected evenly. "Lyra forbade it."

Tanwen paused in stuffing her supplies into her pack. "That hardly seems her right to decide." She frowned.

"She's the only family he has left," her mother replied, pointedly. "It would be selfish of him to go and throw himself into such clear danger after what they survived. There are bounties on their heads in Galia—just as there still are on Mütra."

The kitchen fell into a taut silence.

Though it wasn't the mention of danger that lashed out at Tanwen; it was what else her mother had said—*She's the only family he has left.*

Guilt wrapped around her throat like a noose.

It would be selfish of him to go.

Was that what her mother thought of *her*?

Thought of her choices?

"You think I'm selfish for going?" she asked softly, unable to mask the hurt in her voice.

"No," her mother replied quickly. "I just don't think you have to. This peace meeting—"

"Could be the last one we ever get between our races," Tanwen cut in. "It could decide all our fates—whether we fall into war or find peace. I *cannot* sit that out. Not after everything I've helped accomplish so far. If that makes me selfish, so be it. But everything I've done since the day I first set foot on Galia was for this family. Everything since has been for *us*." Frustration now flared in her chest, hot and unsteady. "For you and Father. For Thol—for his death not to have been in vain. So much of my life I have spent hiding, staying quiet when I wished to have fought, to have spoken. Now, I have that chance. I have a chance to stand up for what *I* want in this world, for me and future generations. And to voice this to a new king."

The kitchen swallowed her words, silence settling heavy until her mother murmured, "That's exactly what holds my fears. Before, you could move about unnoticed in Galia. Now you'll be walking into enemy territory—a known Mütra—in broad daylight. And the last time a Volari king had one of my children . . ." Her voice faltered, her face growing ashen.

Tanwen's anger left her in a rush, replaced by a sharp ache in her chest. "Mother," she said softly. "Your fears are valid. But King Zolya is *not* King Réol."

"Is he not?" her father cut in, his tone edged. "He threatened the Süra recruits at the last peace meeting, if you recall. He abducted me and your brother, allowed Thol to be tortured—"

Nausea knotted in Tanwen's stomach at the mention of Zolya's past indiscretions. A hot, desperate need to defend him rose in her throat, but how could she without revealing more than she dared about their relationship?

She shot Azla a pleading glance.

Her friend seemed to catch it, for she stepped in smoothly. "And all of those were under my father's orders," she said. "Not that it excuses them, but even you, Gabreel, followed King Réol's commands when you clearly opposed them."

Red shame flushed across her father's face.

"You know how impossible it was to disobey him," she continued. "Now think how it must have been for his son. Despite how Zolya may have appeared when my father was alive, I can guarantee you, he is *not* my father. He has always believed differently—progressively. Calling this peace meeting so soon after Réol's death proves that. It proves he wishes for change in our world. And he will honor the safety of every guest while they're on Galia."

Her parents exchanged a look, skeptical but silent.

"May I also remind you," Azla added, brows raised, "he helped your family escape Galia. Helped *me* escape. If nothing else, doesn't that say something about his character?"

"It speaks of his inconsistency," Gabreel muttered. "And I don't trust inconsistencies."

A derisive snort came from Aisling then, and all eyes turned toward her.

"What?" Her father's frown deepened.

"What of your inconsistencies, Gabreel?" she asked coolly. "If you are condemning the contradiction of others, you may as well start with yourself."

Silence fell.

Tanwen held her breath, her heartache splitting open her chest as she watched the silent battle happening between her parents.

"When will you forgive me?" asked her father, tone stony. "When will you accept that I did *everything* I could to protect Aberthol? I lost a child too that day." His voice faltered with his rising emotion, cracked. "I *too* am grieving. I watched him fall, dammit, Aisling. *Fall!*" He pounded his fist on the table, making the room jump. "And I could do nothing. I am his *father*, and I couldn't protect my son. I wish it had been me . . ." He buried his head in his hands, a sob breaking free. "It should have been me . . ." His words trailed off as he wept.

Tanwen hastily wiped the tears from her cheeks and crossed to him, resting a gentle hand on his shoulder. His frame trembled beneath her touch, racked with sobs.

It gutted her to watch—his grief laid bare, raw and unguarded, and all she could do was stand there, choking on her own sorrow.

Besides the day her brother died, he had not cried, at least not publicly.

Gabreel had been stoic, a quiet pillar of support beside her mother—whenever she allowed him to be, that is.

A faint whimper came from Loji outside. The kitchen was tightly wound.

Then, slowly, Aisling reached out, sliding her hand over her father's.

Gabreel's breath hitched as he looked up, meeting her gaze.

"I'm sorry," she whispered, her voice raw. "I've been so consumed by my own pain, I forgot that you're grieving too."

"*Of course* I'm grieving," he said, tone rough. "He was my—"

"I know." She tightened her grip, her features pained. "I know."

Tanwen's father took a shaky inhale, seeming to do his best to regain his composure. "I have been grieving losing you too," he said.

Aisling's brows pinched in anguish. "You haven't lost me," she whispered. "I lost myself."

"I did too," he admitted. "But please, let us find each other again, together." He pulled her hands to his chest, a desperation stretching across his face. A plea.

She took a hard swallow, nodding.

Tanwen's gaze remained locked on their still-joined hands. Relief swirled in her veins as a fractured piece of her heart thumped with hope.

As if blinking from their intimate moment, both her parents straightened as they seemed to sense the room of onlookers.

"Forgive us," said her father.

"There's nothing to forgive," Huw said, from where he leaned against the counter. "We may not share blood, but we're your family too. And families face things—messes and all—together." He offered her parents a soft smile, one they returned with quiet gratitude. He then turned to Tanwen, his smile growing pointedly saccharine. "Now. Let's finish discussing how to keep this one from marching off to Galia."

Tanwen shot him a glare. "That's not amusing."

"Wasn't meant to be," he replied, tone hardening. "I agree with your parents—going back there is reckless."

"Then the three of you can spend your time while I'm gone being disappointed," she said, voice sharp. She snatched up her bag. "Now if you'll excuse me, I have packing to finish."

She walked out of the kitchen without looking back.

By the time Tanwen stepped from her family's den, the sun had begun to set. She descended the winding staircase to the forest floor, her travel sack slung over her shoulder, weighty but bearable.

The canopy overhead was bathed in a soft orange glow, light spilling through the leaves like liquid gold. Shadows danced gently across the moss and roots, all of Drygul hushed in the quiet beauty of dusk—serene.

What wasn't serene, however, was the sight waiting for her at the base of the stairs.

Her parents, Azla, and Loji stood side by side at the edge of the garden path. Waiting.

She slowed, eyes scanning instinctively for Huw—her heart sinking slightly when she didn't find him.

Was he too angry at her to say goodbye? Or worse . . . finally done trying to convince her that what she was doing was foolish?

She approached her parents, apprehension growing. "You can't keep me from going," she said, a bit too defensively.

"That is not why we are here," said her mother.

"We have talked more," explained her father. "Talked further with Azla regarding her brother . . . and, well, we accept your need to go. We support it."

Tanwen blinked, caught off guard. "You do?"

"Yes." Aisling nodded. "We let our fear of losing you cloud the truth of who you are—and who we raised you to be. You and Thol . . . you are just like we were once. Bold and relentless in your convictions. Your father and I never got the support of our families, but still—we left them behind to follow what we knew was right." She paused to take a shaky inhale. "We don't want you to sacrifice our approval for the sake of your purpose. Not when we believe in it too."

Emotion surged in Tanwen's chest, hot and rising fast. Tears brimmed in her eyes.

"We know how capable you are," added her father. "What you did in Galia to free me and your brother . . . what you've done for the Rebellion, for Both . . . Tanwen, you are clever, capable, and brave. If anyone should be afraid, it's those who try to stand in your way."

"Thank you," she whispered. "You have no idea what that means . . . Your support—it means everything."

They reached for her then, and she collapsed into their arms without hesitation.

Loji gave a soft whimper beside them, nuzzling her head into Tanwen's shoulder. Only Azla remained a few steps away—until Aisling extended a hand and pulled the princess into their embrace too.

They stood like that for a long, quiet moment. No words. Just the rustle of leaves overhead and birds calling in the trees.

When Tanwen finally stepped back, the sun had dipped lower. Brynn would be waiting.

She looked once more at her parents. Her chest was full—relief, joy, love . . . and the ache of goodbye. But there was comfort too: in the mending she saw between them, and in the gift of their blessing to go.

"Look out for one of my messenger birds," she said. "I'll send word whenever I can."

"Be safe." Her mother gave her arm a gentle squeeze.

"And smarter than the rest of them," said her father.

Tanwen smiled. "Always."

She turned to Azla, wishing they'd had more time to talk. So much had happened in the past two days, and she never truly got to ask how her friend was coping with the return of her mother. But time was rarely generous.

"If all goes well," said Tanwen, "I'll see you soon."

"Yes." Azla offered a steadying smile. "I'll see you soon."

Tanwen gave one last lingering look to those she loved—though her eyes involuntarily searched for the one face missing. Huw should've been there. She swallowed the ache of that disappointment as she turned.

"I'm going with you!" a breathless voice called out.

Tanwen spun, watching as Huw came running, pack thumping against his back.

"What? No—you can't." She frowned.

"Of course I can," he said, undeterred.

"You weren't invited."

"I have a feeling you'll charm the king into letting me be your plus-one," he said with a pointed look.

Tanwen's stomach tightened, but whatever was hiding in Huw's tone she wasn't ready to unravel.

She also understood that once Huw—like herself—set his mind to something, there was no dissuading him. And if she was being honest with herself . . . she was glad to have his company. It would be a comfort, having someone she trusted at her side as she faced the unknown.

"You must *promise* to keep your complaining at a minimum during our travels," she insisted.

Huw huffed his incredulousness. "I will do no such thing. I never make promises I can't keep."

She couldn't help but laugh at that.

If he's coming, then I'm coming, came Loji's sharp snort at her side.

"No, absolutely *not,*" said Huw, not missing a beat. "Three's a crowd." It appeared he didn't need to know Loji's thoughts to know the wolf's intentions. "They may be welcoming Mütra—but they would *never* allow—"

"*Huw,*" Tanwen cut in, flashing him a silencing glare before turning to Loji. "I'm sorry, friend," she began, gentler now. "Huw is right in that you'd never be allowed to roam free in Galia. You belong here, not up there."

You belong here too, Loji argued, glowing eyes narrowing.

Perhaps, Tanwen agreed. *But you must understand, the last animal companion I allowed to come to Galia with me—* She swallowed past the sudden rise of grief in her throat.

Eli, Loji said gently, knowingly.

Yes, Eli. Tanwen nodded. *And he was small enough to hide. As much as I wish for your company and aid, I cannot risk it. You can help more here. Looking after my parents and Azla. Can you do that for me?*

The wolf huffed her irritation but relented. *I will protect them while you are away.*

"Thank you," said Tanwen, smiling as she stroked the wolf's thick mane, feeling ever grateful for her friendship.

"Not that I'm eager to rush this foolish mission," Huw said, "but we should get moving."

Tanwen nodded.

"We'll be together again soon," she said, forcing her voice steady as her gaze lingered on her parents.

Her mother's eyes shimmered with unshed tears as her father slipped an arm around her.

They stood unified, and Tanwen had to swallow down another rise of emotion at the sight.

It was an image Tanwen tucked deep into her memory as she and Huw walked away.

The one she would summon in the darkest moments ahead, to remind herself what she was fighting to return to.

PART III

Reunion

16

Habelle stood poised beside her son, bearing witness to history.

Horns of every shape and size fanned out in front of them, a tapestry of colors and textures reflecting the diversity of the Rebellion delegates. Wide eyes and parted lips betrayed their awe as they took in the towering columns, shimmering mosaics, and gleaming white marble.

Yet, still, their uneasy shuffling echoed through the vast throne room, the gilded chamber amplifying the absence of the Volari court.

Despite this monumental arrival, it was not to be a spectacle for their nobility. Not today.

Her son had insisted on a private welcoming.

He would not risk souring his accomplishment so quickly.

Unsurprisingly, Galia had been in turmoil ever since Zolya's announcement that he would host the next Cādra peace meeting.

Outrage had rippled through the conservative factions like a thunderstorm, their fury clashing with an unexpected groundswell of progressive Volari and bold recruits.

Habelle had enjoyed every tumultuous moment.

It spoke of change, of democracy taking root beneath a monarchy.

Something that *never* would have been tolerated under her husband's rule.

But just as she had welcomed healthy debate with her son, he now welcomed it among his subjects.

"It is an honor to have you in Galia." Zolya's commanding voice carried over the gathered crowd.

He was not perched high upon his throne—as tradition dictated—but instead waited at its base, grounded and purposeful. A subtle yet powerful message to their guests.

I meet you on equal terrain.

"I am grateful that you have accepted our invitation," he continued. "I understand the risk you each have taken to be present here today, but I give you my word as king—your safety will be respected and upheld." Though he addressed their guests, the declaration also seemed aimed at every kidet and kidar in the room. "I hope for us to be productive in the coming days as our two parties discuss the future of Cādra. To prove my good faith, with you and my Royal Council as witnesses"—he gestured to the council members standing nearby—"today, I take the first step toward fulfilling one of your key requests to end these uprisings. I will repeal a law enacted by my father—the ban on Mütra."

A ripple of shock spread through the delegates, murmurs of disbelief rising as a scroll was brought forward and unfurled before Zolya.

As he took up the quill, Habelle noticed several councilmen stiffen, their disapproval thinly veiled.

They may have backed his vision for peace—faced with a war they could ill afford—but they had not all agreed to this bold, unilateral move, especially without negotiation or concessions from the Rebellion party.

Among the dissenters was Osko Terz, lead royal kidar and new council member. He was perhaps the most verbose opposer of the abrogation of this law.

It was hardly surprising for a Volari aristocrat, but still disappointing to realize her son's oldest friend was so deeply rooted in his prejudice.

Osko remained silent now, however, though the tension in his clenched jaw betrayed his discontent as Zolya bent to sign.

With a single stroke of his quill, centuries of genocide enforced by her husband were ended. Though, the effects, she knew, would take far longer to heal.

Gasps rippled through the assembled guests.

Stunned disbelief as a surge of exhilaration shot through Habelle's veins.

"Mütra are no longer outlawed," Zolya announced, his voice resolute.

As he spoke, his attention momentarily became fixed on a single point in the crowd.

Anyone not watching closely would have missed it, but Habelle didn't.

Curiosity stirring, she followed his line of sight to a woman.

At first glance, she seemed unremarkable—pale skin, dark hair, horns of the eastern clan, yet unease still curled in Habelle's gut. It was the way the woman stared back at her son—unflinching, unabashed, and with a burning pride.

Intimate.

Panic flashed icy cold down Habelle's spine.

She snapped her gaze back to her son, but the moment had vanished.

Zolya had returned to addressing the crowd, and whatever private connection she had glimpsed scattered like smoke.

She prayed it was merely a meaningless glance, a fleeting illusion—but no, recognition now clawed at her as she studied the woman once again.

She knew her.

From the reports: Tanwen Coster—revealed as Tanwen Heiro—daughter of Gabreel Heiro, Mütra infiltrator who had become atenté to Princess Azla. Who had disappeared the same night her father, her brother, and the princess had.

When Habelle had first noticed Ms. Heiro's name on her son's guest list, she'd only thought of the political scandal to invite her—not this.

She had never thought that the girl might be a threat in a more personal matter.

Habelle pressed her lips together, silently fighting the concern crackling within her veins, stirring her magic.

How many times had her son's and Ms. Heiro's paths crossed when she served within the palace?

Surely it could not have been many.

After all, Zolya was not one to indulge in docüra to need her services.

Plus, he had never paid much attention to servants, *especially* never to seek pleasure.

Habelle had even chastised him on his snobbish behavior toward their staff.

With a forced steadying breath, she attempted to calm her spiraling thoughts.

She knew her son.

She was merely being paranoid, afraid that the power she had sacrificed so much for could be taken from him. Just as quickly as it had once been taken from her.

"And we shall work in our sessions on how best to integrate Mütra." Zolya's voice drew her back to the present. "I understand this change will not occur overnight, nor will this erase the historic trauma done to your kind." He looked to the few Mütra in the room. "Many injustices remain, but I hope that you have seen here today I am the king who is prepared to confront them."

The stunned silence still lingered.

Apprehension and distrust.

What trick may this be? the group's collective quiet seemed to say.

But then as the scroll remained signed, intact, as it was held up for the crowd to see, there was an eruption of applause.

Like thunder, cheers and joyous cries filled the chamber, the Rebellion crowd swept away by the king's actions, his promise of change, and their witnessing such a monumental moment in Cādra history.

Despite the moving moment, however, Habelle's expression stayed neutral beneath her mourning veil. Her gaze held on Ms. Heiro.

She was smiling, caught in a celebratory embrace with a blond companion, tears streaming down both their cheeks—until, as if sensing being watched, she hesitated.

Habelle's and Ms. Heiro's eyes met for a fleeting second before the girl turned away, disappearing into the crowd.

It was enough.

Suspicion curled around Habelle's shoulders like a shadow.

She tightened her grip until her knuckles paled, her gaze shifting sharply to Zolya, who now graciously greeted a line of guests.

He was a vision of benevolence, smiling warmly as he offered up encouraging words.

Though he bore his father's likeness, his mind was fiercely opposed.

A truth that had always reassured Habelle but now troubled her.

Because no matter how passionately he ruled, some laws could not be so easily overturned.

There were limits, even for royals, but certainly for kings when it came to matters of the heart.

Habelle understood the cost of forgetting that truth.

Which was why she didn't trust easily—not rebels, not allies, and sometimes, not even her own son.

17

Despite the cause for celebration, Tanwen could not recall a more awkward dinner.

The dining hall felt like an awaiting battlefield rather than a place for breaking bread.

Perhaps it would have been best—for their first meal, at the very least—if the assigned seating had left the two parties, well, parted.

Instead, beneath the warm firelight, stretching along an endless dining table, Volari Royal Councilmen sat stiff backed beside Rebellion delegates. Each of their faces was composed in careful neutrality as gazes remained sharp with mistrust. Conversation came in clipped sentences, forced politeness punctuated by the clink of silverware.

Both sides were clearly waiting for the illusion of civility to fracture into conflict.

Though, more unsettling than the tension surrounding her was the fact that Zolya sat at the head of the table—at the farthest end from where she was placed.

The only way she could steal a glimpse of him would be to bend awkwardly over her plate, peering through the elaborate table decor and towering displays of food—hardly subtle.

Which was what kept her gaze fixed forward, rigid in her restraint.

This, of course, did nothing to keep the longing from thickening in her veins, her grip tightening around her fork, fingers clenched.

The last they had parted, he had been angry with her.

The last they had spoken, his words had been heavy with hurt and betrayal.

She ached to be alone with him, to rebuild the trust she had fractured. Convince him she did not think their love so fragile that truth had to be hidden merely to avoid discomfort.

She was desperate for his forgiveness.

And then there was his repeal of Mütra banishment!

A shock that still vibrated through her core. Still had her heart beating in quick rhythms of elation and disbelief.

It had taken every fiber of her being not to fall to her knees in a sob before running to Zolya in the throne room and kissing him senseless.

Years of her fears and anger and pain, born from a life spent hiding, self-loathing, endlessly moving, and forced into silence and obscurity—had crashed into her like a comet plummeting from the night sky. The terror of merely existing, of knowing that a small misstep could mean her death, had defined her for so long.

And now, it was over.

She was free.

Free.

Though she knew the wounds of their past would never fade—and the prejudice against Mütra would be prevalent in certain groups for generations—this was still a monumental step toward hope that her people hadn't seen in over two centuries.

A miracle of miracles.

The deep timbre of Zolya's voice slid over her then, from where he spoke to those seated nearby.

The dining room came back into focus.

Tanwen forced herself to concentrate on her plate, for her breathing to even.

Yes, to say she was impatient to be alone with Zolya was an understatement.

"I say," Huw called out to a passing servant, catching Tanwen's attention—along with that of a few nearby guests. "I could use a refill."

Tanwen held in a cringe as he waved about his goblet. "I don't think you are meant to announce that your glass is empty," she murmured.

"I wouldn't have to if they were better at keeping it full," he quipped, flashing a sickly-sweet smile as a servant satiated his bidding. "Thank you, good fellow."

The waiter's lips pressed into a thin line as he backed away.

"They don't seem to enjoy serving Mütra," she admitted.

"Mm," Huw agreed, though he hardly seemed bothered as he took a hearty swig of his drink.

"You're okay with that?" she asked.

He huffed a laugh. "My dear little fawn, we are dining at the *palace*, at the table with the *king*, as his *guests*. If enduring the snobbery and prejudice of a few staff is the price for not being hunted, tortured, or killed—so be it. Besides, half of them seem just as irritated to be serving their own kind."

Tanwen glanced around the vast hall, unable to argue with him there.

Servants pressed against the columns. Some fought to contain their excitement, no doubt eager to be witness to this historic dinner. Others barely masked their unease—or worse, their disdain—at being forced to serve the Rebellion delegates.

Tanwen had almost forgotten how snobbish the palace recruits could be.

Or perhaps their contempt lay in what the Rebellion had forced them to lose—their connection with their loved ones on the continent.

Communication and compensation to the mainland remained severed, just as the Rebellion's grip stalling trade with Galia held firm.

Despite the abolishment of the Mütra law, there was much still to do while here.

"It is a marvel how warm it is on this island," said Brynn, bringing Tanwen's attention back to the dinner, to where Brynn sat across the table from her and Huw. She was flanked by two Volari councilmen but held more muscle on her person than the lot combined. "I'd have assumed it would be windy and cold so high up, especially at night."

When neither of her seat companions appeared willing to reply, merely continued to eye her four wings with unease, Tanwen stepped in.

"There are wind and heat wielders all around the isles and the palace," she explained. "It's what keeps the temperature the same night and day."

"Volari who work?" Brynn's brows met her hairline.

"Of course we work," huffed one of the councilmen. "We work here in Galia as well as in Cādra. In the harvest fields, in the timber yards and the quarries. We are soldiers and business owners. How else would we afford to live?"

"Off the labor of others, of course," answered Brynn, gesturing to the staff.

"All recruits here are compensated," he replied in clear offense.

"I know that, but—"

"And where might we get the funds to pay our employees but with our own work," he interjected, furthering his point.

Brynn blinked, reassessing the man. "Huh, so you are not all aristocratic sluggards?"

"No, we are not." He bristled. "My family owns a textile business in Fioré. We are very hands on with the day to day. I, myself, work our looms when creating new designs to be replicated, and encourage our staff with bonus incentives for sharing manufacturing or pattern ingenuities."

"Well," Brynn exhaled, glancing across the table to Tanwen and Huw. "Today has certainly been enlightening, hasn't it? Dare I say, I'm even excited for what tomorrow may bring." She turned back to her seatmate with a smile. "I might just prove to you that I'm not an abomination." She cackled at her own joke, jabbing the man with an easy elbow. To his credit, he did not recoil from the touch.

"I voted in favor of repealing the Mütra ban," he said evenly. "I have always believed it to be a barbaric and unjust law. I'm glad to see it gone."

A shocked hush fell over their group as the councilman took a sip of his drink.

Tanwen, of course, knew not all Volari were like minded in their Mütra prejudices, thinking of Azla and certainly Zolya, but still—to hear one of them admit it outright, and a councilman at that . . . without a trace of fear in his eyes . . .

Well, it was a revelation.

"Careful, my lord," Brynn drawled, a smirk tugging at her lips. "You might just catch my fancy."

The man surprised them further by barking a laugh, unfazed by the attention it brought him from nearby guests.

Lifting his glass, he clinked it against Brynn's.

It was, perhaps, the most promising development of their dinner so far.

That and the miraculous fact that Mütra were sitting here at all, sharing a meal with Volari nobles. She'd come to learn there were two more of their kin invited for these meetings, Mütra hiding within Süra clans.

Tanwen shook her head, still astonished, as her chest swelled with an overwhelming and unfamiliar sense of happiness.

Zolya had done what he had always sworn to do when king.

Mütra were free.

Would it ever feel real?

A soft smile played on her lips as she glanced around the table.

While the guests were remaining civil, what would the rest of Zolya's subjects think of this repeal?

How would their world celebrate it?

She wished she could be there to give the news to her parents. Hold them, cry with them, and scream into the treetops in exhausted relief.

Everything they hoped for, were fighting for was slowly becoming a reality.

Now more than ever, she was glad she had come, that she had convinced her parents that she *needed* to come. To be part of this history.

The pressure of tears burned behind Tanwen's eyes.

Her desire to look at Zolya washed over her again, stronger and more demanding.

"Are you not going to eat that?" Huw forked some of her vegetables from her plate, redrawing her attention.

"I could have said I was going to." She frowned.

He helped himself to a few more bites. "You could have, but then you'd be lying—and you're not a very good liar." He gave her a long, pointed look. "You've barely eaten anything. Which is sinful given how much effort we know the palace cooks put into preparing these feasts."

"Much has happened today," she said by way of an excuse. "My appetite hasn't caught up with me."

"Really? I get hungrier when excited." As if to validate his statement, he finished off the last bit of food from both their plates. "Ah," he sighed with satisfaction as he leaned back in his chair. "I fear I must now find the lavatory. The wine has gone straight through me."

"I'll accompany you," said Tanwen, suddenly desperate to leave the dinner. She was dreadfully tired and wasn't certain how much longer she could abstain from looking at Zolya.

"One of the footmen can escort me," Huw said with a dismissive wave. "No need for you to bother. We're not employed here anymore, remember? Stay and enjoy the dessert. Or better yet, save me yours for when I get back." He leaned in slightly, a sly grin curling at his lips. "Though, to be honest, I might be detained. There's plenty of gossip I'm eager to uncover from the staff. I can only imagine the whispers happening downstairs now that we've arrived as guests." His smile was serpentine. "Madame Arini is probably beside herself!"

"I won't impede on your gossipmongering," she replied with an eye roll, already standing alongside him.

Two footmen rushed to pull out their chairs.

She hesitated, unsure how to navigate such formal decorum—especially when it was directed at her. But the moment was fleeting.

Huw was already moving, and she hurried to catch up, her discomfort forgotten as they stepped into the open-aired path.

Large flaming bowls lined the walkway, their flickering light casting warmth over the marble floor, otherwise bathed in Nocémi's night.

Tanwen nearly sighed in relief, ready to savor the small victory of surviving their first day—and dinner—without a misstep.

But then, Zolya's deep and familiar laugh cut through the space between two columns.

Like a hummingbird drawn to nectar, she turned toward the sound.

An azure storm barreled into her.

The palace, the night, the stone beneath her feet dissolved as Zolya's piercing gaze locked onto hers despite the great distance between them. Despite her standing in the shadow of the columns on the far end of the room.

He saw her.

Watched her, even as he feigned interest in whatever the Süra elder beside him was saying.

Emotions flickered in his eyes, too swift to name, but the connection sent a jolt to her senses.

She tore her gaze away, forcing herself to move forward before anyone else noticed where the king's attention lay.

Her skin hummed, a quiet anticipation building.

As she listened to Huw's idle rant beside her, she tried to steady herself, tried to calm the stampeding thump of her heartbeats despite the heat pulsing through her veins.

She didn't know what this peace meeting would bring.

Didn't know what dangers lurked in her return to the palace.

But Tanwen knew with certainty what she would do to Zolya the moment she had the chance.

18

Clouds draped around Tanwen, a silken whisper.

The hum of insects serenaded her dreams as a tepid breeze from her open window traced its fingers over her exposed skin—light, fleeting.

Until its touch deepened, grew warmer.

Grew real.

She gasped awake as a heated breath skimmed her neck, followed by the low rumble of a familiar voice at her ear. "You left dinner early."

She lay still as her pulse quickened.

Zolya. Her heart leaped.

"It was a long day of travel," she reasoned.

He pressed his body against her back, solid and unyielding. His scent of bergamot and night slid over her senses like a caress. "Do you wish to keep sleeping?" he asked. "I can leave."

"No." She turned quickly, panic rising in her chest—until it evaporated in a rush the moment her gaze landed on him.

Zolya lay beside her, bathed in the moons' light streaming through the window. It caught the sharp planes of his face, his white hair glowing ethereal where it fell loose to his shoulders. A broad chest rose and fell with his steady breath, the embroidered collar of his coat unbuttoned to reveal the strong lines of his neck.

Heat bloomed in her belly, then traveled lower as she studied him and he studied her.

◆ ◆ ◆

Eyes like storm light roamed her features, bright yet unreadable.

Slowly, he lifted his hand, tracing the curve of her cheek, then her chin, then the shape of her lips, like he was memorizing them all over again.

She closed her eyes, an ache racing up her throat. *Gods*, how much she had longed for his touch.

"Zolya," she said, her voice thick with emotion. "I truly am sorry. I should never have kept my role in your father's poisoning from you."

The words were bitter on her tongue—but she forced them out before her courage slipped away.

"I can't express how much I regret not telling you sooner. If I could go back . . . If I could—"

"I know." He gently quieted her. "I understand why it was hard for you to tell me."

She blinked. "You do?"

"You were grieving your brother," he said, his gaze softening. "You still are. I understand. Your heart was where it needed to be. I couldn't expect you to be thinking of my father then. And then you had Drygul. The Rebellion. Just as I was consumed here. I don't like that it was my sister who told me the truth, but . . . I want to believe you would've told me yourself, eventually."

"Yes," she said quickly. "I would have. I kept turning it over in my mind, waiting for the right moment. But I should've known—there's never a good time for something like this."

"No," he agreed. "There isn't."

"I do want you to understand how it happened," she said. "Bosyg made me a deal. Protection for my mother while I was in Galia. I couldn't leave her unguarded and alone. Not after you took my father and brother—"

"I understand," he cut in, knuckles brushing over her cheek once more, eyes dark with his own regrets. "Of course I do. You do not need to explain yourself further. Like I said, I merely needed time with it."

A rush of relief surged through her, loosening something tight in her chest. She leaned into his touch.

"Then . . . you forgive me?" she whispered.

"My wildflower," he rumbled, "I could never stay long angry with you."

Her restraint snapped.

She tangled her fingers in the hair at his nape and tugged him to her lips.

He went willingly, taking her mouth in long, sweeping kisses.

Fire coursed down Tanwen's body as a moan slipped free.

Though awake, she fell back into her dreams—where Zolya was always waiting.

Yet, now, his mouth was real against hers, his weight solid, his scent alive and intoxicating with every breath she drew.

After their long parting.

The unknown of when they'd be together again.

If he'd ever forgive her.

The long travel here.

Topped with what had been done when they had arrived—what *he* had done—the freeing of Mütra . . .

Tanwen was overwhelmed by the magnitude of it all—by the heaviness of her emotions, of her love for him—this incredible, noble, fearless, loyal, loving, and empathetic man.

Her grip tightened in his hair, eliciting a pleased rumble from him as she attempted to claim him as he had already claimed her heart.

They were both breathless when he finally broke away, his gaze dark with desire as he stared down at her.

"May I ease the long pains of your journey here?" he asked, his voice a silken temptation.

She could only nod before holding in a shiver of anticipation as his hand skimmed down her stomach to the hem of her night shift.

Achingly slow, he drew it up, his fingers eventually slipping beneath.

Her breath quickened as he massaged her thighs to part.

The entire time he watched her, that intense, observant blue gaze of his seeming to worship and relish her every reaction to his touch.

But then his fingers reached her most sensitive bud, and she nearly cried out.

He caught the sound with his lips, skillfully working her into a frenzy.

He slipped a finger inside, taking his time to play, prolong, draw her to her wettest, until she nearly growled in frustration.

She gripped his wrist, forcing him in fully as she rubbed against his palm.

"My wildflower," he rumbled, a light tease in his voice. "You don't wish to go slow?"

"We haven't lain together in over a month," she reasoned, tone a pitiful whine. "No, I don't wish for slow."

A low chuckle filled the darkness.

But Tanwen was far from amused.

Sitting up, she pushed against Zolya's chest, forcing him back just enough to straddle him.

Her guest quarters were modest—a small bedroom with an adjoining lavatory. Yet, she had reveled in the accommodations because they were hers. Private.

More than enough for her, but with Zolya also here, with his greatness and muscles and wings, it shrank to a box.

But his mind seemed furthest from the size of her abode.

Efficiently, he shucked off his coat and tunic, his wings stretching without the burden of his clothes. All the while she ground against him, feeling the hard proof of his desire between her thighs.

Zolya moaned, the deep sound reverberating down her spine, a delicious cascade.

She grew frantic, unbuttoning his trousers, freeing him. And then she swallowed as she gripped his thickness, glorious and hers.

A raindrop landed on her shoulder.

Tanwen frowned, confused, as she glanced up.

Her pulse stuttered. "Zolya," she breathed. "Is this you?"

He followed her gaze to the swirling storm darkening her ceiling, biting out a curse.

"My magic," he muttered. "It's been temperamental since my coronation."

Taking a deep inhale, he worked to steady himself. With each of his exhales, the storm slowly dissipated, the lingering droplets vanishing into the air.

"Ré passed on a kiss of his gifts with his blessing," he explained. "I'm still adjusting to the power."

"Should we stop?" she asked.

"No."

His emphatic response made her laugh.

But it was quickly cut off by her surprised yip as he spun her beneath him. Zolya hovered, a mass of muscle and strength as he held her wrists to the bed. "I will learn to master this new power," he said gruffly, slowly grinding his length against her opening. Her eyes nearly rolled to the back of her head from the pleasure. "Just as I learned to master my magic as a boy. I merely need to practice."

"Do you need an assistant for these lessons?" She wrapped her legs around his hips, her smile playful. "Because I will gladly offer my services."

His eyes flared, a flashing shadow of hunger. "How magnanimous." His voice was a velvet drawl. "But I should warn you now, I like to train rigorously."

Tanwen gasped as he slid inside her.

He let go of her wrists so she could grip his shoulders—so big, so full, all hers.

He kept his hips still, allowing her to grow accustomed to him inside her as he pulled down the straps of her nightdress. He bared her breasts before taking one of her nipples into his mouth.

She groaned, the heat of him searing through her, setting fire to every nerve.

Then—finally—he began to move. Slow at first, savoring her, before plunging deep with deliberate, glorious thrusts.

The weight of him was a balm to the ache of their separation, his licks and kisses and caresses a remedy to the fever of her longing.

Tanwen was desperate to cry out, to let her pleasure crest uninhibited, but she bit her lip instead.

They kept their groans hushed.

Not just for fear of Zolya's magic slipping, but because they were in the palace now.

No longer were they hidden beneath a secret gondola, wrapped in the safety of seclusion.

They both seemed to understand this.

Understand the ears that lurked beyond these walls, the servants and kidets prowling the halls.

But the risk only heightened the pleasure, sharpened every sensation, sending sparks with every touch.

As the night dipped forward, they consumed each other like a sacred secret—like a whispered prayer in the dark.

19

Tanwen's eyes were heavy, but she refused to let them close.

Her body was spent, her limbs liquid and useless as she lay nestled in the crook of Zolya's arm. One of his wings was draped over them like a velvet blanket, his fingers tracing lazy patterns over her bare shoulder.

Even now, she couldn't help but marvel at him—at the man holding her. How could someone so full of goodness have come from a ruler like King Réol?

"You did it," she whispered, unable to stop the tear that slipped down her cheek. "You freed me."

Zolya's brows knit together, his features bathed in moonlight as he reached out, brushing the tear away with his thumb. "We did it," he corrected gently.

"Yes, but you repealed the law without asking for anything from the Rebellion in return."

"I made a promise to you," he murmured. "If I was ever king, it wouldn't be my law. I meant it. What has been done to Mütra . . ." He swallowed, agony clear in his features. "I'm sorry, Tanwen. I wish there was more I could do to right the wrongs that have been done."

Her heart squeezed with gratitude.

No one had ever been able to promise her safety—not even her parents, despite all their sacrifices. Being Mütra had always meant living in fear.

But now, there was a future. A real one.

Because of Zolya.

Because of his loyalty to her, his vow to her kind, and his compassionate heart.

Zolya helped her feel safe—truly safe—for the first time in her life, and the realization hit so hard it stole her breath, a sob of relief catching painfully in her throat.

"You've made it possible for the next generation to live born free." She worked desperately to steady her voice as she cupped his jaw. "To not be scared or ashamed of who they were born. That is a *great* wrong righted."

His smile was small, but it was there. "Thank you," he said.

She frowned. "For what?"

"For helping me always see the potential of our world. For making me a better man. I hope one day I can be worthy of the miracle of your love."

Emotion swelled in Tanwen's chest. "Well, you're doing a fine job of working toward it," she teased.

He rumbled a laugh before he pulled her close. He kissed her slowly, reverently, and it threatened to bring more tears to her eyes.

When they settled back against the bed, Zolya exhaled, his fingers threading absently through hers. "I can make such changes now," he said. "I had to be reminded of that. My council is there for guidance, to voice the needs of my people, but the final say of what's put into law rests with me. It's unsettling, actually—how much power one person can wield. How much a king can change, for good or for worse."

"Yes," Tanwen agreed. "It is rather terrifying."

"It makes me uncomfortable," he admitted.

She tightened her grip on his hand. "You will not abuse it."

His frown deepened, shadows flickering in his gaze.

"What's wrong?"

"My ascension to the throne was not exactly . . . clean," he replied.

A pang of guilt twisted in Tanwen's stomach. The poison. The king. The role she played.

"If this is about the poison, it was not you who planned—"

"I wasn't speaking about that," he said, cutting her off.

She frowned. "Then what?"

Zolya hesitated for a moment. "Bosyg hasn't been the only god meddling in mortal affairs. It seems Nocémi did not support my father. Or rather, she didn't support who her husband favored."

"What does that mean?"

"Nocémi helped us kill him." His voice was low, grave.

Shock rooted her in place. Her comprehension slow.

Nocémi helped us kill him.

Kill the king.

Tanwen felt she was tumbling into another realm.

By some miracle, she kept her tone composed, unjudging, as she tentatively asked, "Us?"

"My mother and I," Zolya admitted, his gaze growing distant as he looked toward the ceiling. "Nocémi came to my father's bedside, offered a godly blade for my mother and I to do the deed. Said it would appear as if he merely died in his sleep, the poison finally claiming him."

The bedchamber hung silent like a tomb with his admission.

Tanwen held her breath, sensing there was more he wished to say.

"I was prepared to do it." He met her gaze then, eyes sharp, clear. "But my mother stopped me. She took the knife in the end."

For a long moment, Tanwen couldn't speak, could hardly think.

She could not judge him or his mother, of course.

Not when she had been willing to do whatever it took to rid the world of the old king.

It had also been clear Zolya understood King Réol was a cruel tyrant who needed to be stopped—but this . . .

To be willing to commit patricide.

She did not know the queen in the least, but right now she was eternally grateful toward her. That she was the one to take up the blade rather than allow her son.

Tanwen did not doubt that Zolya would have done it—but it would have cost him greatly.

A vital piece of his heart would've frozen in that act—lost forever.

And knowing this was what brought her to say "I'm sorry, Zolya. Despite who he had become, I understand how hard that must have been."

There was a hard swallow to his throat.

"It's okay, you know," she said softly.

His brows pulled together. "What is?"

"To mourn your father." She placed a hand to his chest. "To mourn who you wished he had been."

Zolya's jaw tightened, his expression growing dark. He gripped the hand that lay atop him, as if it were holding him afloat, keeping him from drowning. "Thank you." His words came out a rough whisper.

She squeezed his hand in return.

"How is your mother?" she asked after a beat.

Zolya finally let out a deep exhale. "Don't let her mourning garb fool you—she's thriving. Dare I say, happy."

"Well . . . that must be a relief for you, at least."

Something softened in his expression as he turned fully toward her, clasping both of her hands in his. His gaze earnest and open. "I don't want secrets between us," he said, his voice quiet but firm. "Not anymore. Now, more than ever, we need to be honest with each other. There is too much at play, too many forces working in the shadows. And with the gods showing interest in us . . ."

His words trailed off, but Tanwen understood.

They were standing on the precipice of something far greater than either of them had planned.

The gods are fickle with how they move us around their celestial board.

Lady Esme's words from so long ago echoed in her mind then. How true they still remained.

"Ridi has involved himself in the uprising," Tanwen explained. "He seems rather enthusiastic about helping the Rebellion."

"That's hardly surprising." Zolya's tone carried a note of resignation. "I only hope he's the last god to interfere, though I doubt we'll be that fortunate."

Tanwen hesitated. There was more she wished to say.

Her journey to Both Island.

What they had uncovered there.

But to reveal this went beyond remaining truthful to one another.

It would be breaching her loyalty to her people.

Zolya wanted honesty between them, as did she. But this news wasn't hers to share—it belonged to the Rebellion. To her council. To Lady Callia and those who had fought and schemed and sacrificed to gain what little leverage they had.

She trusted Zolya. Of course she did.

But like he always reminded her, they still stood on opposite sides.

And there would be a time and a place for her to broach this topic with him.

In an official way.

When the Rebellion was ready to play such a hand. Until then, she would hold her tongue. As she'd expect Zolya to, as well, regarding whatever his party had planned for these peace meetings.

Because this—*this*—wasn't the time for politics.

Not when they were here, tucked close in the quiet of the night, speaking not as king and rebel, but as two people clinging to something rare. Something fragile—time together.

A precious, precarious commodity.

At the thought, she urged their conversation to a subject that could only be addressed privately.

"Let us speak no more of gods or rebellions," she said. "We'll have plenty of meetings for that. What I want to know, *Your Majesty*, is—what is it like being king?"

Zolya's expression grew thoughtful. "It's . . . different," he admitted. "A lot more people to see. More expectations to meet. I barely have a moment to myself."

"I imagine trying to stop an impending war keeps a king occupied."

"Mmm," he hummed in agreement, his expression remaining pinched. "I'm hardly a moment without my guards or another summons. How we'll be able to find time together will be . . . different from before."

"Yes," said Tanwen, the weight of her earlier thoughts tightening her chest.

"We need to be especially cautious," he warned. "In fact, I should probably return to my chambers soon."

Her fingers tightened in his. "Can you not stay a little longer?"

His brows drew together, the conflict evident in his face. "It was nearly impossible to come here tonight," he said, voice low with regret. "I had to fight Osko just to allow my guards leave from my quarters while I sleep. He was . . . less than thrilled by my demands." His lips twisted with his clear annoyance. "I had to remind him who was king."

Tanwen bit back the remark fighting up her throat.

Osko Terz.

She had come to learn how close he was to Zolya. And it unsettled her. The two men seemed opposing in every conceivable way—yet somehow Zolya seemed to value the man's counsel.

"I'm not sure how often we'll be able to steal these moments," he admitted, irritation and remorse flickering across his face.

She reached up, smoothing the tension from his brow with her fingertips. "We'll have our time when this is over," she said softly, though even as the words left her lips, she knew it was more of a wish than a promise.

Despite how hard she tried to suffocate her doubts, they always found a way to roar free.

Could there ever be a world where a king could be with someone like her?

A commoner.

A rebel.

A Mütra.

The world might have been ready for change—but whether it would ever embrace her love with Zolya remained uncertain.

Perhaps—even if their world found peace—these stolen moments would still be all they ever could get.

Hidden.

Secret.

Just like your existence once demanded.

The taunting hisses filled her mind, clenched invisible fingers around her throat.

She had fought so hard to crawl out of such an existence.

Yet, despite the new freedom of her people, she might still find herself shackled.

Forced to hide because of who her heart chose to love.

With a rush of panic, stronger than she could control, she pulled Zolya closer, capturing his lips.

She prayed he didn't feel her desperation in their kiss, didn't sense the way she clung to him—not just for warmth, but also for escape. For one blissful breath where the world beyond these walls ceased to exist.

He answered her passion with his own, hands encircling her, allowing her to disappear into their cocoon of dreams—offered her the safety she so desperately craved.

Tanwen knew then: If these moments were all Zenca, the High Goddess of destiny, would allow, then she would take them.

Because the alternative—a life without Zolya—was far worse.

20

Zolya's head throbbed.

A familiar affliction these days.

But the two men arguing in front of him in his private study were certainly not the cure any meddyg would prescribe.

"We are being too lenient," Osko said, arms crossed so tightly over his chest it seemed as though he were bracing for battle.

"We haven't agreed to anything," Lord Vincent countered from his seat in front of Zolya's desk, his tone measured. The late-afternoon sunlight caught the tight curls of gray at his temples, his weathered plumage in need of a good molting. "This was our first meeting with the Rebellion. Each side was meant to present their grievances and requests. That is how negotiations begin."

Osko scoffed. "A majority of their grievances were preposterous."

"Perhaps," Lord Vincent conceded, "but may I remind you—our treasury—"

"—is collecting dust," Osko cut in, his tone laced with irritation. "Yes, yes, you remind us with every breath you have left to take."

Lord Vincent shot him a withering look.

Unlike Osko, he had no interest in posturing.

As the long-standing master of the treasury—for more than three centuries, in fact—Lord Vincent's concerns were purely practical. His allegiance was to the kingdom's coffers and whichever path filled them. It was one of the reasons Zolya had chosen to keep him on the council after his father's passing.

"Then it won't be out of character for me to remind you of our position again," said Lord Vincent. "Your offense will not keep our treasury from running dry. Hearing out our opposition and what we might financially gain from them, however, will. After all, if war is what you wish, Kidar Terz, we still need the funds for one."

"There will be no war," said Zolya, his voice calm yet final. He hadn't wished to engage in their debate, but if speaking would end it, so be it. "Listening to the Rebellion's side is not leniency." He eyed Osko sharply. "It's patience."

"Or weakness," muttered Osko, jaw tight.

"*Careful*, Kidar Terz," warned Zolya, his magic jumping in his veins with his annoyance. They might have been childhood friends, but Osko's attitude was bordering on insolent.

"I apologize, Your Majesty." Osko inclined his head just enough to show deference. "I only meant that we must present ourselves as strong in Galia. Otherwise, the Rebellion will believe they have the upper hand, and what leverage will we have then? Appearances matter, sire."

"I do not disagree," replied Zolya. "And as the head of our armies, your desire for us to project strength is understandable. But strength is not measured solely in brute force. Power also lies in the ability to persuade. What purpose would there be in provoking tension during our first meeting? Especially when we have taken such care to show both the Rebellion and Cādra that Galia is willing to negotiate?"

"Negotiate," Osko scoffed. "An act King Réol would never have entertained."

Zolya nearly winced at the blow, his skin chilling as his magic thrummed like a windstorm in his veins. It took a great deal of effort not to loose a crack of lightning right where Osko stood.

He might have once shown esteem for his father, but those days were gone. *He* was now king, and he would no longer tolerate the failures of his predecessor—nor would he endure being unjustly measured against him.

Through clenched teeth, he forced out, "Which is exactly why we are in this position. *King Réol* bled our treasury dry with his bullheaded pride and appetite for war. To follow in his footsteps would not only be foolish—it would be the final ruin of our kingdom's wealth."

A tense silence settled over his study, thick as storm clouds.

Lord Vincent remained unruffled, however.

He observed the two men with a detached sort of interest—no doubt having witnessed far more dramatic clashes between a king and his council over the centuries.

"And I must say, Kidar Terz," Zolya continued, voice quieter now—more dangerous. "Your lack of faith in my rule is concerning. Tell me, if you are to compare me to my father, what punishment do you think he would have delivered for such free speech in his presence?"

Osko paled, the weight of the words settling on his shoulders.

"The way I see it, you should be thanking Udasha that I am *not* him. Not only for your own sake, but because I intend to return Galia to its true strength—not a hollow illusion of it." Zolya kept his voice measured, but the warning behind it was unmistakable. "That is why I will continue to tread these negotiations carefully, and why your fellow councilmen will as well. We'll obtain what we need to restore the treasury, and we'll do it without bloodshed. In the meantime, I advise you to practice patience."

Osko's lips pressed into a thin line, his displeasure evident, but he bowed nonetheless. "Yes, Your Majesty."

It gave Zolya no pleasure to see his friend forced into agreeing with him. Instead, it cleaved open his chest, filling it with woe—with loss.

They had been estranged since his signature repealed the Mütra law—a signature that had become an invisible border between them. Osko's prejudice ran deeper than Zolya had ever wanted to believe, but he now realized his friend harbored a profound hatred for those unlike himself. And it was blinding him.

Osko spoke of weakness, but what was weaker than lacking the strength to open his mind beyond the narrow confines of his bigotry?

In the following thick quiet of his study, Zolya could sense Lord Vincent's assessing gaze lingering, calculating. Weighing.

But he had no energy to entertain whatever conclusion the old man was drawing.

With a dismissive flick of his fingers, he said, "You're both excused."

The moment his door shut behind them, Zolya allowed himself a long exhale.

But the reprieve was fleeting.

"Your Majesty, the queen dowager requests an audience," announced his usher.

Zolya didn't bother looking up from his desk as he declared, "No."

"Zolya?" His mother's hurt voice cut through his room.

He glanced up, finding her already standing there.

Regret tugged at him, but exhaustion overpowered it.

"I'm sorry, Mother," he said, standing, his wings tense and restless at his back. "I don't have the energy for whatever this visit might entail."

Concern pooled in her gaze.

But his disappointment in Osko currently sat heavier on his chest than his mother's worry. It curled inside him like a familiar ache. It was a sorrow he recognized—one he had felt the day he realized his father was not the great man he had once believed him to be.

And now, Osko. A friend. A trusted figure.

It was another fracture in his foundation.

One more loss to bury.

"I will call on you later," he offered gently, though even as the words left his lips, they felt like a delay rather than a promise.

His mother didn't argue. She only nodded.

Zolya turned away before the guilt could further settle too deeply.

Striding onto his veranda, he spread his wings wide and leaped into the open air, the wind catching him instantly.

While his mother did not follow, his guards did.

And that, above all, only deepened his frustration.

Even in the skies, he was never truly alone.

21

Tanwen regretted not bringing her hat.

She had forgotten how relentless the light remained on Galia, despite the setting sun, the Royal Gardens offering little relief. The trees—decorative and sparse—provided only slivers of shade, their presence overshadowed by the abundance of manicured hedges and sprawling flowerbeds.

She and Huw walked side by side, the air thick with the scent of jasmine and the buzzing serenade of insects.

"Gods, it feels good to be outside," Huw exhaled, stretching his arms as though shaking off the weight of their recent meeting. "You'd think, with all the wall-less buildings in this palace, they'd pick somewhere less suffocating to hold our negotiations."

"I believe it's by design," said Tanwen, the gravel path crunching with her steps. "To keep what's discussed as private as possible."

"Well, I wish some would do a better job of keeping their *bad breath* private," Huw grumbled. "After so many long-winded speeches today, I thought the air itself in that room might smother me."

Tanwen laughed, the sound foreign even to her.

Not for the first time, she was grateful that Huw had forced his way into these peace meetings. He had an uncanny ability to lighten even the heaviest moments—a skill she had leaned on more times than she could count over the past months.

The weight of their uncertain future had been pressing down on her for so long, her shoulders felt bruised.

Yet, now, despite the pain Galia represented—that weight was shedding, being replaced by a salve of possibility.

Of progress.

Of change.

And this change was only reinforced by where they now walked.

They turned down another footpath—familiar, yet foreign. They had once trodden these lanes in silence as servants. Now, they navigated them as guests. *Mütra* guests.

It was a shift that felt both surreal and triumphant.

Especially given who else strolled these gardens.

Courtiers lingered nearby, their reactions to her and Huw's presence mixed.

Most cast them aside with the same practiced indifference as before—others recoiled in terror upon encountering rebels on the same lane, hastily taking to the skies, but a few, a very rare few, offered nods of acknowledgment.

It was subtle, but it was there.

And that was enough to send another ripple of hope through Tanwen's heart.

Zolya was proving that if Galia could follow one king's beliefs, it could follow another's.

Despite so many Volari still clinging to old ways, perhaps there were enough willing to learn new ones.

A small smile tugged at Tanwen's lips as she lifted her chin, now basking in the golden warmth of the setting sun.

For the first time in a long while, peace settled over her.

Then—

"You." The sneering voice sent Tanwen's stomach plunging.

She snapped her eyes open to find Gwyn standing in their path.

A storm of emotions crashed into her—shock, fear, sorrow—but the one that lingered, burning hot and unwavering, was anger.

Here stood the monster who had taken her Eli.

Who had filled his final moments with terror and pain.

Who had wedged a dagger into both their hearts.

Tanwen forced her breaths steady as her magic writhed within her, restless and seething. The sheer force of her ire startled even her.

Everything she had buried in the days after Eli's murder—all to stay focused on freeing her family—now surged to the surface. It growled and hissed and kicked, hungry for vengeance.

Nearby fowl chirped in distress, sensing her heightened emotions.

Fleetingly, she thought of Loji—how the wolf would've bared her teeth, hackles raised with Tanwen's distress. Gwyn would've likely shrieked and fled, dress soiled in fear. The thought brought her a flicker of satisfaction, though she knew it was better Loji wasn't here. Tanwen wasn't sure she could've—or would have—stopped the wolf from doing exactly as she pleased.

Pushing the daydream away, she kept her attention pinned to the glaring woman in front of her. Gwyn's fingers were clenched around her gardening basket, her neatly styled curls framing a face marred by a pinched scowl.

Beside her stood another atenté, unfamiliar to Tanwen, yet she mirrored Gwyn's disapproving stare.

"I didn't want to believe the rumors"—Gwyn sneered, her gaze raking over Tanwen and Huw—"that you'd be foolish enough to come back here. To be arrogant enough to defile this sacred ground again. *Mütra.*" She spit on the ground between them.

Specks landed on Tanwen's open-toed sandal, and something inside her snapped. She took a step forward, but Huw's voice cut through the tension, stilling her.

"Ah, ah, Gwyndolyn," he tutted. "That's hardly the etiquette Madame Arini taught you. Is that really how you greet the *king's* guests?"

Gwyn's rich-brown complexion paled with her rage. "I will *never* bow to you," she seethed. "I'd rather be transferred to the Shadow District."

"I'm sure that can be arranged," offered Huw, smile sharp. "After all, we do have the ear of some very influential lords these days."

"How anyone found you charming is a miracle," she ground out before turning her venomous glare back on Tanwen. "And you—how *dare* you serve a royal with your tainted hands. You desecrated our princess with your presence and corrupted tonics."

"Nothing about my tonics was impure," Tanwen shot back. "They were for headaches and menstrual cramps, Gwyn. The most basic meddyg—"

"I will not be fooled by your Mütra mind tricks!" she spit. "Princess Azla would never have left on her own or have abandoned her king and country. That was *your* doing. Your filthy magic twisted her mind, just like you've twisted others into tolerating you."

"What are you talking about?"

"How else could you stand here unpunished when the law demands your throat be slit?"

"Oh, haven't you heard?" asked Huw. "The laws changed."

Gwyn's lip curled. "More Mütra mind tricks!"

"You're mad," Tanwen bit out.

"And *you* will always be abominations," she hissed in return. "Ones who never know when to stay gone."

Tanwen stared at her, momentarily speechless.

She had seen her angry before—of course she had—but never like this. Never brimming with such raw, unhinged hate.

Cautiously, Tanwen eyed the gardening shears resting in Gwyn's basket.

"Your prejudice is so uninspired," sighed Huw. "Why don't you run along before you add more frown lines."

Gwyn's eyes bulged with her fury. "You have no idea the pain you've brought upon us here," she snarled, unmindful of the courtiers who had begun to gather, drawn by their commotion. "The suffering your foolish Rebellion has caused. I haven't been able to reach my mother or sister in weeks." Her voice cracked slightly at the admission. "None of my wages reach them. Who will pay for my sister's medication now? Hmm? Will you, *Mütra*?" Her gaze was a poison-dipped dagger flung at Tanwen. "Will you erase the pain of our interrogations? Yes, that's right," she added, catching Tanwen's expression of confusion. "It was not well met that the royal atentés had been employing mixed-bloods to serve aristocrats. Madame Arini was terminated because of the two of you! And we were each brought before an evaluator. The court wanted to ensure there were no others hiding among us. And let me tell you"—her voice dropped, bitter and tight—"their examinations were *thorough*."

Tanwen stiffened, guilt pooling in her gut to hear of Madame Arini and sickened by the thought of anyone being tortured because of her actions.

How could such cruelty unfold under Zolya's rule? But then she reminded herself that, at the time, Galia would have still been under King Réol's corrupt council.

She swallowed the bile rising in her throat, unsure how to navigate the tangle of her emotions. It was like unknowingly stepping onto a snake's nest, being instinctively ready to defend herself yet painfully aware she was to blame for disturbing its habitat.

Not to mention the reveal of Gwyn's family, of her caring for a sibling.

It was perhaps more disturbing than her current aimed hatred—twisting further complication into their exchange. That Gwyn could love *anything*. Could think of someone besides herself . . .

It made her seem a little less soulless.

Unwanted empathy bloomed in Tanwen's chest.

"Since the moment I met you," Gwyn continued, her fury continuing to froth over, "you have only brought suffering into my life."

Tanwen flinched.

Not at the accusation but at the sheer hypocrisy.

Her empathy vanished.

"*You* speak of suffering?" she scoffed, a bitter laugh escaping her. "You, who have been nothing but cruel and spiteful to anyone who doesn't bend to your will? You speak of a sibling—well, did you know that mine was tortured here?"

Gwyn blinked, momentarily stunned.

"Tanwen—" Huw touched her shoulder, his voice a gentle warning.

She shrugged him off.

She was too far gone now.

Too lost in her braid of pain and guilt and remorse.

The grief of losing those she loved to this island clawed at her chest, snarling to be free.

This island that was so blinded by light it couldn't see the world it was burning. Couldn't see how it turned its own citizens against each other.

"Have you ever had to bathe the blood from your sister's body?" Tanwen demanded, her voice trembling with her fury, her magic thrumming in her veins. "Reset her shattered bones while she lay limp in your arms? Have you ever pulled a knife from your best friend's heart?"

Gwyn parted her lips, but Tanwen wasn't finished. She was letting loose the years she had been forced to be quiet, small, forgotten in front of her tormentors. She was finally fighting.

"How quick you are to cry victim when you have always been the bully."

Gwyn's expression flickered—hesitation, doubt. "I never tortured your brother."

"No, but you took my Eli. *My* Eli." She could still see his blood on her sheets. His small body impaled. Her magic cried and hissed through her veins. "I know it was you who killed him," Tanwen whispered, rage thick in her throat. "You call us abominations, but only a monster could do what you did."

For a beat, something passed over Gwyn's face. Remorse. Surprise.

But then she uttered the words that shattered Tanwen's last tether. "It was a mouse."

"He was my *friend*," she bellowed.

"Tanwen," warned Huw again.

But she hardly heard him.

Her powers were pulsing in her head, her darkest desires whispering in her ears. *Pain, pain, pain. Give her your pain.*

In her periphery she could sense the animals, their slithering and skittering and whooshing. They were gathering beneath the hedges and landing on nearby branches.

And with them came the muffled distress of guests.

Gwyn's gaze flickered with unease, taking in the swarming creatures as she stepped back. "You Mütra are freaks," she whispered.

"You have no idea," Tanwen purred, her grin curling like a blade. *Go,* she thought.

The animals lunged.

Snakes struck. Lizards leaped. Beetles flittered. Birds dived from the trees.

Gwyn screamed.

She dropped her basket, hands flailing as she tried to shake them off.

The courtiers gasped, horrified.

But Tanwen was too consumed with watching Gwyn writhe and shriek to care.

Until a rush of wind cut through the chaos.

A shadow fell over them.

The king landed in the lane behind Gwyn like a comet—blazing and sudden—his guards fanning out at his back.

"What is the meaning of this?" Zolya's deep rumble sliced through the mayhem.

The garden went still.

Even the animals scattered.

As if on instinct, everyone bowed.

Tanwen dropped to one knee, gravel pressing against her skin. Her breaths were ragged as she forced her magic to settle, curling back into her veins.

Despite keeping her gaze lowered, she could sense Zolya's attention pinned to her, his anger.

It sent her pulse racing with unease.

She knew she should feel shame.

She should feel regret.

But she didn't.

She felt satisfied.

22

The gardens had been cleared.

The courtiers sent away.

Gwyn and her companion dismissed.

Only the king and his guards remained, staring down at where Tanwen and Huw stood, hands clasped in front of them, heads hung in contrition.

Within the long stretch of silence, Tanwen's guilt had finally snuck in.

If etiquette hadn't forced her to avert her eyes, she wouldn't have been able to meet Zolya's anyway.

He was furious. And worse yet—he had every right to be.

"I will not tolerate attacks on my staff," said Zolya, voice low, stern. "As guests of the crown, you represent me, and the behavior I have just witnessed is nothing I would ever condone."

Remorse gnawed at Tanwen, though it tangled with a petulant frustration. Gwyn had started it. But how could she say that without sounding like a child?

"I humbly beg your forgiveness. Your Majesty," she said, her head still bowed. "It was never my intention to act in a manner unbefitting to your grace and rule."

"Yes, Your Majesty," added Huw. "My sincerest apologies."

A tense silence followed. The kind that pressed down, weighted and expectant.

"In case you were unaware—or have forgotten," Zolya went on, "there are strict laws in place regarding the use of magic on Galia that every Volari must abide by. You may not be Volari, but you certainly both hold such gifts. I suggest you reacquaint yourselves with these laws."

"Yes, sire," they answered in unison.

"You will also write a formal letter of apology to Ms. Allyga."

Tanwen flinched. Not at the reprimand, but at the unfairness of the demand, *and* that he seemed to know Gwyn. At least enough to know her surname.

Heat flared beneath her skin, ugly and irritated—jealousy.

"You are displeased by my request, Ms. Heiro."

She looked up, not enjoying that her feelings had been so clearly on display.

Zolya regarded her evenly, his broad shoulders and tucked-in wings alight with the setting sun.

A formidable king.

She hated that they were once again back on uneven footing. He her superior, she his subject, unable to speak her mind fully. But these were the parts they were expected to play, the masks they were forever forced to wear in public.

She only wished Zolya didn't wear his so bloody well.

"I only find it displeasing, sire, that Ms. Allyga is not required to write one as well."

A single white brow arched. "And what apology do you seek from her?"

Tanwen's anger stirred again. "Well, sire," she began carefully, "I trust you understand my actions were not without provocation."

He waited, silent, expectant.

"My companion and I"—she gestured toward Huw—"were walking these paths in peace when Ms. Allyga chose to verbally accost us. It seems, sire, that some take offense at having once worked beside Mütra."

Zolya's expression remained unreadable, but a muscle in his jaw twitched.

Beside her, Tanwen could sense Huw's unease, no doubt wishing she had left it alone. Part of her wished the same, feeling like a kid tattling, but she was tired of swallowing the bigotry, or of bearing its weight in silence.

Let the tormentors finally be held accountable.

"And you believe using your powers against former peers will change their prejudice?"

Her cheeks burned.

Embarrassment tangled with her frustration that he would call her out like this.

"You and your fellow Mütra were invited here to represent your kind, Ms. Heiro," Zolya continued, his voice measured. "To show that peace between our people is possible. I understand that it is unfair to hold you to a higher standard than others, but that is the reality of your position. While here, you will be expected to rise above these petty provocations. By clashing against others' hatred, you do not weaken their blade—you sharpen it. You prove their slurs and prejudices true."

He let the words settle, his disappointment pressing around her throat like an unseen grip.

"You have earned your seat at my table," he added. "I ask that you do what is necessary to keep it."

His gaze was searing as it held to hers.

Tanwen's pulse pounded, a storm in her veins as she wrestled with a maddening mix of mortification and frustration knowing he was right.

Her conflicting emotions had her wishing to shove him, while also desperate to kiss him. Incredibly irresponsible of her to even think, she knew.

He was just so near, so commanding, and so off limits.

But then, with a sudden rush of wind, he and his guards were gone, leaving her and Huw bowing in their wake.

PART IV

Schemes

23

Habelle stood at the railing of her veranda, ill at ease.

She had personally requested that her rooms face the Royal Gardens—a favorite haunt of the court, perfect for strolling, being seen, and collecting gossip.

From her perch Habelle had the pleasure of watching without being watched.

But today, she gained no joy from what she had witnessed unfold below. Her son dressing down Ms. Heiro and her companion.

She could not exactly name what troubled her, she only knew something did.

Call it a mother's intuition.

For as she eyed the two Mütra hastening back inside, she understood that any interaction between her son and that woman was an interaction too many.

"Ma'am," came a soft voice to her right. "We are ready to dress you for this evening."

Habelle turned to find Ms. Sonja, her head of staff.

"This evening?"

"Yes, the court reception that is tonight, ma'am."

"Oh, yes, that," she replied absently, her gaze drifting to the woman's horns—so like Ms. Heiro's.

Ms. Heiro, who had demonstrated an impressive strength with her unique magic just now in the gardens.

Ms. Heiro, who had caught the attention of her son, yet again.

What Habelle had glimpsed in the throne room no longer felt like a fluke. Not after catching Zolya's attention flickering in Ms. Heiro's direction during the Rebellion dinner. Not after watching his focus linger on her during today's peace meeting. Not after today—when he had looked upon the woman not just with disappointment but also with a known expectation of more.

If Habelle wasn't watching for it, she wouldn't have noticed. If she hadn't known her son so well, she wouldn't have been able to interpret the meaning behind his carefully composed expression.

But she was watching.

She *did* know him.

And a warning bell tolled in Habelle's chest.

She bore no ill will toward Ms. Heiro or her kind—she and her people deserved their freedoms and future.

But that was a far cry from condoning her becoming a part of the royal household. The court would never accept it. The gods least of all. Such scandal would put not only Zolya's reign at risk but also his life.

Habelle held in a shiver of disquiet as she looked toward the sky.

It was hard to predict how close the High Gods watched them, but surely with Nocémi's recent visit and the turnover of Volari kings, they'd be paying closer attention than usual.

Her thoughts churned.

Young love, she thought mulishly. *Always foolish.*

Because unfortunately she knew it was love, not merely lust.

Lust she could ignore. Lust she would have gladly welcomed instead.

For she knew lust fizzled and faded and died after time, after growing comfortable.

No, what she saw in her son's gaze when he looked upon Ms. Heiro was something fiercer—protective, reverent.

He was not a man who gave himself to anything lightly.

Still, before she spoke to him, she needed to be certain.

"Ma'am?" Ms. Sonja asked again. "Do you not wish to attend tonight's event? I can dismiss the staff at once."

Habelle glanced toward her open veranda doors, where shadows of servants lingered at the threshold to her bedroom.

They were forever tucked in corners or behind columns, quiet adornments of the palace, ever waiting for a noble's beck and call.

"How long have you served as head of my staff, Ms. Sonja?"

A flicker of unease crossed the woman's face. "Three decades, ma'am."

She considered her a long moment. "And they have been three decades of faithful service for which I am truly grateful."

Ms. Sonja bowed, visibly moved. "It has been the greatest honor of my life to serve you, Your Majesty."

"I'm honored to hear it," Habelle replied. "Because what I ask now will require a different kind of service."

Her head of staff straightened, attentive.

"I need your help, Ms. Sonja, but you must swear on your life this remains between us."

Ms. Sonja blinked, momentarily surprised, before her expression settled into one of steady loyalty. "Of course, ma'am. My obedience to you is the very purpose of my service."

Satisfied, Habelle stepped in close and bent to whisper her request in the woman's ear.

24

Zolya would never have agreed to this gathering if not for the relentless pressure from his court.

It's not like they had the funds for such frivolity.

Nor did he particularly trust his nobles to behave hospitably toward the rebel party.

Still, he understood the necessity. The court needed to see the people he and his council were to negotiate with daily—the ones shaping the kingdom's uncertain future.

They needed to feel included.

Needed to believe their opinions held sway.

Despite the farce of it all.

Our court are like children, his mother had once told him. *So long as they believe you are paying attention to them, they will leave you alone.*

And so far, her advice has appeared sound.

None had done more than offer a perfunctory greeting before returning to their posturing, more than satisfied to be included in this historic mingling.

So far, they were behaving.

The great hall blazed with warmth, firelight spilling from bronze bowls hung high along the vaulted ceilings. Through the columns, the star-strewn night sparkled, and within the golden glow of the room, nobles glided about with practiced elegance. Some smiled as they brushed shoulders with the infamous rebels, though Zolya surmised more for the thrill than any true goodwill.

Others lingered with barely veiled disgust, clearly attending only to collect grievances they could later parade at court.

Zolya sipped his wine more from habit than thirst, his gaze inevitably drawn—again—to Tanwen.

But how could he *not* look at her?

She stood across the room, tucked into the far corner like a reluctant flame.

She wore a dress in the Galian style: off-white silk that clung to her curves, cinched by a broad gold-hammered belt. Her hair was braided up, her horns tipped in gleaming gold.

She was radiant.

But his quiet admiration soured the moment Huw joined her.

They were rarely apart, these two, and as always, the sight of them together sent an unreasonable jolt of jealousy through him.

Not because he suspected anything beyond friendship between them but because *he* wanted to be the one beside her.

Instead, he stood here—on the opposite side of the hall, watching like a sentry rather than a suitor, tension tightening his wings anytime a sharpened glare turned her way.

She and the other Mütra were the easiest targets tonight. Openly different. Openly resented.

But each of them seemed to be taking the mixed attention in stride.

Tanwen held her head high, shoulders back in quiet defiance, meeting each curious or scornful gaze without flinching.

In contrast, she hadn't looked at Zolya once all evening.

He knew why, of course.

And it had nothing to do with the fact neither of them should be sharing glances in the first place.

She was still angry at him.

Though, perhaps it was for the best.

Safer.

Still, it stung.

Just as it had earlier, when she'd acted out so recklessly in the gardens. Attacking a servant was bad enough. But to use her Mütra magic violently—and so publicly? It was foolish. Thoughtless. No matter how provoked she'd been by Ms. Allyga.

He, of course, understood the burden of restraint in the face of injustice—he'd been raised under a tyrant, after all.

But his fury at her actions wasn't born of disappointment.

It was fear.

Fear for her safety in a palace teeming with enemies. Fear that another outburst would only paint a larger target on her back.

As if the gods wished to prove his dread justified, his mother slid to his side. "I heard there was an incident in the gardens today," she said, her voice smooth and low. "With the inventor's daughter."

"There was." He forced himself to reply evenly despite his flicker of irritation. "But it was handled."

"Clearly not handled well enough."

He turned to his mother. "What does that mean?"

"My ladies-in-waiting were endlessly abuzz about the incident while I dressed. I'm sure my ears are still ringing."

"Your ladies are notorious gossips. I'm surprised you haven't developed the skill to tune them out by now."

"Usually I can," she replied lightly. "But they were discussing details regarding Ms. Heiro that I hadn't heard before. It caught my attention."

He arched a brow at her. "You do not need to spin such dramatics, Mother. If you have something to say, say it."

"Did you know she can command animals?"

Zolya lifted his glass, affecting a casual sip as he turned his gaze back to the hall. "I did."

When his mother remained silent, he looked back to her, catching the scrutiny in her eyes.

"I know the abilities of every Mütra rebel invited here," he explained. "Information that was given willingly once the law against them was repealed."

Her frown only deepened. "Why was this not shared with the council?"

"It was if a council member asked."

His mother remained silent, face brooding.

"You don't approve of Ms. Heiro's form of magic."

She scoffed. "I couldn't care one toss about her magic."

"Then what is the point of this anecdote, exactly?"

Her tone turned sharp. "Can a mother not have a conversation with her son?"

"Not if that mother is you."

She gave a soft huff of offense.

"You always have a point hidden in your conversations, Mother. Some warning, or lesson, or challenge."

"I'm simply pointing out that Ms. Heiro has stirred quite a bit of attention since arriving."

Zolya's protectiveness surged. "All of the rebels have," he said. "Mütra, especially."

"Yes, but she's Gabreel's daughter. She infiltrated the palace, served the princess, freed her family from your father's dungeons. When it comes to stirring, she's practically a storm."

He didn't reply. Didn't let his rising of unease show.

"Why her?" she asked suddenly.

It took everything in him not to drop his glass. His pulse thundered as he looked down at her. "Excuse me?"

"Why bring Ms. Heiro back?" she pressed. "It's clear her presence is a distraction to the court, her display in the gardens not helping matters. Notoriety has as many disadvantages as advantages, Zolya. I fear her being here may inhibit progress in our negotiations."

He kept his voice even as he said, "How curious that these grievances of yours were not voiced before sending out our summons. May I remind you, Mother, you reviewed and approved my list of candidates."

She pursed her lips with clear displeasure at his point.

"But if I must extrapolate, your newfound objections *are* the reasons she was invited," he continued, "all which were carefully outlined for both you and the council to look over."

He'd provided full reasoning behind every name on his list, not that he had needed to. He was king—explanations weren't required. But after demanding the next peace meeting be held in Galia, he'd wanted to reassure the council of his clarity.

Tanwen's inclusion had been, on the surface, simple.

Yes, she was Gabreel Heiro's daughter, but also a growing leader in her rebel chapter. She had experience living as a Mütra in hiding while also working inside the palace. She had served a Volari princess, even befriended her, lending herself a point of view of compassion for both sides. She was living proof that peace between races was possible. In more ways than he could outwardly admit to.

And so far, she had proven each of these points during their first meeting.

Tanwen had been brilliant today in the room, showing that she was a master negotiator whenever rising to speak. She had displayed her sharp mind and empathetic heart.

And yes—as his mother accused—it had honestly been bloody distracting.

But, he'd assumed, mainly for himself.

During the negotiation Zolya had found himself hungry to snatch her from the room and soar them straight to his bed. Taste her smart mouth and pull forth the sweet sounds of her moans.

He blinked back to the room, ignoring the heat sliding down his body with his errant thoughts.

He knew he had quite thoroughly explained Ms. Heiro's value in being here.

Which made his mother's line of questioning seem all the more deliberate.

"I must say," he began slowly, "this conversation is beginning to feel more like an interrogation. What is this really about?"

"I was simply curious," she said, voice light, though her eyes remained sharp as they stayed locked on where Tanwen stood across the room.

Something twisted in his chest. He didn't like her interest—nor her curiosity.

But he'd been trained by the best debaters. He knew how to steer conversations away from dangerous waters.

"You do bring up a good point, though, Mother," he replied, casually, taking in the great hall. "Perhaps a stir is what our court needs."

"What do you mean?"

"They clearly need distractions." He gestured to the mingling court. "Something other than bribing my councilmen for details of our negotiations. Tonight is certainly proof of that. If we give them a story, perhaps they'll stop making up their own."

She blinked, thrown.

But Zolya merely smiled, lifting her hand and bowing over it. "Forgive me, but I believe I'll take a turn about the room."

She stared at him, startled. "You loathe taking turns about rooms."

"True enough. But kings sacrifice in many ways for their kingdoms." He swept his gaze over the crowd. "And I think I'll start with the Mütra rebels. That should give the court enough to talk about for the fortnight, don't you think?"

With that, he stepped away from his mother and walked straight toward Tanwen and her companions.

25

Tanwen decided she wasn't fond of parties.

At least, not palace ones.

They felt less like celebrations and more like performances—pompous parades wrapped in silk and slow music.

Everything was too polished, too pristine.

Even the wine felt like a risk, with gowns this expensive.

The conversations were even worse. Thinly veiled criticisms disguised as compliments, or questions that were merely sharpened curiosity.

Still, she had promised Huw she'd stay at least until one dip of the moons.

So here she lingered in the corner of the ballroom, doing her best to wedge herself between a column and a decorative planter. Fewer people could corner her here.

Though she wasn't alone in her discomfort.

Despite the evening's supposed purpose—to mingle and integrate—most of the Rebellion kept to the edges like wallflowers at a village dance.

Though Brynn and Huw appeared at home, flittering around the room.

Brynn was making a game of unnerving the more uptight courtiers. Huw, meanwhile, was happily breaking social norms by chatting with palace staff and slipping drinks to anyone who looked bored.

Until, inevitably, he came back to pester her.

"Are you planning to sulk here all evening?" he asked, stepping into her refuge with an infuriating grin.

"I'm not sulking," she replied, chin lifting.

"Then what do you call this?"

"Observing."

"All right, then. I'll bite. What have you so far observed?"

"That the palace hasn't changed. It's still filled with coddled courtiers and layers of untouched excess."

Huw clicked his tongue. "That sounds suspiciously like a *sulky* observation."

She shot him a sharp look.

"Seriously," he said, lowering his voice. "You've been in a mood since the garden incident. I thought we'd moved past that."

"We have," she snapped, a little too quickly.

Huw arched a brow. "Then come dance with me."

"No one is dancing."

"Which is exactly why we should. It's not a real party until someone starts the dancing."

"No, thank you."

Whatever Huw was about to say next was lost as a sudden hush swept the room.

The shift in energy was immediate—like a ripple through still water.

Tanwen followed the line of everyone's gaze . . . and saw him.

Zolya, striding toward her, trailed by a small cluster of guards.

Oh no, she thought. *What is he doing?*

She had purposefully avoided looking at him all evening . . . because, well, yes, fine, she *was* sulking, but also out of self-preservation.

Her heart ached just seeing him, the longing almost too sharp to bear.

Zolya was his usual overpowering self. His warm-brown skin glowed under the amber light of the hall, and his deep-navy coat clung perfectly to his frame, every gold button and embroidered detail catching the light. Behind him, his wings cascaded down his back like snowcapped waterfalls.

He was beautiful and devastating and still heading their way.

Next to her, Huw straightened, the playfulness draining from his features as the king came to a stop before them.

"Mr. Lew. Ms. Heiro," Zolya greeted, his tone even as they both bowed. "I trust you're enjoying this evening's festivities."

"Very much so, Your Majesty," Huw answered smoothly. "In fact, I was just attempting to convince Ms. Heiro to dance."

Zolya's expression darkened just slightly as he turned to Tanwen.

"And what was your answer, Ms. Heiro?"

Her pulse fluttered. The weight of his attention, the air between them—it was too much.

"I prefer to remain still this evening, sire," she replied.

"And why is that?"

"I think she's still upset about what happened in the gardens, Your Majesty," Huw added cheerfully.

Tanwen's eyes snapped to him, furious.

But he only continued to smile sweetly at the king.

Zolya didn't look away from her, an unreadable emotion playing in his gaze. "I hope that hasn't permanently strained our relations, Ms. Heiro. I trust someone as intelligent as you understands the need for my correction."

"I do, sire," she said tightly. "I assure you, I've moved on from this afternoon. Please forgive my friend—he tends to prattle when he's nervous, or drunk."

Zolya's eyes flicked briefly to Huw, a spark of amusement lighting his features. "Pray tell, Mr. Lew, is it myself or Ms. Heiro who makes you nervous?"

"For his own safety," Tanwen muttered, cutting her friend a glance. "He'd be smart to say me, sire."

Zolya smiled at that—a slow, radiant thing that set butterflies loose in her belly. "I would agree, Ms. Heiro. You are quite formidable."

A beat of charged silence followed. Tanwen's reply stuck in her throat as the air between them stretched tight with unspoken things, the kind that made words feel too small.

Then, with perfect composure, Zolya broke the moment. "I hope you enjoy the rest of your evening." He nodded to them both.

As they bowed, he moved to greet the next-nearest group of rebels.

Tanwen tried to steady her breath as she straightened, tried to hide the blush she could feel staining her cheeks red, and—by the gods—she tried desperately not to follow him with her gaze.

"Well," Huw murmured at her side. "I've never felt that much sexual tension in my life."

Tanwen turned on him, brows hitting her hairline. "What?"

"Come off it, little fawn," he said, expression unamused. "I know."

Tanwen's stomach dropped, her blood draining from her face.

Fear pulsed through her, a wave of sick panic. She felt suddenly trapped, as if the whole ballroom had vanished and she were standing alone on a cliff's edge.

"Know what?" she asked, forcing her voice even.

Huw gave her a long look—one that clearly said, *Do you really wish for me to say it out loud,* here*?*

With her heart racing, she grabbed his elbow and dragged him out and into the covered walkway just beyond the hall.

The night air slid over her shoulders—not refreshing, but bracing. Warm and clammy. A warning.

She pressed them up against the outer banister, the glittering sky stretching endlessly on the other side.

"Oy." Huw tugged his arm free. "You'll wrinkle my shirt."

"What do you know?"

He smoothed the front of his tunic with theatrical care. "I'm not mad you didn't tell me," he replied instead of answering. "Even though I *am* your closest friend and have saved your arse more times than I can count."

Tanwen said nothing, but her glare demanded more. Her pulse hadn't slowed.

This is bad. Really bad.

"I saw you two together," he finally admitted. "Meeting at that little gazebo of yours right outside Drygul's borders."

"Oh gods," she croaked. "You . . . followed me?"

"Of course," he replied lightly. "My magic's made me terribly nosy over the years. Besides, what choice did I have? When I caught you sneaking through the woods in the dead of the night? Nothing innocent happens at that hour."

"Then what were *you* doing out at that time?" she snapped.

"Headed to a tryst of my own, naturally."

Tanwen stood frozen, her heart galloping through all the worst-case outcomes.

"Calm yourself," Huw said. "I'm not going to tell anyone. Obviously."

She blinked at him. "Then . . . Wait, you're not . . .?"

"What? Mad? Shocked? Scandalized? Devastated by your betrayal?" He shrugged. "Sure, at first. But after some time, I understood why you didn't tell me. I mean—let's be honest—it's completely insane what you're doing."

Tanwen swallowed the lump in her throat, ignoring the flicker of offense.

"Not that I don't get it," Huw added with a grin. "I mean, it's the king. He's disturbingly attractive. And those shoulders, and *wings*." He let out a low whistle that made her cheeks flame. "Tell me, is he a generous lov—"

"Huw!" she hissed. "Please. I'm begging you. Stop."

"What? I thought you'd be relieved you could finally talk about him with me."

Tanwen hesitated. "I . . . am," she admitted, surprised by the truth of it. Even with the danger, it felt good not to hold it alone anymore. "I just—how are you taking this so well?"

"Probably the same way you're able to take him so well—"

"Oh my *gods*." She turned away, facing the open night. "You're impossible."

Huw leaned on the rail beside her, his tone softening. "And you're in over your head, little fawn."

She said nothing for a beat as the knot of unease in her chest tightened. "Is it that obvious?" she asked. "Him and me?"

"Not unless you're looking for it."

"Not very reassuring."

"I'm not here to reassure," he explained, tone turning serious. "What you're doing . . . It's dangerous. Extremely forbidden, even now. Not that I don't get the allure of forbidden, believe me. But this? This is different, Tanwen."

"I know."

"So—you and him . . . started when we worked here?"

She nodded.

"And it's love?"

"It is."

Huw gave a slow, exaggerated sigh. "Well, then, that settles it. I now require every sordid detail."

Despite herself, Tanwen let out a soft laugh, shaking her head. "I wouldn't expect anything less from you."

"I'm a simple creature, really." He winked.

For a stretch of time they stood in companionable silence, the night settling around them as the low hum of the party drifted through the columns at their backs.

Then, softly, Tanwen broke the quiet. "Thank you," she said.

"For what?"

"For keeping this secret. For accepting it."

Huw held her gaze before slipping his hand over hers, giving it a squeeze. "It's beautiful, really. The son of a tyrant, in love with the very creature his father hunted."

"You make it sound tragic, not beautiful."

"Aren't they the same thing?"

Tanwen said nothing, the weight of his words settling too heavily in her chest for her to answer.

"I'd tell you to be careful," Huw began, after another long pause. "But there's nothing careful about this. Just . . . don't get caught, *again*."

And with that, he headed back inside, the glow of the ballroom spilling faintly out behind him.

Tanwen remained where she was, gripping the railing, her gaze lifting toward Nocémi's night. The goddess of dusk—the one who survived each day the sun set.

She and Zolya would survive this too.

They had to.

Azla knew of them. Now Huw did too.

And both were willing to accept their union.

Tanwen forced herself to see this as a good omen.

Proof that love could be seen beyond race and bloodlines, beyond fear.

She tried to believe it.

But her conviction faltered as she recalled Gwyn's hateful glare and the hundreds of courtiers who still mingled behind her, more of their gazes tipped predator than friend.

Tanwen was skilled at many things, lies most of all, but while she could weave falsities for others, she had never been able to fool herself.

26

"Huw knows."

Zolya had barely climbed through her window before Tanwen rushed him.

"What?" He staggered back a step, startled.

"My friend—Huw." Her eyes were wide and wild with panic. "He knows."

"Knows what?"

"About us."

Her words sank into him like acid.

He'd come tonight hoping to smooth over what happened in the gardens, maybe even reconcile. But that hope was quickly replaced by a far more pressing dread.

"How?"

"He followed me. Back in Drygul." Her voice was thick with regret. "I don't know how I missed him. I was looking, I swear, but . . . I'm so sorry. He told me tonight." Her voice dropped. "I'm so sorry," she said again.

"It's all right," he replied automatically, though it didn't feel all right—not yet. But he hated the fear in her eyes, the guilt in her voice.

He wanted to ease it, even if his thoughts were still spinning. "How did he react?"

She hesitated. "A bit like Azla did."

"Mad?"

"No, not exactly. Disappointed at first—mostly because I didn't tell him. But he thinks we're in over our heads."

Zolya couldn't deny that. But it didn't change how he felt, what he wanted, with her. "So . . . he accepted it? He accepted us?"

She blinked. "Yes. I suppose he did."

"And you trust him?"

A long pause followed. His wings tensed, muscles twitching, ready to fly from her room that instant and deal with Huw himself.

But finally, she nodded. "I do."

"Are you sure?" he asked again, his tone quieter this time. A looming threat to Huw if he was to be a problem.

"Yes," she said, more firmly. "I trust him with my life."

Some of the tension bled from his shoulders.

He nodded, though a small sting of jealousy pricked him. She had a friend who knew and accepted their union while Zolya had no such luxury. But he pushed thoughts of Osko's ire from his mind, as there were more pressing matters.

"While we're on the topic of being in over our heads," he said, his voice shifting, "my mother asked about you tonight."

"Your mother?" Her eyes flew wide.

"It seems the incident in the gardens caught more attention than just my court's."

He didn't mention the full extent of the queen dowager's suspicions or objections.

In all honesty, he had no energy for such a conversation tonight.

Tanwen sank down onto the edge of her bed, burying her face in her hands. "Gods, I'm so sorry, Zolya. I was foolish. But I just couldn't let Gwyn's cruelty go unanswered—not again, not after . . ."

"After what?" He crossed over, sitting beside her.

She hesitated, then spoke softly. "She took someone from me."

Zolya stilled, watching her carefully.

"Eli," she said. "He was a mouse—I know how it sounds—but he was more than that. I loved him. He helped me find my father and brother. He was my companion when I had no one else. Gwyn saw us together, and the next time I saw him . . ." Her voice cracked. "She'd put a dagger through his heart."

Zolya cursed under his breath, rising sharply. His magic stirred, hot and furious under his skin.

"Where are you going?" Tanwen asked, alarmed.

"To take care of Ms. Allyga."

"No—" She stopped him at her window. "You mustn't."

He glared down at her. "Why in the Eternal River not? She murdered your pet—"

"She has a family," Tanwen interrupted. "A sister who's sick. As much as I despise her and her actions, I can't bring more pain to people who had nothing to do with it."

"What are you talking about?"

"The Galia recruits haven't been able to reach their families, send them their funds. That's punishment enough."

Zolya exhaled hard, jaw tight. "That'll be resolved soon through our negotiations."

"Still—please, Zolya. Let me handle Gwyn."

He pressed his lips together, brow furrowed with his frustration. "I can't promise that," he said finally. "But I give you my word—her family won't be harmed."

"Zolya—"

"I will not allow cruelty to thrive in this palace," he cut in, voice edged with steel. "That ended with my father's reign. Ms. Allyga will be dismissed. Sent home to Cādra. With a generous severance to support her family while she seeks other employment."

Tanwen's shoulders dropped, her expression shifting. "That is . . ."

"—more than she deserves," he finished, his tone clipped.

Tanwen didn't argue. But her gaze slipped to the floor, her thoughts clearly drifting. "You were right," she murmured. "In the gardens. I shouldn't have lashed out."

"No, but I understand now why you did."

A quiet moment passed between them.

"And now your mother has her eye on me. That can't be good."

Zolya couldn't deny that, but he also couldn't allow Tanwen to carry any more weighted guilt tonight.

"I'll handle my mother," he said gently. "But I should . . . stop coming here. For now." The words dragged across his chest as he forced them out. "It's grown too risky."

Tanwen's expression mirrored his pain, her mouth tightening, eyes dimming. But she nodded. "Yes. That's probably best."

They both knew what was at stake. If their relationship came to light, it would unravel everything—every step of progress, every fragile negotiation lost in the fallout.

To protect the peace they were building, a few stolen nights could be sacrificed.

But knowing that didn't dull the ache.

As their eyes locked, the air between them pulled tight, a quiet, painful tether—because they both understood this would be their last night together for a while.

Zolya reached for her, desperation in every line of his body as he pulled her into his arms. Tanwen didn't hesitate. She folded into him like she always did—like home.

And when he kissed her, it was with everything he couldn't say.

She clung to him, just as greedy, just as wanting.

The scent of her filled each of his inhales like a heady vapor, sending heat to his groin.

He groaned, hunger erupting in his core as he walked them to her bed.

She pulled him down with her, onto her silken sheets, as he slid between her legs.

Zolya's vision blurred as he felt her heat against him, cupped her breasts in his hands.

Tanwen whimpered, a pleading sound that had him rushing to undress them both.

As skin slid deliciously against skin, he finally allowed a relieved breath.

Allowed a slip of euphoria and peace to settle into his heart.

He needed them to forget the weight of tomorrow, if only for tonight.

So, he reclaimed her mouth, and just for a little while—he made sure that they did.

27

Zolya hadn't anticipated just how consumed his days would become once king.

But maybe that was the price of caring.

He was stubbornly determined to clean up the chaos his father had left behind—a courtesy King Réol had never offered anyone. He had been like a spoiled child refusing to tidy the mess he'd made of his nursery.

Except his toys had been his subjects' lives and livelihoods.

From dawn until dusk, days on end, it seemed Zolya's presence was demanded in every room, listening to one grievance after another.

Today was no exception.

Not two hours after concluding tense negotiations with the rebel party—a daily occurrence this past week—he found himself sequestered in his study yet again, navigating the complaints of his Royal Council.

Half of them were arrayed before his desk, droning on about how the peace meetings were failing to address their *real* concerns—foremost among them refilling the treasury.

"Reopening trade routes is all well and good," said Lord Vincent. "But that revenue will trickle in slowly. We need a more substantial down payment in the meantime."

"I don't disagree." Zolya thrummed his fingers on his desk. "But what exactly do you propose? The rebel party cannot give what they don't have."

"What of a mine?" Lord Vincent offered.

Zolya stiffened. "What of it?"

"We're still holding the leftover funds your father set aside for the north coast expansion. We could invest in opening a new one."

Zolya's jaw tightened. The old man was grasping. "And where would you have us dig, exactly?"

The planned site—which had become his father's eventual downfall—had been consumed by the sea. Orzel's tiring wrath had battered the cliffs with unrelenting waves, causing most of it to fall away, any precious minerals lost with it.

No, that option was gone.

And even if it wasn't . . . the thought of returning to those practices made his stomach turn.

"We have no viable location," he added.

"Well, *something* must be done," Lord Vincent pressed.

"A comment as helpful as ever," Osko muttered from nearest Zolya's desk.

The treasurer scowled at the kidar, lips drawn thin, but any retort of his was cut short by the sudden appearance of Zolya's usher in the seam of his door.

The gold caps on the young man's horns glinted in the afternoon light as he offered a tight bow. "Your Majesty, several members of the Rebellion Council request an audience. Shall I inform them you are unavailable?"

"No." Zolya waved a hand. "Let them in. In fact, why not allow the entire court to sit council with me today. Perhaps we'll finally find a unanimous solution to everyone's grievances, eh?"

His council clearly didn't share in his humor.

Moments later, six members of the rebel party entered. Three Süra elders, Brynn, Huw, and—Zolya's pulse stuttered as he drank in Tanwen.

She met his gaze furtively—bright, electric—before lowering it in perfect etiquette.

He hated the distance their stations imposed in these moments.

Hated more that in every room like this, she had to bow when all he wanted was to fall to his knees before *her*.

Briefly, his eyes caught on another—Mr. Lew, who stood beside Tanwen, his expression watchful as he glanced between her and Zolya.

I know your secret, he imagined her friend saying with that look. It was one that was rather too smug for Zolya's comfort.

Unease trickled into his wings.

Though Tanwen said she trusted Huw, he'd still need to prove himself to Zolya. Until then, he'd be keeping a close watch on him.

"Your Majesty." Eldoth Yin bowed with the others, his shoulder-length gray hair spilling forward as he bent. He had become the Rebellion group's spokesman as of late. "We apologize for the intrusion. But following this morning's debates, we've come with a proposal—one that may benefit both our parties."

Zolya leaned back, intrigued. "How fortunate. My council has been discussing solutions all afternoon—with little success. You may have the floor."

"The subject is . . . delicate," eldoth Yin hedged, casting a wary glance at the nobles standing nearby. "We'd prefer to discuss it with you in private."

Predictably, his council erupted with murmurs of protest.

Zolya lifted a hand, silencing them.

"I'll need more than vague assurances to dismiss my entire council," he warned.

"It concerns the location of a rich ore deposit," the elder explained carefully.

The room stilled, along with Zolya's heart.

It felt like the work of Udasha, goddess of luck—or perhaps Ridi and his mischief—for such a perfectly timed solution to appear just after he and his council had voiced the very need.

Which of course set unease to creeping beneath his skin. *What godly scheming is this?*

"That's excellent news." Lord Vincent sat straighter, eyes alight. "Where is it?"

"It is not *our* location to give," eldoth Yin explained. "There is someone we wish to bring to the palace. Someone who . . . claims the rights to the site and is willing to assist both parties. But only under strict conditions—their identity, for the moment, remaining private from the Royal Council being one. If we break that promise now, we then also break the deal."

Zolya's instincts stirred. He glanced at Tanwen. She gave the slightest nod.

That was all he needed.

"Leave us," he demanded of his council.

"Sire, you cannot be serious," Osko began. "We cannot leave you unguarded with this lot."

"Their only way out is through that door—where you'll be standing," Zolya reasoned, gaze locking with his friend's. "I'll call you if needed."

It took another tense moment, but eventually, Osko and the rest of the council filed out.

One by one, their wings brushed the doorframe as they passed, his usher shutting the door with a gentle click.

Zolya turned back to the rebels, his gaze catching on Tanwen again. "Now," he said quietly. "Tell me—who is this person you believe can help us?"

28

Tanwen quickly discovered how difficult it was to write a letter with an audience.

It didn't help that the desk she sat behind belonged to the king himself—an immense, imposing piece of furniture that seemed to hum with his power and carried Zolya's scent in the grain of its wood.

Sunshine and bergamot.

Longing and desire.

Each inhale only further flustered her.

Worse yet, she could feel Zolya's gaze—as he loomed by her side—like a heat pressing along her neck, unwavering, intense.

Annoyed.

Since they had revealed their request to him along with their needed guests—and the reason for the secrecy—he had gone disturbingly calm.

Too calm.

Like a lion crouched low in tall grass. Calculating. Waiting.

Tanwen's stomach twisted.

In front of her, the rest of the rebel party stood quietly, watching.

Huw's presence—usually a welcome one—now only set further upset to her nerves. He no doubt was enjoying every moment of witnessing her and Zolya's formal charade.

In short, the quiet in the room was suffocating—broken only by the scratch of her quill on parchment.

"There," she finally said, leaning back. "How's that?"

Zolya took her offered letter, eyes sweeping over the lines with a steady, unreadable expression. His brows were drawn, his mouth tight.

She knew his silence came from more than the shock of who they were inviting. It came from the knowledge that she had kept this from him. After he had asked for honesty. For openness.

But she hoped he understood why. This wasn't her secret to share.

It was politics, not personal.

This was the Rebellion Council's last hand to play—a *very* specific agreement made to another, held in reserve for when the odds were stacked too high against them.

After this past week of peace meetings, the odds had never felt steeper.

Both sides were running out of time, with the negotiations soon coming to an end.

Which, Tanwen suspected, only added fuel to the fire simmering beneath Zolya's calm exterior.

He'd been backed into a corner—

Because what they were offering was a solution too good to ignore: a fix to his kingdom's bleeding treasury in one clean stroke.

It was a solution, however, that came with risks—a whirlwind of them.

But nothing of worth ever came without cost.

Zolya, of all people, would know this truth intimately.

Which was no doubt why—after an excruciating silence, his magic having chilled the room to near freezing as he processed their proposal—he had finally said yes.

Tanwen sat with held breath as she watched her letter be passed from Zolya through the rebels' hands, praying to the Low Gods this version would finally suffice. It was the fifth one she'd written, and her fingers cramped from the effort.

Blessedly, the last eldoth nodded in acceptance before handing the letter back to Tanwen.

"You may send it," Zolya said at last, voice low and gravel edged.

His gaze was gripping, a searing promise as it met hers. *We will discuss this later.*

Tanwen's stomach twisted, but her resolve remained firm.

Standing, she moved swiftly to the open doors of his veranda.

Bright light flooded her vision as she stepped outside, the sun making her squint.

She sent a silent request into the wind. *I have a summons to send.*

Moments later, a colorful-feathered falcon descended from the sky with a piercing shriek, answering her call.

I will take it, the falcon said in her mind.

"Thank you," she murmured, offering the bird her leather-bound wrist on which to perch. She tied the scroll to its leg. "It's very important this letter is received."

The falcon blinked its black eyes at her, giving another shriek before it launched itself skyward.

Tanwen watched it disappear into the horizon—carrying with it not just a message, but also the fate of their future—toward Princess Azla.

29

"Sire, this is absurd," grumbled one of Zolya's councilmen, his wings twitching with irritation. "Surely by now we can be told what's going on?"

"We've been waiting for nearly an hour," another chimed in, voice edged with impatience.

Zolya sat at the head of the two long tables, posture rigid, jaw tight. They were gathered in one of the more secure negotiation rooms—his council, the rebels, and the walls growing more stifling by the moment. Which was why he could not fault his council's frustration—he shared it. Even knowing what was to come brought him no calm, not here, trapped in such a confined space.

"How much longer?" he asked, turning a sharp gaze on eldoth Yin. "I agree with my council. This is becoming unnecessary theater."

To his credit, eldoth Yin appeared genuinely distressed. "We apologize, Your Majesty. Our party should be arriving any moment. Then we may—"

A bird swooping in through the only open skylight stalled his words and cut the tension with a rush of wings.

It landed beside Tanwen, head cocked, eyes gleaming.

A silent exchange passed between them. She nodded, murmured her thanks, and released the bird back into the sky.

She gave eldoth Yin a single steady nod.

Zolya braced himself as the elder faced the room.

"Your Majesty, esteemed council," he began, "we thank you for your patience. I assure you, today's negotiations will conclude with both parties satisfied."

"We shall be the judges of that," muttered a noble.

Yin pressed on. "There exists a mine—untapped, rich with ambrü and gems, more accessible than any site previously on Cādra."

Zolya momentarily met Tanwen's stare.

The connection tense but fragile.

They hadn't had a chance to meet privately before today, for her to explain how this came to pass.

Which was why he was still smarting from this surprise, as he loathed surprises in any form.

But this move was more than a shock; it was a checkmate.

Though, he understood that it was not by her hand, but by those who stood with her.

Which was why, begrudgingly, he forgave her keeping this close to her chest.

It lay beyond the bounds of their promise of transparency—falling into the realm of politics, not the intimacy of their relationship.

Well . . . to some degree.

"The owner of this site is willing to negotiate with the Volari council," Yin continued, bringing Zolya's attention back to the room. "So long as her subjects may once again live among us freely."

A hush.

"*Her* subjects?" Lord Vincent asked, brow furrowing.

"Yes." Yin gestured toward the far wall, where telescopes had been set up along the north-facing windows. "We ask that you look."

The room erupted in movement as councilmen surged toward the lenses, robes rustling, wings fluttering, and chairs scraping against stone. The Rebellion party remained seated.

As did Zolya.

As did his mother.

Her brown eyes found his across the room—confused, concerned, searching.

Guilt twisted in his gut.

She was the one person he wished he could have told beforehand. But his hands, like the Rebellion's, like Tanwen's, had been tied.

Tied to an agreement that seemed soaked in revenge.

In retribution.

In justice.

Though he could not fault such desires from someone who had been so thoroughly discarded and left for dead.

Still—he wished it wasn't he or his people on the receiving end.

Gasps echoed in the room. Startled cries. One councilman stumbled back from his telescope, pale as Maja.

Zolya didn't move.

He had already seen.

Beyond the glass stood the impossible.

Creatures pulled from myth and bedtime stories. Centaurs. Satyrs. Cyclopes. Minotaurs. Thousands of them. Living. Breathing. Real.

All standing near the northern coastline of Cādra. They mixed with an impressively large Rebellion horde, spreading out and covering the land like a dark splash of paint.

An army.

When taking in the scene, he had been paralyzed with his own disbelief—learning that such beings had not been lost to time but exiled. Forgotten. Surviving as prisoners on a cursed island.

Never had the sins of past Volari kings felt so damning.

Shame gripped his chest, wrapped sharp claws around his throat.

How many souls had been discarded beneath the weight of their throne?

Too many.

Far too many.

"What you see," eldoth Yin declared to the shocked room, "are new allies to the Rebellion. And to Cādra."

A ripple of murmurs surged.

"A promise of security," Yin continued. "Should Volari choose peace. A warning, should you not."

The air shifted—tension snapping taut like a bowstring.

"What—are they?" a nobleman whispered, eyes wide.

"I believe you mean '*Who* are they,'" said a smooth, commanding voice from the chamber doors. "For they are certainly not things."

Heads snapped toward the new arrival.

Queen Habelle lurched to her feet, letting out a strangled gasp as her eyes locked on the woman entering. His mother's complexion grew ashen, as if she were witnessing a spirit rise from the Eternal River.

Zolya resisted the urge to go to her, to steady her; instead he remained rooted, forcing composure as he took in the scene by the doors.

At the threshold, Osko stood rigid, duty bound and tense—his presence a confirmation that he'd obeyed Zolya's order, even if it meant escorting a fugitive and an exile into the heart of Galia.

Princess Azla's sudden arrival had brought forth a wave of outcries.

But it was the woman beside her who then struck the room silent.

She was tall, arresting, her midnight waves tumbling loose and untamed to her waist. Her gown mirrored that wildness—stitched together in jagged blacks like torn shadow—but it was her wings that caught the eye: limp, clipped, the amber sheen faded like dying firelight. A brutal scar curved down one pale cheek, disappearing into the line of her throat.

A history written in flesh.

Yet she carried herself like a conquering queen—undaunted, chin high.

"Hello, old friends." Lady Callia swept her gaze across the stunned room, her grin satisfied, sharp—a weapon. "Have you missed me?"

PART V

Reckoning

30

Habelle might have loved her sister, but they had never been friends.

And Callia's dramatic return to Galia was a perfect reminder of why.

Sitting in her private parlor, she, Zolya, Azla, and Callia pretended at casual civility over tea. As if one of them wasn't charged as an accomplice to treason and the other presumed dead.

Guards lined the room, discreetly stationed at the columns.

A quiet reassurance for Habelle.

For her sister was, in a word, chaos.

Unapologetically individualistic.

Ambitious to a dangerous degree.

In truth, she'd always been better suited to King Réol than Habelle ever was. A far more fitting queen for a ruthless king.

But that was not the fate Zenca had woven into either of their lives.

A twist of destiny Callia had never let her forget.

Habelle, the sister who stole the crown.

Stole the power.

Stole their parents' pride and their people's love.

It was only fitting, in the end, that Callia would find a way to steal a seed of her husband.

Defy a death sentence.

And eventually claim a crown, not by marriage but by might.

"I must say, Sister," Callia remarked, sipping her tea, the large ambrü in her crude stone circlet catching the afternoon light filtering into the room. "I would have thought you'd be more pleased to see me."

"I am." Habelle lifted her chin, fighting a frown. "I merely . . ."

She merely was what?

Still in shock.

Dismayed.

Relieved.

Angry.

Confused.

She was sitting across from a sister she had thought dead. A woman she had made peace with losing decades ago. The Callia before her held faint echoes of the woman she'd once known—but in truth, she felt more like a stranger now.

And not merely in presence.

She held a wild, volatile energy, like the charged stillness before a lightning strike. The steely glass surface of water before a sea beast snapped. Her gaze now more cunning than caring.

It perhaps unsettled Habelle more than learning her sister lived.

But their world tended to harden those who survived it long enough.

Especially those from Both.

Habelle finally settled on "I thought you were dead."

Callia huffed a laugh while placing down her cup. "Yes, well, in many ways the girl you knew is. Both has a way of chiseling one away like stone, leaving only what's necessary to survive."

Guilt surged in Habelle's chest.

Her eyes drifted to her sister's wings.

They were still striking in their beauty, like Callia herself, yet robbed of flight. Their freedom clipped as her sister's wings had been.

"I'm sorry you were ever sent there." The apology slipped out before she could stop it.

Words over sixty years in the making, ones that she immediately regretted as Callia's eyes flashed—sharp steel. But she blinked it away a beat later, her fury buried under a practiced composed mask.

"Certainly, that was a path of my own making," she said coolly. "What use did Réol have for me once I failed to bear him a son like you?"

The air snapped taut.

Habelle straightened, irritation flaring and dashing away her earlier remorse.

The princess flinched beside her mother, the sting of her words playing plainly across her face.

"Oh, don't fret, my darling." Callia patted her daughter's hand—catching her discomfort. "That was not your fault. Plus, you've avenged my death with your father's. That is no small gift."

Zolya cleared his throat—eyes flicking toward the guards.

The mentioning of the princess's rumored involvement in King Réol's poisoning would not help her case.

While Callia's appearance had been a shock, the princess's was an affront.

Shouts for Azla's arrest had risen at once, but kidets hesitated, waiting for the king's command.

Instead, Zolya had immediately sequestered the royal family into Habelle's chambers after calling a recess to their negotiations.

There was no hope for meaningful talks after her sister and the princess's explosive return.

Too much had been upended.

And with Callia wielding the treasury's salvation with her supposed island of riches, future diplomacy would become a performance more than a process—one Zolya currently played with restraint.

Much to Habelle's mix of pride and frustration. She didn't enjoy her son being beholden to anyone.

"Aunt," he began, tone measured. "We are, of course, relieved to find you alive—and that your unjust exile, along with your people's, was survived. Had I known you still lived and what souls had been banished to Both, releasing you would have been among my first acts as king."

Callia studied him. "Instead, you freed Mütra. Surely, an equally noble act, Nephew. And bold. Clearly you are not to follow in your predecessor's footsteps."

The true meaning of her words was not lost on any of them, least of all Habelle.

You are not to be as your father.

"There is much we can learn from the past to create a better future," replied Zolya evenly.

Callia let out a low, throaty laugh. "How tactful. You have raised him well, Sister."

"My son's accomplishments are entirely his own," she replied coolly.

Callia's gaze flashed along with her grin. "Indeed."

"You, of course, know," Zolya pressed on, seemingly determined to stay on task, "what you have brought to Galia is of tremendous aid to our kingdom."

"I'm glad to hear it," she said. "Our discussion can move swiftly."

Zolya hesitated, gaze flickering to the princess before settling back on Callia. "I'd prefer that, yes. Though, I do fear the style in which you arrived—and the revelations that followed—will take some time to settle within my council and court." He turned to Azla then, voice softening. "Despite the risk, I am glad you came back."

"I don't want to run forever." Azla held a determined pinch between her brows.

She wore Süra-clan garb of a tunic and trousers—a clear message of where her loyalties now lay—though for all her visual defiance, she had been quiet, almost demure, until this moment.

Habelle couldn't blame her. She no doubt was waiting for the chips of her future to fall.

"You won't need to run," Zolya promised. "But we will have to hold a tribunal, as is customary."

"I understand."

"As do I," added Callia. "But I hope *you* understand, Your Majesty—our deal depends on her absolution."

A muscle along Zolya's jaw flared as he held her stern gaze. "You've made your terms quite clear, Aunt."

Callia nodded. "Good."

"Let us allow things to settle," he continued. "We'll resume talks in a few days. I'm certain all parties will benefit."

"You are king," Callia replied, eyeing him questioningly. "If you want to agree to my and the Rebellion's terms, you merely need to agree to them. Your father certainly never bent to his people or council."

"*Callia*," Habelle warned.

"I only speak the truth," she countered.

"As you've noted, Aunt," Zolya interjected with forced calm. "I am *not* my father. His legacy—as I'm sure you've seen—has left little to defend."

Callia tilted her head, watching him anew. "You really aren't like the others," she murmured, half to herself. "Réol would've had my throat slit the moment I set foot on this island."

None of them appeared to know what to do with that.

Least of all Habelle.

There was a time she had truly despised her sister—not for the affair, which was all too common with her husband, but for choosing ambition over their bond.

And yet, even then, even when shouldering the humiliation at court for being cuckqueaned by her own family, Habelle had never wished her sister's death.

"Yes, you're very different, indeed, sire," murmured Callia. "Which is why I have faith we'll come to terms. Zenca has tied our fates together. My people will no longer be prisoners. My daughter will be cleared of her charges. And your treasury"—her eyes gleamed—"will thrive. You've seen what I've brought—ambrü the size of fists, gems like plums. All of it and more, in exchange for a place for myself and my people in Cādra."

Habelle studied her son. The glint of hope—and hunger—that lit his gaze. It all sounded so simple, utopic, the way Callia framed it. But she knew it wasn't so easy. And so did he.

Territory within Cādra would need to be ceded to make room for these new citizens—a likely source of tension between clans. And beyond that loomed the daunting work of integration: legislation, infrastructure, food distribution, trade, materials to build homes and businesses. The list was endless.

"Let's hope my council and court see it that way," Zolya replied. "For now, you must both be tired from your travel. I've arranged secure accommodations." He turned to Azla. "Your old quarters have been prepared."

Azla frowned, a slip of tension to her shoulders. "While I appreciate the gesture, sire, I'd—prefer not to stay in my old rooms."

Zolya eyed her with confusion.

"Essie . . ." Azla began, voice hoarse with sudden emotion. "She's everywhere in them."

"Of course." Zolya's expression instantly softened with his understanding.

"If it suits, I'd prefer to stay in the same wing as the Rebellion and my mother." Azla looked to Callia, who gave her a soft, steadying smile, her hand drifting back to rest over her daughter's.

It was a simple touch, but one that hit Habelle like a spear through the chest.

For all her sister's steel-edged composure, it was easy to forget what she had truly lost the day she was exiled.

Not just her wings.

But also her child.

Her baby, not yet four months old.

Habelle's throat tightened. The image of her own son as a newborn flashed through her mind, the mere thought of losing him unbearable. Never seeing him again, its own form of death.

Her magic sparked in her veins, a surge of cold rain wishing to be freed as a silent flare of anguish bloomed beneath her skin.

For the first time since her sister's return, she wished to embrace her.

A most unsettling urge, to be sure.

For when was the last time they had held one another? Affection was never well met in their childhood home.

"Consider it done," said Zolya. "I'll have a new room prepared for you within the hour."

"Thank you," said Azla.

"Of course." He nodded, before his expression grew strained. "Even when you're cleared, I must warn you, returning to court may not be easy. I'll do what I can—"

"I won't live here, Zolya," she interrupted gently.

Shock flickered across his face. "What do you mean?"

"You can't be surprised, Nephew?" Callia said, brow arching. "She hardly had a life here to return to anyway. Few Volari women do."

"That's changing," he argued. "New training has begun for those who wish to explore abilities beyond their delicate magic. We've even scheduled flights off island for those interested."

Azla's eyes widened. "Zol . . . that's incredible."

"You helped inspire it," he said. "You still can."

She shook her head, frowning. "I'm sorry. After everything I've seen—experienced—since leaving Galia, I can't live here again. Not when"—she looked at her mother once more—"there are those I wish to get to know better."

Callia held her daughter's gaze, a proud smile stretching across her face.

"I want my freedom, Zolya," Azla continued, turning back to him. "And I won't find it here. Not when I know how much more I am out there." She gestured to the sky beyond the columns—toward Cādra.

The princess's words landed sharper than expected.

Because they were true.

Habelle had never known true freedom—not under her parents' oppressive expectations nor beneath the iron grip of her husband. Only on her private isle had she glimpsed something close to peace, and even that had come at a price—most dearly, time lost watching her son grow.

Even now, with Réol gone, the chains of royal life still clung to her: heavy, invisible, inescapable. All the scrutiny. Expectation. Endless demands from court, country, and gods.

But such were the weights that came with a crown—and as she'd taught her son, they were to be carried with dignity.

So Habelle sat straight, said nothing, and quietly swallowed the bitter tang of envy curling at the back of her throat as she listened to her niece speak of the life she could have beyond this palace.

"This, of course . . . saddens me," said Zolya, a pinch to his brows. "But, I understand. And I respect your wishes."

Azla's gaze shimmered with emotion as she reached out to grab his hand. "Thank you for your blessing. I told you you'd be a great king, and you are. You are healing our world."

"I'm not quite sure about that," he huffed. "I merely wish to end the centuries of hurting in the effort to build some hope."

Callia's husky laugh pulled the group's attention. "How extraordinary to hear such words from Réol's son. Despite your resemblance to your old man, clearly you inherited more from your mother—or are all you rainmakers this sentimental?"

Zolya's posture straightened—but Habelle replied before he could. "Our magic certainly requires more emotional nuance to control than merely setting things ablaze," she snapped. "Or do I need to remind you of all the careless fires you started in our nursery with your tantrums and *I* being the one forced to put them out?"

Callia tsked. "Over sixty years apart, and still you haven't forgiven me for those transgressions? May *I* remind *you* that I was a child."

"Was?" Habelle's retort hung in the air like a spark over dry kindling.

But she wasn't sorry for it.

She only regretted how childish it sounded.

Damn Callia for pulling her back into such sophomoric behaviors.

As if sensing her sister's distress—and savoring it—Callia grinned, a slow, sharp curve of delight. "I can see my time here will be more than fruitful for my people," she declared, gaze locked on Habelle. "And perhaps it will also give us the chance to settle quarrels from the past."

Habelle bit the inside of her cheek, forcing down the reply burning on her tongue. For the thought of revisiting the past—especially one entwined with her sister—left her with an urge she hadn't felt since the night she caught her husband and her sister in their betrayal.

The urge to run.

31

"Well, I'm officially offended," Huw announced, turning in a slow circle and craning his head back to admire the fresco of a sun-drenched garden painted on the ceiling. "Your room is much nicer than ours."

Azla offered a subtle shrug from where she reclined on a lounge, her long legs clad in black trousers, crossed neatly at the ankles, her wings a luminous white. "I am the king's sister."

"A fugitive sister," he corrected breezily.

"*Huw*," Tanwen warned as she stepped farther into the room.

Though, in truth, Azla's quarters *were* nicer than theirs.

The setting sun filtered in through the two-story windows, catching on the pale-gold trim of the lavish chamber. An opulent bed could be glimpsed behind a partition, along with a silk-clad seating area and a marble connected lavatory.

Guards remained stationed outside—Tanwen and Huw having been searched for weapons upon arrival—but once within the room, the space was theirs alone.

While happy for Azla's accommodations, Tanwen couldn't help the flash of anger that flared in her chest as she took in the rooms.

Despite being, technically, a prisoner, Azla's stay at the palace was unfolding far differently from how her father and brother's had.

Not that she wished her friend harm—but the injustice of it, the memory of what had been, stung fresh like a reopened wound. But that was a time when a different king had ruled.

"What?" asked Huw, feigning innocence. "It's not like her charges are a secret."

"Would you rather visit me in the dungeons?" Azla asked him flatly, stirring unease in Tanwen's gut—her words echoing too closely to her unspoken thoughts.

"Gods, no." Huw made a face. "Prison bars clash with my complexion."

"Did you miss us?" Tanwen asked dryly as she joined Azla on her sofa.

"Only some of you."

Huw let out a dramatic harrumph as he collapsed into the lounge opposite them.

"How are you?" Tanwen studied Azla. The princess appeared as composed as ever—her brown complexion flawless, her hair braided and coiled atop her head. But if Tanwen lingered too long on her eyes, or the faint downward curve of her lips . . .

"I'm tired," she admitted. "And nervous."

"I know it was a difficult decision for you, coming back here."

"I didn't have much of a choice."

Tanwen's guilt churned, but before she could speak, Azla—seemingly reading her discomfort—placed a gentle hand on her knee.

"I didn't mean it like that," she reassured. "Just . . . if I want the life I'm fighting for, I need this behind me."

"Yes, but you didn't have to be a part of the negotiations."

"I want to be useful," she reasoned. "And I need to face this. I need to finish what Essie and I started—what she gave her life for. I can't run forever. Essie wouldn't have wanted that either."

The words hit Tanwen hard. Sharp claws.

She knew all too well the ache of running, the terror in hiding.

"Your mother seems to have everything in hand," Huw piped up as he idly played with the lace lining his shirt. "Your charges will be dropped in no time."

"That seems to be the general opinion—my brother's included."

"That's all the assurance you need." He waved a hand. "If the king wants it done, it's done. Or should I say, if your mother demands it."

"*Huw*," Tanwen admonished—again.

"What?" He mimicked her tone.

"Even though the guards remain outside," she whispered harshly, "doesn't mean they can't hear what's happening in here."

He had the good sense to glance nervously at the doors. "Well, it's not as though we all don't see she holds the winning hand. Wasn't that rather the point of the Rebellion joining up with her? The king and his council would be foolish to argue." Huw sighed, staring off whimsically. "Can Callia adopt me? She's magnificent."

"She's certainly that," Azla agreed with a huffed laugh.

"How has it been going?" Tanwen asked. "Being with your mother?"

Azla tilted her head, thoughtful. "It's . . . nice. And an adjustment. I guess when I imagined her alive, I thought of the woman who would have remained here. The mother she would have been if she had never been sent to Both."

"You mean not the fierce exiled warrior queen who just verbally backhanded the entire council?" Huw grinned.

"Please ignore him," Tanwen grumbled. "I do."

"I'm impossible to ignore," he countered. "Unless, of course, I wish to be." He blinked out of existence then, the sofa now sitting empty.

"Let's hope that's permanent," Tanwen muttered. "Ow! Hey!" She winced, rubbing her arm where an invisible pinch had landed.

Huw reappeared, smugly lounging in the same spot.

"I'll get you for that," she hissed.

"No, you won't."

She narrowed her eyes at him. "I'd check under your sheets tonight. I'd hate for something to bite those pretty pale legs of yours when you crawl into bed."

He gasped, sitting up. "You wouldn't dare sic your creatures on me."

"Oh, I'd dare."

"You two have the strangest relationship." Azla cast a raised brow between them.

"Don't worry," said Huw, reclining once more. "You'll get there."

"Anyway." Tanwen turned back to Azla. "You were saying—about your mother?"

Azla shook her head. "It doesn't matter. I'm just looking forward to getting to know her more. And I know she feels the same."

"You're lucky to have her affections," said Huw. "Did you see her today? When they challenged her claim on Both?" He laughed gleefully. "I thought it was Hyfel who had descended from the heavens, come to land justice on those soft-handed noblemen. I got chills!"

How could any of them forget that moment.

The council had tried to undermine Callia's claim, citing the island as crown property.

Callia had countered with calm, icy precision. "The prisoners who inhabit it beg to differ. Unless, of course, you care to set foot on it yourselves without my permission? And take your chances surviving the wrath of those you've exiled there."

No one had seemed capable of responding to that.

"She's fearless," added Huw.

"Your obsession with her is noted," said Tanwen.

"Don't be jealous."

"I'm only jealous that she's not suffering your company right now."

"Should I leave you two so you can squabble in private?" asked Azla.

"I'm sorry." Tanwen turned back to Azla, her voice softening. "Now you see why I didn't want him coming with me. We're here to visit you, not argue." She shot Huw a pointed glare—a silent plea for good behavior.

He raised his hands in mock surrender.

"I've been meaning to ask," said Tanwen, returning her attention to Azla. "How are my parents?"

"They're worried, of course," Azla replied. "But the letters you've sent have helped. They're comforted."

She let out a breath she hadn't realized she was holding. "Good."

"They also seem . . . better," Azla added gently. "The two of them, together."

A wave of quiet relief passed through Tanwen, her shoulders loosening. Her parents would survive this. And after Thol's death, it was a greater healing than she could have expected.

"Thank you," she murmured.

"Of course." Azla gave her a soft smile.

"And the rest of Drygul? How's the clan been getting along?"

"Honestly? The rest of the refugees have been inspired. With Both's survivors joining the cause, the might of them, nearly all the clan has now pledged their support. Especially with more Low Gods showing up."

"Truly?" She sat straighter, pulse skipping. "Which other gods?"

"It seems Bosyg's close relationship to Nen—and all her rivers flowing through her forests—has been fruitful in drawing the Low Goddess's support. Thryn also has pledged her aid if ever healing is needed in any future battles. It's been quite an exciting time on Cādra, actually, and why there were so many more than expected along the coastline, joined with the other Süra clans."

"That's incredible," Tanwen breathed, a renewed sense of hope filling her chest. "We actually might win this."

"Let's hope without needing Thryn's help, though," said Huw. "I'd like these peace negotiations to end peacefully. We've all had our fair share of escaping death. I'd rather not test Maryth's patience as she waits for my soul in the Eternal River."

"King Zolya will not allow violence to come to his palace," reasoned Tanwen, a bit too defensively.

"A promise he's made to you, now is it?" Huw raised a brow at her.

She felt her cheeks redden. "A promise he made to us *all* when we arrived."

"Yes, but I'm sure his oath was *really* meant for one of us."

"Am I missing something here?" Azla glanced in confusion between the two of them.

Tanwen let out a defeated sigh. "He knows."

A beat of silence.

"Excuse me?" Azla frowned.

"He *knows.*" She meaningfully met the princess's gaze.

Her brows lifted as the words sank in. She peered over at Huw.

"Oh, yes." He wore a honey-sweet grin. "I've known about our friend's juicy secret for some time."

"How come you didn't tell me?" She turned back to Tanwen with an accusatory stare.

"He only told me he knew recently," she argued.

"That's because I was waiting for *you* to tell me yourself," he quipped. "But that clearly was never going to happen."

"Of course it wasn't," she hissed, furtively eyeing the closed door, all too aware of the guards still stationed outside. "Because no one should know."

"I can't believe this," said Azla, her shocked expression seemingly permanent as she turned back to Huw. "We could've been talking about this behind her back the whole time."

"We still can," he countered, eyes lighting up. "In fact, Tanwen, you should leave. Azla and I need to make up for lost time."

"Okay." Tanwen sliced the air with her hand. "Enough."

"Enough for now," Huw mock whispered to Azla, eliciting from her a giggle.

Tanwen crossed her arms over her chest, annoyance flaring. "I'm glad my position is amusing for you both."

"I'm sure not nearly as amusing as the positions he gets you in—"

"*Huw!*" she scolded.

"Gross." Azla's face scrunched.

Huw was in a fit of laughter across from them.

Gods, I need to get out of here, thought Tanwen.

She stood. "I believe that's my cue."

"Oh no! Don't leave," whined Huw, sobering quickly. "I was only trying to lighten the mood. The Low Gods know we could all use a laugh, given the current state of things."

"Well, excuse me if I don't enjoy having my love for someone turned into the arse of your jokes."

"Tanwen." Azla's gentle voice cut through the moment, pulling her attention—and with it, the sharp sting of tears she'd been holding at bay.

She hated how raw she felt.

Hated how easily her composure was fraying.

This week had been more brutal than she'd let herself admit.

Returning to a place soaked in a mix of her darkest nightmares and brightest joys—memories of her brother's frail form, her father's haunted exhaustion; thoughts of Eli, of his loss, of Gwyn, of the other atentés. The crushing weight of walking these halls as a known Mütra. The constant eyes of guards, the sneers from courtiers. The negotiations, forever looming like storms on the horizon, deciding whether they would leave here triumphant . . . or in shrouds.

Zolya had been her only refuge, her only breath of calm amid it all.

The one space where she felt safe, truly seen, allowed to unravel in the arms of someone who understood her and shared her dream for the future.

And now, even that comfort had been stripped away—for their own protection.

It had only been a few days since the last night they spent together, but being so close to him, seeing him in each of their meetings knowing there would be no later relief—it was a mounting frustration in her heart, which was near bursting.

So, yes, perhaps she was cracking—but she had good reason.

Here she was, with the only two people who knew her secret—one that could see her executed—and they were laughing at it.

"Please," Azla said gently, reaching out a hand. "Come sit. We're sorry."

"Yes," Huw added, expression sobered. "I didn't mean to upset you."

"Well, you did."

"I apologize."

Tanwen exhaled, weariness sinking deep in her bones. "It's fine." She eased back beside Azla. "I'm sorry too. Being here . . . It's harder than I anticipated. For all of us, I'm sure."

"The negotiations are nearly finished," Huw offered with a hopeful smile.

"Yes." Azla rested her hand over Tanwen's. "Once the tribunal ends, so does this chapter."

"And then we'll be back on solid ground," said Huw.

Tanwen knew they meant to soothe her. But their comfort only widened the ache inside her heart.

Once she left the palace, there was no telling when she'd see him again.

While the Rebellion might leave bearing hope for Cādra's future, the future she and Zolya dreamed for themselves would still remain far out of reach.

32

The night sky stretched endlessly ahead as Zolya flew, the cool air skimming over his wings like a steadying hand.

He banked left around the palace's northern rim, wishing—not for the first time—that his guards weren't trailing behind.

Were he alone, he might have flown until Ré's light burned the edge of the horizon, beyond even Cādra's last coastline.

Flight was his salve for the static weight of royal duty—days spent seated, tethered indoors.

Tonight, it had nearly purged his headache, nearly dissolved the tension wound tight along his shoulders from the negotiations and upcoming tribunal.

Nearly.

Because only one person could truly unmake his burdens—dissolve the weight of the day with a simple touch, a lingering kiss.

Zolya shook his head, scattering his thoughts like birds from a tree.

He and Tanwen had only days left before the Rebellion's departure.

A handful of fleeting moments.

It should have steeled his resolve—to keep his distance, avoid the risk of being seen slipping into her chambers.

Instead, it only sharpened the ache to be near her. Alone.

Only Zenca knew when—if—they'd be together again.

The thought stirred something hot and furious in his chest.

He clenched his jaw, wings tensing as he veered hard around the southern towers and shot toward the Royal Gardens, wind lashing against him like an insult.

Behind him, the soft pulse of his guards' wings.

By the Eternal River, he groaned inwardly—they tailed him like his nursemaids did when he was a boy.

Insufferable, but necessary.

His mind returned to the day's events, to everything that had been revealed.

His aunt's promised bounty was one thing, but the gathering of creatures—beings once thought to be myth—standing with the uprising, claiming the land as the Volari claimed the sky.

It shifted the balance in a way no one could ignore.

Fury burned along his skin.

Anger only toward the old kings.

How shameful. How cowardly.

To lock away what they didn't understand, as if fear justified control.

To believe they had the right to decide who got to live freely and who didn't. Who could live or die. They might be children of the High Gods, but they were not gods themselves.

Which prompted the question—why had the gods allowed them to rule for so long?

His mind drifted to Nocémi—her reason for wanting King Réol dead.

Because he is my husband's favorite.

Games. Entertainment.

Could all this truly be for immortal amusement?

Whatever the answer, Zolya had had enough.

There was only one way forward that would avoid a war—one path that wouldn't burn them all.

And yet he knew his people would not see it as peace, but surrender.

They would question his crown, his loyalties.

Still, Zolya would endure it.

As he had endured many hardships, one beat of his wings at a time.

He only hoped that once they were nestled again in the warm cradle of a replenished treasury, their grievances would retreat—tucked away between lavish courses at dinners he wouldn't attend.

As he swooped back toward the palace, a figure at the far edge of the gardens caught his eye. She sat alone on a bench near a night-blossom bush, the gentle pulse of lightning bugs spinning around her shoulders. Her companions.

Zolya's heart leaped, breathing quickening.

Tanwen.

His thoughts cleared as a new resolve formed.

He cut a hard right, speeding toward his royal wing.

As soon as he touched down on his veranda, he dismissed his guards with a stern command. "I'm heading to bed. Off with you, now."

His men hardly fought him, their breathing ragged from where they hovered in the sky at his back—clearly exhausted from their flight. Soon they were gone, heading to the barracks to change posts.

Once inside his rooms, Zolya tore off his kingly attire, layers upon layers of restrictions. He then dismissed the staff before slipping into the black garb he had worn when out scouting as a kidet.

When he still could do such things more freely.

Then—ensuring no one was near—he leaped back into the air and toward her.

Gravel crunched under Zolya's boots as he landed, drawing Tanwen's attention.

She turned on the bench, the lightning bugs that were dancing around her shoulders scattering.

Her brows lifted with her surprise. "Zol—sire." She stood quickly and gave a respectful bow.

"That won't be necessary," he said. "No one is around."

Tanwen eyed their quiet surroundings, apprehension clear.

"I wouldn't have come to you otherwise," he added, drawing nearer.

As their gazes locked, something tightened in his chest. Her skin, pale and smooth, caught the dappled moonlight, and her dark hair framed her face in soft, loose waves. She wore the traditional garb of her clan, the fabric wrapping snugly over her figure.

For a moment, she looked just as she had the first night they met—measured and watchful, with a steady confidence beneath the surface.

A sudden rush of heat flared along Zolya's skin, his magic humming quietly in response. Desire curled low and steady, a protective pulse.

"Even though I'm glad I've found you alone," he said, stopping just a little too close, "you shouldn't be."

"I'm not," Tanwen replied. "You're here."

He gave her an unamused look. "It's late. Most of the palace is asleep."

She glanced toward the far-off glowing windows behind him, before turning her attention back to the view she had been enjoying before he had landed. "I forgot how bright the sky is from up here," she said, voice almost wistful. "How the Kaiwi River lights up when both moons are full. The atentés will be out harvesting jadüri tonight."

"I've missed you." His declaration came out ragged, unguarded.

Her eyes found his again, her expression softening. "I've missed you."

Zolya's fingers twitched at his side. He swayed, drawn by her nearness, her scent, her everything.

Gods, he wanted to pull her into his arms. Kiss her.

But even here, surrounded only by hedges and moonlight, the risk was still too great.

"You're not . . . mad?" she asked, hesitancy stealing her smile.

The question cooled the blood pounding in his ears. He blinked. "You mean, regarding the fact that my aunt is alive and brought a sack of riches to the table, along with an army?" He raised a brow. "I would have, of course, preferred more of a warning, especially given how shocking it was for my mother, but I understand the position you were in. I would not have told you either if our roles were reversed."

"Thank you," she breathed, shoulders loosening. "Her terms were so specific, her support hinging on your council being genuinely surprised. If there hadn't been genuine surprise in the room, she would've noticed. She's . . . honestly, kind of terrifying."

"I won't argue with that."

"How is your mother faring?"

"She's feigning indifference while also clearly having an internal war. I've honestly never seen her this . . . ruffled. The strife between her and my aunt seems to run deeper even than the affair with my father."

"I'm sorry." She frowned.

"Please." He closed the space between them to gently take her hands. "Let's not waste tonight talking of my mother or my aunt. What's done is done. This may not have been how I wanted to refill the treasury, but it's not the worst outcome. Callia's island provides the safest form of mining in Cādra's history."

She blinked up at him. "Wait, so—you'll agree to the Rebellion's terms?"

"I will." Saying it out loud solidified the weight of it in his chest. It brought relief—but also dread. The storm it would stir among his people, his court. But it *was* the right choice. For now and for later.

His legacy would not be a repeat of old kings'—not one of wars and strife, but harmony—even if that took time to grow on Galia. Change did not instill fear in his heart, but evoked excitement.

"Oh, Zolya." She threw her arms around him, hugging him tightly.

It was like slipping into a warm bath, a relief, a poultice, peaceful, right.

Mine.

His composure snapped.

His arms encircled her, breathing her in. His magic surged, a possessive yearning.

Finally, it sighed.

"You are changing the world," she said, eyes shining as she looked up at him.

"*We* are." He brushed her cheek with his knuckles.

Her lips parted, drawing his gaze to them.

Want coiled in his gut, raw and familiar, a quiet ache. It was the need to be close to her, to let down the armor he wore everywhere else but when with her.

Yet neither of them moved.

Closer or apart.

They were still out in the open.

Still were risking everything by merely embracing.

They continued to fight what they knew would be inevitable—holding back.

Until Zolya couldn't take it anymore.

With a low growl he leaned down, angling toward her mouth—

A rustling came from a nearby hedge.

In a flash, he spun, shielding Tanwen as his senses flared sharp. "Someone's here."

She let out a soft, startled sound behind him.

"Don't move," he told her as he strode forward, sweeping aside a thick hedge branch.

A stout woman with tall straight horns crouched within, frozen, eyes wide as a startled hare's.

For a heartbeat, they simply stared at one another.

Confusion flooded Zolya, until recognition dawned.

Then all he felt was rage.

Cold, consuming rage.

"Ms. Sonja," he said, his voice sharp steel as he glared down at his mother's head of staff. "I don't suppose you'll enlighten your king as to why you are hiding in this bush."

33

Oh gods! Tanwen tore through the palace corridors, breath sharp, feet fast.

After Zolya had revealed the servant hiding in the bushes, he'd told Tanwen to go.

She hadn't hesitated.

Panic chased her from the gardens and back inside.

She had risked only one glance over her shoulder—finding a fuming Zolya staring down at the woman who had stumbled from the hedges to throw herself at his feet.

A flicker of pity had bloomed in her chest, hoping he wouldn't do anything rash, despite the woman—Ms. Sonja, he had called her—having been obviously spying.

Tanwen didn't know how long she'd been there. Or why, but the fact that she was there at all . . .

Really, *really* bad.

They'd nearly kissed, for Ilustra's sake!

And she'd been the one to throw her arms around *him*. The king!

Stupid, stupid, stupid. Tanwen clenched her fists as she rounded a corner, passing flickering torch bowls that tossed shadows up tall columns.

Why did I have to hug him?

Because he's him, came a taunting voice. *Because you wanted much more than to hug.*

Tanwen groaned with a mixture of mortification and frustration.

Of course she wanted to do more than hug! Zolya had just told her he would be agreeing to the Rebellion's terms. Pardoning Azla. Paving the way toward a new, rich, diverse Cādra.

The emotions that had overwhelmed her then.

Love.

Relief.

Need.

Need to not merely feel his arms around her but—

Tanwen stopped, her gaze running over her stone surroundings.

Her pulse tripped into a new quick rhythm.

This was not the way to the guest quarters.

She'd been so lost in thought she hadn't seen where her feet had taken her.

The soldier barracks.

A spike of fear shot up her spine as she bit out a low curse.

She spun to leave—and smacked into something solid.

"Lost, are we?"

The voice slid cold over her cheek like the edge of a blade.

Blood drained. Fear spiked.

She quickly backed away.

Kidar Osko Terz gazed down at her, eyes hard, dark uniform a looming shadow that matched the great drape of wings at his back.

"Sir," she said automatically, bowing from old habit—one she instantly regretted.

He didn't deserve that.

Kidar Terz had made his dogmatic beliefs regarding Mütra *very* clear during their negotiations.

"What brings you out so late?" His eyes cut over her, his gaze too long, too invasive. "Spying on my unit?"

She straightened. Stiff. Defenses flaring.

"To what purpose would I need to spy? As you witnessed today, we have more than enough leverage to help our cause."

It was reckless, provoking, but gods did it feel good.

To finally stand with shoulders back and face a bully without flinching.

Even if that bully towered over her by two heads, with a blade at his hip and heat magic humming under his skin.

She blamed the events in the garden—the servant witnessing her and Zolya. The way Tanwen's entire future now felt like it was cracking open beneath her feet.

"You forget I am still your superior." Kidar Terz's voice dropped low, icy. "Your freedom does not improve your rank, *Ms.* Heiro." He twisted her lacking title mockingly. "You are still the lowest of the low, and you always will be."

"Then what does that say of you, standing here, conversing with such a lowlife?"

His lip curled. "The king was wrong about you."

Unease twisted in her gut. "Regarding what?"

"We never should have spared your life. You should have gone to Maryth with the rest of your family."

Tanwen stiffened but didn't cower under the threat. "Clearly the king doesn't seem to fear me as much as you do."

His face darkened, rage flaring as his wings began to unfurl.

Tanwen had a moment of regret, until his next words robbed her of breath. "You know, your brother feigned the same sort of confidence in the beginning."

She froze as blood drained from her, nausea churning.

"But I broke him eventually," he said, voice a low rumble. "Like I break all your kind. I just needed the right instrument to heat up." He lifted a hand, his fingers glowing red—fire rolling beneath his skin.

Something inside her snapped.

Rage invaded each of her quick breaths. A delirium of fury and devastation.

"You monster." She stepped closer, shaking, vision warping.

Thol.

All this time she'd blamed only the king.

But of course Terz had been there.

Of course he had taken part.

He had commanded their army.

Despised Mütra.

A thought awoke ugly and painful in her mind then.

Had Zolya known his friend had been involved?

Had he known and still done nothing?

Tanwen's breath hitched.

Heart tearing in two.

No.

She refused to believe it.

She couldn't.

Her hands trembled. Her magic pulsed, screamed for her revenge.

"Do it," Kidar Terz murmured, smile like a knife as he leaned in. "Try what you're burning to try. Then I'll finally be allowed to do what I want to you, *Mütra*."

Her magic howled again. Her heart pounded.

Don't, came a sharp warning cry within her mind.

Birds nesting in the columns high above cut through her fog of devastation and ire as they beat their wings, sensing her desires.

Don't, they screamed. *Too strong. Too sharp. Don't. Don't. Don't. Run.*

Tanwen's breaths continued to come out in harsh bursts, each one stoking the fire burning beneath her skin.

But by some miracle—she listened.

Tanwen stepped away.

She swallowed the fire clawing up her throat, enough to say in a low, cold voice, "One day you will see the reckoning of your hatred, Kidar Terz. And I pray to every god that I'll be there as witness."

She didn't run, despite wishing to flee.

She didn't look back, despite her fear that he might follow.

She kept her head held high as she calmly walked away.

Every step a battle.

Not until she reached her room, bolting the door behind her, did she collapse against it, sliding to the ground.

Her entire soul trembled, overwhelmed by the weight of everything that had happened tonight.

And rising above it all—fear.

Fear that her and Zolya's one mistake would be their downfall.

Fear that everything they had fought for could vanish by morning.

Fear that those like Osko, and the hatred he carried, might win in the end.

That final thought shattered her thinly held composure.

With her face buried in her hands, Tanwen bent forward and wept.

34

Zolya sat a statue, fury radiating from every line of his body.

Morning light flooded his mother's chambers, pouring in through the wide-open curtains. The veranda beyond offered a sweeping view of the sky and manicured Royal Gardens, golden with the early sun.

But the beauty did nothing to soften his mood.

He had come here first thing, only to be told by her usher that the queen had already left—off to some breakfast engagement with one noble lady or another.

The usher, however, had taken a quick look at Zolya's dark expression and had obeyed his every command without question—not that he wouldn't have otherwise. He was king.

Still, it had been with a fervent haste that the man had cleared out all the queen's staff within her rooms.

Now Zolya waited—alone.

A quietly brewing storm.

He had dealt with Ms. Sonja—as best as he could without taking her life. Not that that option was off the table. He only hoped, for her sake, the weight of a king's threat along with a heavy purse would keep her tongue.

She also reported to him now. Keep enemies closer and all that.

Ms. Sonja's first task had been to slip an unmarked note beneath Tanwen's door. A simple, cryptic line of correspondence that said *All is well.* For he was determined to make it so.

He could imagine Tanwen pacing, sleepless in her panic, her thoughts spiraling like his had all night.

Frustration bloomed beneath his ribs. He hated the thought of her distressed.

All because someone couldn't leave his affairs alone.

His rage stirred, sharp and impatient.

"My dear?" came the smooth voice of his mother when she finally entered. "I had not expected a visit from you this morning." She slid out of a silken shawl and handed it off to a trailing servant, before her brows gently furrowed as she glanced about her chambers. "Where is my staff?"

"Leave us," Zolya commanded of the young man behind his mother.

He vanished at once, nearly tripping in his rush out the door.

The queen turned back to him, frowning. "What is the meaning of—?"

"Why are you having me followed?"

She hesitated—just slightly—her step catching as their eyes met.

"I'm not having you followed," she said, voice even.

"Do *not* test me this morning, Mother," he warned, tone dropping low. "I have had words with your Ms. Sonja after I found her concealed within a hedge grove."

The queen lowered herself onto a daybed across from him, smoothing her skirts with deliberate care. "How interesting." Her expression remained unreadable. "And what exactly were you doing near this hedge to discover her?"

"Mother." A low rumble echoed through the chamber—his fury leaking out with his magic.

"As I said," she replied, seemingly unfazed by his display of power. "I'm not having you followed. I was having followed Ms. Heiro."

Silence.

Zolya stared at her, the full weight of the admission sinking in like frost creeping through bone—quiet, gradual, painful.

He dared not breathe.

"Which is why I find it interesting," she repeated. "If you found Ms. Sonja, that means Ms. Heiro must have also been nearby."

His jaw clenched. "Why are you having Ms. Heiro followed?"

"I do hope you go easy on Ms. Sonja," she continued, ignoring his question. "She was only listening to a queen's command."

"Stop evading," he snapped.

Her eyes clung to his, a drawn-out moment.

"When it comes to where you seek your pleasures," she began. "I've never been a prying mother, have I?"

"I sense a contradiction forthcoming."

"But *this* cannot come to pass."

Zolya's unease laced tightly around his lungs. "I don't know to what you are referring."

She gave him a pointed look. "Ms. Heiro."

He remained silent—refusing to entertain it. Terrified to.

"*Zolya*," she pressed. "Others may not see it, but I'm your mother. And mothers see everything. And from what I've observed, it's clear you care for the girl. While I've certainly encouraged your broader view of the world, your challenge to old ways, *this*"—she shook her head—"this goes a step too far."

"A step too far," he repeated, rising to his feet, his outrage finally breaking through. "You are such a hypocrite."

She frowned. "How so?"

"You call yourself a progressive. A champion of equality. You have called me a snob, lectured me on the importance of honoring all bloodlines—yet now, when another threatens to touch your own, you disapprove?"

"Oh, Son," she breathed, expression falling. "So . . . it's true."

Claws dragged across his heart as he turned. "Don't look at me like that."

Zolya couldn't bear the sorrow in her eyes. The disappointment.

It tore at him—because his own disappointment in her was too heavy to carry.

Losing respect for his father had been one thing.

Réol had ruled through fear and force, had only earned Zolya's devotion through his son's desperate hope that somewhere beneath the cruelty, a father still existed—a man who saw him not merely as his future successor but also as his child.

His mother, however?

She was supposed to be different.

She had been the one to help fight his demons, to teach him the strength in knowing himself, in owning his voice.

To lose faith in her now felt like losing the last of who he was.

"Do you love her?"

His mother's question redrew his attention.

He replied without hesitation. "With my entire soul—on every plane of existence."

She closed her eyes, expression pained. "Oh, Zolya. How did this happen?"

"Does it matter how?"

"She can never be your queen."

The words landed like a blade.

Deep, fatal agony.

He had known this truth. Of course he had.

But hearing it from her lips—from the queen dowager herself—shattered something in him all the same.

"She doesn't want to be queen," he argued.

In truth, they hadn't discussed such an outcome. But he knew Tanwen was not with him for power or title or crown.

"Then what future are you imagining for the two of you?"

"Only one where we can be together."

"It's impossible."

"Why?" he demanded, voice sharp. His magic jumped along with his outrage, a flash of lightning overhead. But he no longer cared to control his power; he let it howl like he wished to. "Our world is changing. She and I are changing it. We aren't the first of our kind to be together."

"You are *king*, Zolya," his mother reminded him, tone admonishing. "You most certainly *are* the first of your kind to engage with a Mütra. What of your heir? Our lineage?"

"Our *lineage*?" he repeated, indignant. "I expected your hesitancy if ever you found out, but I didn't expect you to be so closed minded, so like . . . *them*." He gestured beyond their rooms—to those in their court and kingdom who scowled behind fans and shrouds of silk, who remained so bigoted in their beliefs. "You are just like father, to only care about the purity of a bloodline."

"Son." She rose, agony painting her features as she went to him.

He stepped back.

The action caused his mother's expression to fall, along with her outstretched arm.

"*All* I want is your happiness," she said gently. "I want you to love whoever your heart chooses—of course I do. But I also don't want everything you've worked for, everything you've endured, to come undone. Most of all, I want you safe. And our world . . . It hasn't changed as much as you believe."

"I disagree," he said, voice tightening, along with his wings at his back.

"If that were true, you wouldn't feel the need to hide your relationship with Ms. Heiro."

"That's not fair," he bit out. "I don't hide her out of shame—I hide her to protect her. To protect what we have."

"Exactly," she said softly.

Zolya's frustration surged—anger, exhaustion, grief all blurring together.

Loving Tanwen was so easy. So natural. So right.

Why wasn't that enough?

Why did love have to come with conditions? Why did it need to please others to be accepted or allowed? The right to their union didn't belong to anyone but them.

Gods, he hated how naive he sounded.

Like the wishful thinking of a boy, not the seasoned judgment of a king—a king trying desperately to keep a war from erupting between races.

"I do not argue that strides still need to be taken for the world to accept our union." He held his mother's gaze. "But I don't believe it's far away. When the time is right, we'll make our relationship public."

Her eyes filled with pity then, and he hated it. Hated what it meant.

"I need you to accept who I love, Mother." He loathed how his voice trembled on the edge of command and desperation, but *by the twin moons*, he *was* desperate. "I need you to accept Tanwen. Because if you can't . . . then you and I will have no future."

She looked at him for a long, aching moment. A dozen emotions passed through her gaze—shock, sorrow, anguish—until it landed on a blaze of determination.

She stepped forward then, and this time he didn't move away.

She reached for his hand, and as he let her take it, a single tear slid down her cheek.

It was nearly his undoing.

"My child," she whispered, grip tightening. "I will *always* accept you. Just as I will always support you. If she is the one you choose, then so be it."

A tidal wave of relief crashed through him, so fierce it nearly buckled his knees.

His eyes burned, his throat tightening as he swallowed hard against the surge of his emotions.

"Thank you," he said, voice thick.

She gave him a small, encouraging smile—one that faltered almost immediately. "It's not my approval you'll need, however, for this union to come to pass." Her gaze clung to him, heavy, fearful. "It will be the gods'."

PART VI

Faith

35

Within the royal temple of Zenca, Habelle lay prostrate, the marble floor a cold, unyielding kiss to her forehead. But the chill was nothing compared to the anguish tearing through her chest, or the storm of worry thrashing in her blood.

Her magic hissed, restless and clawing through her veins, aching to do something—anything—to help.

But nothing could mend what was coming undone.

No power could fix the slow unraveling of everything she held dear.

Why? she implored silently to the goddess of destiny. *Haven't I sacrificed enough? Given enough? What divine plans do you have for my child? I will give more to allow his future to be bright. I will give anything.*

It had destroyed her to witness her son's faith in her slip, to watch disappointment pool in his gaze. She had needed him to understand, her disapproval in Ms. Heiro was not because she was against mixed-blood relations—nothing could be further from the truth; her disagreement came from how this put such a heavier risk on his rule, on his life.

Freeing Mütra and welcoming the newly released beings from Both was already a radical enough shift. But to then fall in love with one of them, to choose a public life with Ms. Heiro—if the first change had left their conservative factions reeling, this would be the final blow.

Though it wasn't their court's disapproval she feared—it was their gods'.

Their creators'.

Their true rulers'.

Would this be too much, too fast?

There was a reason Réol had clung so fiercely to tradition—not just out of prejudice but also from a deep paranoia that any deviation would invite the wrath of the High Gods. Unseating his reign.

From where she bowed, a slow panic clawed up her spine, sharp, cold.

Habelle clasped her hands tightly together, her desperate prayers spilling from her lips. "*Please*, spare him. He is a good king, a passionate and compassionate ruler. A faithful servant. He is worthy."

"I was told I'd find you here." Callia's husky voice cut through the temple, sliding through the incense-laced air like smoke.

Habelle bit back a sigh of annoyance as she briefly closed her eyes.

Despite the interruption she rose from her kneeling and concentrated on finishing her service.

She poured a measure of blessed wine into the goblet resting at the base of Zenca's prayer mantel.

"Still subservient to the High Gods, I see," Callia said as Habelle turned, their gazes meeting.

"And you no longer are?"

"The High Gods never seemed to serve my life."

"It is we who must serve them," Habelle corrected softly.

Callia huffed in distaste. "An imbalance I've never enjoyed."

Her sister, per usual, looked both untamed and regal. She wore another dark wrap dress, understated but refined, and atop her brow sat her rough-hewn stone circlet, the large ambrü in its center pulsing like a heartbeat. Her wings, the same rich amber hue as Habelle's, hung limp at her back.

Clipped.

Flightless.

Habelle's heart always ached at the sight of them, no matter how easily Callia seemed to wear their loss.

"Then who holds your faith now?" she asked.

"My people," Callia replied without hesitation. "They've done more for me than any immortal ever has."

Habelle flinched inwardly at the blasphemy—spoken so casually, so boldly within the temple walls. She strode past her sister and left the chamber, skirts whispering as she moved.

Callia followed while Habelle's guards fell in step behind them.

Outside, the morning sun filtered through the trees, scattering golden light across the shaded path. Gravel crunched beneath their feet, awkwardly straining the silence.

"Did you need something?" Habelle asked, voice polite but distant.

Despite her sister's resurrection, they'd barely seen each other since her arrival—a distance not unlike the one that had stretched between them before her exile.

"Must I need something to see you?"

"Our past proves that you do."

Habelle caught the edge of Callia's frown.

"When will you forgive me?" asked Callia.

She stopped mid-step. "Excuse me?"

"You don't have to pretend with me." Callia's tone was quiet, almost vulnerable. "I know you still hold resentment. For what I did. For what happened with Réol. I'm not asking you to forget it—but I'm hoping we can move forward from that time."

Habelle studied her carefully. "Can *you* put the past behind you?"

Callia straightened, shoulders pulling back. "I want to try."

Suspicion coiled low in Habelle's gut. "Why?"

For a moment, hurt flickered across Callia's pale face—quick, unguarded—before vanishing behind cool composure. "Because we're the only family we have left," she said. "Because I never thought I'd see a blue sky again, let alone you . . . or my daughter. I've been given a second chance at life. I would like it to be different from the one I was living before."

"And what kind of life was that?"

"An angry one," she admitted. "I'm done being angry, Habbie."

The use of her childhood nickname squeezed her heart, threatening to crack open what she'd kept sealed. But she had been manipulated by her sister before.

"You don't need to be angry now," she said coolly. "Because you've won. You and your Rebellion have everything you've wanted."

"And isn't that for the better?" Callia asked. "For my daughter's future and your son's? For the future of our world? Or would you prefer a war?"

"No," Habelle said quickly. "Of course not. I only mean . . . I doubt you'd be so forgiving if you hadn't come out on top."

Callia tilted her head, considering. "No, I suppose not. After spending over sixty years imagining all the ways I could take my revenge, simple forgiveness was never going to be enough. I needed atonement for what was taken from me. If roles were reversed, you would have needed the same."

"That would imply I would have acted as you did, to find myself in such a state," Habelle said coolly. "And that would never have happened."

Callia's eyes flashed before she let out an incredulous huff. "You always did play the pious victim well, Sister. But you're not without blame."

Anger pricked at Habelle's control. She glanced at the guards hovering nearby. "Give us space."

They bowed before stepping back, leaving the sisters alone on the shaded path.

Habelle faced Callia fully, her tone steel edged. "As I recall, I wasn't the one who climbed into *your* husband's bed and bore his child."

"And there it is." Callia folded her arms, eyes narrowing. "Finally."

"I won't do this." Habelle turned and walked away, a storm brewing beneath her skin.

"Do what?" Callia called after her. "Show emotion? You should, Habbie. You'd finally prove you're not made entirely of stone."

She spun back, voice sharp. "You know nothing of me or of what I've felt."

"That's because you never let me know! You didn't even cry, did you know that? Or yell or bat an eye when you found us. You merely stared at Réol and me in his bed and walked out."

The mention of that day, that moment that had torn open the ground beneath her feet and had her falling—it was too much, too vicious. "I left Galia!" she snapped. "And not because of jealousy or even shame of what our court would say—but because my heart had shattered. Not over Réol. Over you. You broke my heart, Callia. *You.*"

She stared, stunned. "I—didn't know . . ." Her words were a whisper of disbelief. "You never even seemed to like me."

"You are my sister! I loved you."

A tense silence stretched between them, their past finally colliding with their present. Painful, messy, inevitable.

"That's why I kept you at arm's length once I was married," she explained, her sadness leaking up her throat. "You have no idea what it meant to be queen to a man like Réol. From the moment of our union, his cruelty knew no bounds. You call me cold, but I had to be. It was the only way to survive. Anything that made me smile, he took. Anything that hurt, he magnified." Her voice wavered, but she pushed through, determined to finally speak the words she had never dared speak before. "As the eldest, I was raised to obey. By our parents, and then by him and what my crown represented. You should be glad you weren't the one chosen for such a role. You have never been good at following anyone's orders but your own. A trait I grew to envy. Callia, the sister who laughed louder, cried harder, stole the attention in every room. It's no wonder we ended up where we did. Mistresses are allowed feelings. Wives are expected to bury them."

Quiet fell heavy between them, pressing against the covered footpath.

"Oh, Habbie." Callia looked uncharacteristically shaken. "I'm so sorry. I knew it wasn't a love match. I mean, you were basically estranged after Zolya's birth, but I hadn't realized the extent of how he made you suffer. Why didn't you tell me?"

"What could you have done to stop it? He was king. To speak against him was treason."

"Yes, but it might have—" Callia cut herself off, her gaze sliding away as frustration tightened her brow.

"What?" Habelle pressed.

Callia's eyes flicked back to hers, guarded. "If I had known what he was before . . . before it was too late, maybe I would have made different choices."

Guilt slammed into her, heavy and crushing. "That's not fair. You can't put the consequences of your decisions on me. I invited you to my isle after you became with child. *Many* times, but you refused."

"I thought you were jealous and wanted me away from him."

Habelle let out a broken laugh. "I was never jealous. I was terrified, Callia, *for you*. And your unborn babe."

"Gods." Her face grew ashen. "I was such a naive twat."

"Yes," Habelle said simply.

Their gazes met, a brief beat before they began to laugh. Great big guffaws.

It must have appeared a rather unhinged scene if anyone were to stumble upon them, two ladies in crowns cackling among the High Gods' temples.

But it was decades in the making, a tangle of shared trauma and old grief and the sheer absurdity that they had both somehow survived. It was a cool salve over stubborn wounds, a fragile promise of relief after the years of pain.

When they were finished, the air around them danced a bit lighter, a bit freer.

Callia wiped at the corners of her eyes. "Good thing I'm nothing like that woman anymore."

The quiet implication sobered Habelle. "Same for me," she said. "Though I would have preferred we'd grown under different circumstances."

Callia's expression hardened. "I'm glad he's dead."

At any other time, with any other company, such a cold declaration would have drawn a gasp of well-bred shock from Habelle.

But standing alone with her sister—under the reign of a far different, far better king—she allowed herself a rare moment of honesty.

She leaned in and whispered, "Me too."

They shared another smile then, small but real, one that felt like a mending.

Perhaps a day would come when she'd tell Callia the truth. How Réol had met his end at the edge of Nocémi's own blade, her hand steady as she dragged it across his throat.

But for now, this moment was enough.

"I'm sorry." Callia reached out to clasp her hands. "Truly. For all of it. How can I make things right between us?"

Habelle held her sister's earnest gaze, taking in the scar that cut down Callia's cheek and the deep shadows under her eyes—marks that no amount of time would erase.

They had always been opposites: in their magic, in their temperaments, even in the way they wore their wounds.

Callia bore hers boldly, unhidden, as if daring the world to look.

Habelle kept hers tucked close to her chest, veiled and private.

But the wounds were there all the same—etched by the same cruel hand.

And now, at last, he no longer ruled either of them.

"Let's start by getting to know the women we've become," Habelle said. "I'd quite like to meet this new sister of mine."

Callia grinned. "I can oblige that."

They set off down the shaded path, steps unhurried, hearts a little lighter, Habelle's guards once again in tow.

"What will you do once you leave here?" she asked Callia.

"If all goes well, we'll establish ourselves on the land we've been promised in Cādra."

"And your role there? Do you believe those from Both will continue to follow you once they are free?"

"I won't force them," Callia said easily. "Gods know, they're a lot who don't take kindly to being forced into anything. We'll likely vote—same as we did when I was first chosen to lead. If I had it my way, though, I'd appoint a council as figureheads. It's a burdensome thing, being the only one carrying the weight of so many."

"Yes," Habelle murmured, her thoughts straying to Zolya.

"Your son seems to be doing a fine job of it, however," Callia added, as if knowing the subject of her mind. "It takes great skill and fortitude to be instilling the changes he is while maintaining loyalties."

Habelle kept her unease from showing as she nodded. "His passion for peace seems just as fierce as Réol's had been for war."

"A poetic justice we can celebrate, isn't it?" Callia mused.

"So long as the poem doesn't end in tragedy."

She felt Callia's curious gaze slide over her. "Has something happened?"

Habelle shook her head, offering a mild smile. "Just a mother's constant worry. Nothing more."

But it wasn't nothing.

Already her fears coiled tight again, threading through her chest—fears she couldn't so easily dismiss.

Yes, Zolya carried many responsibilities—most he bore with strength, but there was one risk that could undo him entirely.

She only prayed Ms. Heiro's love for her son was as true as his love for her.

Otherwise, the girl would have Habelle to answer to.

"Look at us," Callia said lightly, pulling her back to the path they walked. "Two queens thriving without the chain of a husband—our children beside us. Imagine how fun our futures will be."

Habelle smiled faintly, but the hope didn't quite reach her heart.

A quiet exhaustion settled over her like a cloak instead.

It was hard to imagine a future when their present felt so precarious.

36

The courtyard was in an uproar.

Zolya stood on the royal balcony, his face a mask of calm even as his wings remained tense at his back.

His decree had fallen: Princess Azla's charges of treason were dropped.

The crowd was a fractured wave of noise—cheers clashing against jeers, fists pumping, faces twisting in fury or celebration.

Palace staff jostled uneasily along the floor, while the Rebellion and his court were separated in mezzanines.

At the center of it all, Azla remained alone atop the raised marble dais of the accused, where so many before her had met far grimmer ends.

Where her own mother had fallen.

And now, that same mother watched from two floors up, Callia's face a fragile mask of uneasy triumph.

The stone beneath Azla's feet still bore the faint veins of dried blood—her mother's blood, Tanwen's father's, and countless others'.

No amount of scrubbing could erase the history written there.

No cleansing could wash away the pain.

Pain his father had carved into this palace.

Pain the kings before him had allowed to thrive.

But today, Zolya would leave a different mark.

Though, one that still would produce heartache—for himself most of all.

He met his sister's gaze, and she gave him the slightest nod.

It was a gesture of support, of understanding of what next needed to be done, of acceptance.

It did nothing to steel his heart, however, only fissured it.

With a decisive hand through the air, he silenced the courtyard like a falling blade.

"While you are free of your charges," he declared, his voice thundering through the still air, "this kingdom is no longer your home. Let the records be written: Azla Diusé, princess of the Sun Court of the first Sky Isle, is banished henceforth from ever again setting foot on Galia."

The square fractured once again.

More cheers, more howls of anger.

It had been a necessary part of her sentence.

The only way to appease both factions of his kingdom.

The rising emotion of the crowd battered against the marble columns, seeming to tremble the sky itself.

It reverberated the war that raged within his own heart—the mix of relief and grief.

He had saved her life, but he was also losing her all the same.

Soon, Tanwen would follow, leaving with the Rebellion to finish what they had started—ending the uprisings so they could secure Cādra's chance at unity.

Amid the storm, his eyes sought her.

Tanwen.

She stood at the edge of the Rebellion's mezzanine, gaze locked on him.

Despite the watching crowd, despite the queen dowager standing a pace behind him, she remained staring.

And he was glad for it.

She was the steady mast for his sails, the fixed horizon in a stormy sky.

The afternoon light caught her dark hair, which spilled around her pale face, her horns tall and gleaming with gold-capped tips.

Pride shone in her expression, and Zolya's chest squeezed painfully.

They had negotiated peace—without a single blade raised in the palace, without a single drop of blood spilled.

It should have felt like victory.

Instead, it flooded him with exhaustion.

For he knew what came next.

The cracks among his people would deepen before they could heal. Fioré would hear of his decree by nightfall—of Princess Azla's fate and the terms of the new accords—and their judgments would flood in just as divided.

Noble houses would whisper.

Courtiers would plot.

His council would question.

But such was the price of peace.

Even if those he ruled would never understand the nuances it demanded.

What decisions kept them comfortable in their lavish lives.

Sacrifices had been made—were still being made—and he would carry them all.

He would watch Tanwen depart, Azla leave, and he'd stay.

Stay and steady a kingdom that, despite its bruises, had a future again.

Their treasury would be replenished, and with it a kingdom that could flourish.

Change.

This was the thought that finally allowed a fracture of hope to glimmer awake in his chest.

Without the threat of war, change *could* be made, was being made.

No matter what his mother believed, what fear she held of their gods, there would always be hope.

Slowly, his wings loosened at his back as his gaze remained tied to Tanwen's, steady, sure.

If what lay ahead was the cost of such hope—if all the pain they had already endured was the foundation to bear it—he would pay such a price a thousand times over.

For his future, his heart, would always be Tanwen.

Even if their time together wasn't now.

He vowed it would be soon.

37

The grand hall glittered with celebration.

Glasses brimmed and plates never emptied as laughter and music swirled through the golden-lit hall. Outside the marble columns, the night sky shimmered, stars twinkling in time with the revelers within.

Tanwen stood at the edge of the party, tucked into her usual hiding spot—beside a vase overflowing with summer lilies and midnight roses. She nursed a half-empty flute of spirits, not really tasting any of it. Her gaze wandered the crowd—a boisterous mix of nobles, rebels, council members, and even staff invited to join in on the merriment.

It was a curated crowd of those who supported today's verdict and the outcome of their peace negotiations.

A rather sizable and encouraging turnout of their supporters on Galia.

Still, beneath the finery and smiles swam a tension—a fragility that all this would be gone in the morning.

A fear not far from the truth.

Tomorrow they would be leaving.

Azla and her mother were already packed, the banished princess naturally not in attendance. She was being sequestered to her rooms, awaiting her final departure with the rebels, Callia keeping her company.

Tanwen had offered to stay with her as well, but Azla wouldn't hear of it.

"Enjoy your final night in the palace," she had told her. "You must celebrate what you have helped achieve."

But such a directive was hard to obey.

Yes, their negotiations might be over—the Rebellion coming out on top.

And Tanwen should have been relieved. Elated. Dancing among the revelry.

Instead, a thousand conflicting emotions churned inside her, a dozen unresolved worries.

The garden with Zolya, the servant finding them, his mother's suspicions, Tanwen's run-in with Kidar Terz, his cruel words still echoing.

But heavier than all of it was not knowing if she and Zolya would be able to steal another moment alone before she left.

While she was keeping company with the foliage, Zolya was keeping court at the front of the grand ballroom.

Kingly duties and all that.

As she downed her drink in one swallow, she chased the hope that the wine might dull her frustrations, drown her uncertainties. But her heart only pounded harder, each beat a sharp, unrelenting thud against her ribs.

Gods, sometimes her mind was an intolerable place.

A blur of wings twirled past her—Brynn laughing breathlessly as Huw caught her by her waist.

Per usual, the pair had been the livelier ones on the dance floor, but as Huw spotted Tanwen, he excused himself and made his way toward her.

"You must stop pouting," he declared, cheeks flushed, eyes bright, blond curls shimmering in the candlelight. "By your expression you'd think we'd lost."

"I'm merely tired," she reasoned.

"No, you're sulking in a corner again because you'd rather be in the privacy of different company."

Tanwen's cheeks were the ones to now grow red—his assessment so spot on. "That's not true."

"Of course it is," he replied breezily, snagging a glass from a passing waiter. "And I don't blame you, he's looking like Ilustra's muse tonight."

"*Huw,*" she admonished, despite her eyes drifting—inevitably—to the front of the hall, to where Zolya stood beside the queen dowager. He was accepting the congratulations of guests with his impeccable, unreadable mask.

Draped in black stitched with gold, Zolya was a consuming vision. His tailored coat molded to his broad chest, his brown skin flawless as it gleamed beneath the hall's glow. His crown was a glint of gold woven into his alabaster hair as his wings swept regally behind him.

Looking at him was absolute torture.

Because in such a room, with so many people, they were forced to remain as if strangers.

And she was forced to share him.

Forced to accept the smiles he bestowed on everyone but her.

As if sensing her attention, Zolya's gaze found hers from across the hall—blue sapphires locking her in place, stealing the breath from her lungs.

Despite the great distance, the air between them crackled as his features grew dark.

It was a collision of longing and unspoken need, heavy enough to drown in.

"All right, that's enough of that." Huw clapped a hand on her shoulder, startling her back into the present. "I know it's hard, little fawn, but you've made it this far safely. You'll find moments together like you have in the past. Better on Cādra than up here."

Tanwen tried not to shift with her unease.

She hadn't yet confided in Huw or Azla about what had happened in the gardens with Ms. Sonja. If everything continued as it was, she wouldn't either.

No need to get them upset for no reason.

Or give them room to say *I told you so.*

"Come." Huw grinned, placing down his glass on a nearby ledge. "Dance with me. The night is young. Tomorrow's worries are for tomorrow."

Tomorrow.

The word was like a vise grip to her throat.

Huw's caution about safety had been wise, yes—but she couldn't bear to think about leaving without the reprieve of being with Zolya tonight. There was still so much they needed to discuss and *not* discuss.

If she was forced to wait any longer, days stretching onto days—

Her dress suddenly felt too clingy, the air in the hall too thick.

"I will shortly," she said to Huw. "I need some fresh air. The wine has gotten to me."

He eyed her skeptically. "You know I'll come find you if you don't keep your word."

"Nothing in this world is more certain than your persistence, my friend." She flashed him a quick smile before slipping away into the warm night.

Once she was alone, the tension along her shoulders eased slightly.

As she sought a quiet corner of a nearby veranda, her mind was too tangled to notice the shadow that peeled away from the revelers to follow her out.

38

Tanwen spun at the sound of approaching footsteps, her heart leaping with foolish hope that it was Zolya.

Instead, dread coiled through her like smoke.

"Kidar Terz." She greeted the commander coolly.

As he approached, she held her ground, despite every nerve in her body screaming that she should run—because the danger he carried was not merely in the blade at his hip but also in his twisted grin as he gazed down at her. He was a pleased predator finding his victim alone.

Tanwen's magic jumped awake in her veins, a silent cry to any nearby animal.

I may need your help, she warned them.

"Are you enjoying tonight's festivities, Ms. Heiro?" Kidar Terz's tone was anything but polite. "It's quite a scene of merriment, is it not?"

She frowned, studying him more closely. "Are you drunk?"

"I'm celebrating." He waved his arm, spirits spilling from the glass he carried. "Isn't that what we are meant to be doing this evening? Celebrating the downfall of our great kingdom?"

"How exactly is maintaining peace a downfall?" She shouldn't be provoking him—not when he was in this state or when they stood alone with only the faint hum of the party echoing behind—but her disdain for him made restraint impossible.

"*Peace*," he scoffed. "At what cost? To fill our court with tainted blood and our lands with beasts?"

His bigotry bounced off her like stone against steel. "Well, you certainly couldn't afford to continue living within your narrow views anymore, now could you? Not with the state of your treasury. Tell me, Kidar Terz, will your conscience feel as heavy when you spend the precious gems flowing in from our treaty on your army?"

His expression twisted, his rage boiling to the surface. "You are a leech on this world," he spit.

She rolled her eyes. "Your hatred is exhausting. When will you realize that *this*"—she waved a hand toward the celebration behind him—"is Cādra's future, and has been for some time? Why does it frighten you so?"

Wrong thing to say.

His fury ignited like a spark to oil. His glass crashed at their feet as he seized her wrist in a bruising grip, yanking her toward him until she could smell the sour bite of alcohol on his breath.

"The only thing that frightens me," he growled, "is the wrath of our gods. And you—and your kind—are nothing but blasphemy begging to be purged."

Fear jolted through Tanwen like a lashing, but beneath her terror stirred something heavier—sorrow. The kind that came from recognizing hate too deep to unroot, too ingrained to reason with.

It was a rot that festered across generations, as unchanging as the turning of seasons.

"I ask that you remove your hand, sir," she said tightly, forcing herself to hide her panic.

Above, she felt the rustle of wings—birds gathering along the pediments. Below, snakes coiled within nearby garden beds, waiting. Her friends sensed her distress and poised, ready to strike on her signal.

Kidar Terz ignored her request.

His grip tightened, burning hot as his magic leaked through his skin.

She cried out, knees dipping as agony seared her wrist.

"I'll enjoy breaking you," he spit. "Just like I did your brother."

At his words, something molten ignited inside her.

Fury for Thol.

Fury for every hunted, beaten, discarded Mütra.

For every soul who met adversity at the hand of someone's fear.

And for every coward like Kidar Terz who called cruelty *justice*.

Her scream of pain became a roar. With a sharp thrust, she drove her knee into his groin.

He folded with a gasp, wheezing curses. "You *wench*—" His lunge was too fast to recognize until the searing sting.

The slap rang out like a crack of lightning.

Her head snapped to the side, cheek blazing, vision blurring as tears gathered.

Her animals shrieked in response, wings flapping, tongues hissing—but before they could defend, another voice cut through the night, cold and lethal.

"You'll regret ever laying a hand on her." The fury in Zolya's voice was chilling. His expression was as dark as an approaching storm, his grip crushing as he held Kidar Terz to his chest, dagger tip pressed tight to his throat.

39

Zolya's vision bled crimson.

Rage erupted through him like a volcanic torrent, his magic spiraling into the skies, thickening the air with the promise of a hurricane.

"You will stand down, soldier," he commanded, voice honed steel, holding Osko, the blade in his grip steady, deadly, and pointed at his friend.

Osko lifted his hands—slow, reluctant surrender.

Still, Zolya wished to draw blood, wished to land a crushing blow—like the one he had witnessed Osko deliver to Tanwen.

His fury surged again, the image of Tanwen reeling from Osko's strike scorched behind his eyes, feeding the torrent firestorm under his skin.

Osko's breath hitched, causing Zolya to blink back to where his knife had pricked through skin.

A small trickle of red slid down Osko's pale neck—over his tattoo.

With unknown restraint, Zolya let him go, shoving him away to step forward and shield Tanwen.

He didn't look at her.

Couldn't.

One glance at the welt forming on her cheek and he'd forget control altogether.

There would be no pulling back from what he'd do next.

"*Leave*," he commanded.

A flicker of pain flashed in Osko's eyes before it was buried beneath mounting frustration. "This wasn't how it was meant to be, Zolya."

From Zolya's periphery he caught the crowd gathering, guests beginning to spill from the party, drawn by their raised voices and the sudden shift in the air.

Light droplets of rain had begun to fall.

"How was it meant to be, then?" Zolya asked, voice low.

"I've been loyal," Osko said tightly. "I've followed each of your commands, no matter how I might have disagreed. But what you've forgiven . . ." His voice wavered. "You let her *go*. Princess Azla. You pardoned a traitor—one tied to the murder of our king! *Your* father."

Fury twisted in Zolya's gut. "As was discussed," he began tightly. "There was no evidence against Azla. Only her love for the woman responsible—and Lady Esme has already paid the price of her actions."

Osko shook his head violently, eyes wild, disbelieving. "Still, we can't cower to their demands no matter how many riches they promise. It only proves how weak we can be and how dangerous they are."

Zolya's brows snapped together. "What are you talking about?"

"The Rebellion," Osko snarled. "*Mütra.*" He threw a hand toward Tanwen.

Zolya instinctively stepped farther in front of where she was angling around his arm.

"They've infiltrated everything—corrupted our kingdom. They've even got their claws in *you* with their blackmail."

Gasps rippled through the crowd, the air thick with disbelief at hearing Osko speak thus to their king. Osko was committing sedition, and all watched how Zolya would react.

Certainly, they knew how his father would have reacted.

Zolya clenched his fists, his magic burning beneath his skin, the distant thunder sharpening like a blade in the heavens. Still, he forced control, jaw locked.

He was *not* his father.

"You're drunk, Kidar Terz," he said. "You will leave now. We'll speak of this in the morning."

"I don't understand how you can't see it?" Osko raved, spittle flying, as if Zolya had never spoken. "You, the son of the mighty Réol—siding with *them*? You are tainting everything your father built!"

Ire bloomed slow and hot in Zolya's lungs. "You cannot taint what was already ruined," he said, tone a dangerous rumble. "My father left me a kingdom drowning in unrest and a treasury stripped to the bone."

More hitched breaths leaped from the crowd—the first time such truths had been spoken out loud.

But Zolya no longer cared.

Let them hear it.

Let them see the wreckage he had inherited from such a *mighty* king.

"You accuse me of not being able to see," he continued. "But for the first time, my vision is clear."

The tension crackled as the two men held gazes, the sky above them swelling with wind and warning. Zolya's heart hammered, not from fear, but from the weight of what must be done.

"I will not keep a commander who lets hate cloud his judgment," he declared. "I can no longer trust you, Kidar Terz."

Osko's frown deepened. "What are you saying?"

"I will need your stripes, soldier."

Osko froze—shock and fury warring across his face. "You are choosing them over me?" His eyes darted to Tanwen, venomous. "*Her?* This is not you, Zolya. She's cursed your mind with her Mütra—"

"*She* is the woman I love."

His words echoed across the veranda.

The crowd hushed.

The only sound the pattering of rain kissing stone.

"No," Osko whispered, voice breaking. *"No."*

His gaze slipped to Tanwen, to the hand she gripped around Zolya's forearm, to the way he stood as a shield in front of her.

Revulsion twisted his features as realization dawned. "You are not my king!" he roared.

And then he lunged.

Zolya reacted in an instant, yanking Tanwen to the side, her startled cry lost in the chaos. He met Osko's fist strike barehanded, skin searing as flame flared beneath the contact—Osko's magic burning hot.

Zolya staggered back, letting out a hiss of pain.

Osko was already coming again.

And again.

And again.

Each blow carried the weight of treachery, of madness, of a man undone.

Zolya quickly traded his dagger for his sword as he moved defensively, blocking, dodging, retreating. Even now.

Even as his friend attacked with killing intent, Zolya fought the instinct to strike, not wishing to do anything he'd regret. Anything he couldn't come back from.

From the corner of his eye, Zolya caught the glint of armored soldiers gathering—but none moved.

Shock rooted them all. The commander of their army going up against their king.

A king who did not call them to action.

He would not involve them unless necessary.

A flash in the night redrew Zolya's attention to Osko pulling his sword from his hip.

Steel clashed violently with Zolya's as he struck. Magic exploded between them—flame against rain, fire battling storm.

Osko lunged again, reckless in his ire. Zolya twisted and ducked before driving a brutal kick to his friend's back.

Osko crashed to the ground, right at Tanwen's feet.

She stood soaked, gripping the banister behind her, eyes wide with panic.

Osko looked up, features twisted with hatred as he found her there.

He reached for her ankle, drawing himself to his knees. “If he will not send you to Maryth, I will!”

His blade arced upward.

For the first time in Zolya’s life, he didn’t think—he moved.

Lightning streaked across the sky. Thunder clapped.

With his next breath, he had crossed the space.

His sword pierced through Osko’s chest with a wet, sickening crunch.

Osko let out a gargle of surprise.

A drowning agony tore through Zolya as he met his friend’s eyes—saw the betrayal, the disbelief, the pain.

And then Osko’s gaze dimmed.

His sword fell.

His friend’s body slumped in Zolya’s grip.

Lifeless.

40

Shock blanketed the veranda.

Rain—a relentless downpour, covered the scene in a gray sheet of devastation.

Tanwen stood frozen, hair and dress plastered to her skin, her limbs numb, her mind hollow, unable to recognize anything beyond the sight of Zolya—kneeling, cradling the body of Kidar Terz.

"I'm sorry," he whispered to his friend, his voice broken and rough.

He remained in a halo of dryness, his magic curving around him where he crouched, where he mourned.

Pain finally pierced through Tanwen, witnessing Zolya's own, a cleaving to her heart.

She moved—quickly working her way forward, toward him.

But then the veranda splintered.

Chaos erupted in the palace like a dam breaking.

Screams rang out as soldiers surged forward, a shattering of fault lines.

Factions loyal to the fallen commander clashed against those loyal to the crown.

A surge of kidets turned on Rebellion delegates, too many cut down before they could react, others because of their lack of weapons.

Those with powers stepped in to defend, fight back.

Mütra conjured roots, morphed into feral animals. Brynn extended her claws, landing lethal slashes, while noblemen and -women hurled sky magic at soldiers. The delicate magic of ladies proving deadly.

The queen dowager's cry drew Tanwen's attention to where she was shoving through the fray, desperate to reach her son. Her grief was a storm of its own as she flung back guards with her blasts of rain. But too soon she was overpowered by their swarm as they pulled her away to safety.

"Tanwen!" Huw was at her side, throwing her a sword.

As she caught it, he disappeared just as quickly as he had appeared, flashing through the melee. He snatched more weapons from stunned courtiers or distracted soldiers before placing them in the hands of Rebellion allies.

Tanwen's trance shattered when a councilman charged her. But before she raised her sword, she sent out a quick plea in her mind.

Shrieks answered.

A cloud of wings dived from the night sky, a blur of color in the rain. Beaks like blades, claws like knives tore at the man's face.

He screamed in pain, falling to the ground as he clutched his bleeding eye socket—one of the fowl making off with the eyeball.

Tanwen didn't pause at the gruesome display. She sent a quiet burst of gratitude toward the flock as she plunged forward.

But before she could meet her next attacker, a tremor rolled beneath her feet.

A pulse of power knocked her back—along with the crowd.

Lightning tore through the sky, a vicious whip of wind.

Tanwen hit the stone floor, palms scraping.

As she looked up, her pulse was a tornado in her veins, her breath catching.

Zolya stood in the heart of the uproar.

Power rolled off him in waves, light dancing along his skin like fire licking wood. His wings were stretched wide, a white canopy of power as his face was etched in thunder and grief.

At his feet, Kidar Terz's body lay across the marble in a crimson pool.

Awe twisted with a sliver of fear as she regarded Zolya.

Never before had she seen him like this—never had she seen anyone like this.

He looked more god than mortal, and a shiver raced down her spine that had nothing to do with the storm raging around them.

"*Enough*," he boomed, his voice a warning tremor that shook the very foundation of the palace.

No one dared move, breathe, blink.

For a blessed moment all was still.

Quiet.

Done.

Then the heavens split.

Above them, the sky fractured with light, the air crackling, alive, ancient.

Terrifying.

A single beam lanced downward, blinding and pure, cutting through the squall, brighter than any dawn.

Tanwen shielded her eyes, every hair on her neck rising, as she witnessed in the celestial blaze the High Gods descend.

PART VII

Judgement

41

Habelle's knees throbbed their protest from where she knelt on the hard marble floor.

But the pain was nothing compared to the terror held captive within each beat of her heart.

Her worst fear had materialized.

The High Gods loomed above the trembling partygoers, who lay prostrate in what had once been the grand ballroom—now reshaped into a throne room of impossible make. Twelve towering celestial seats glimmered with light and raw power, but those who filled them were the real spectacles.

Ré beamed in the center, highest of all. His form barely perceived—more radiance than flesh. He was a sliver of the sun, caged beneath skin, licks of flames dancing endlessly.

To his left sat his wife, Nocémi, a startling contrast to his light. She was made up of indigo shadows, a body stitched in starlight and void.

Beside her was Naru—a kaleidoscope of colors shimmering like wind over glass.

Ilustra followed, so stunning only lust and jealousy and longing stirred in Habelle's heart when she glimpsed her.

Even Orzel, god of the sea, was present, his form a swirling column of seafoam and current.

Never in all their recorded history had the full pantheon gathered in the mortal realm.

Their collective presence was suffocating.

Their power an oozing that turned the air heavy, thick, torturous.

Habelle's magic quivered in her veins—a strangling.

We gifted you this magic—their power seemed to hiss. *We can reclaim it.*

"Tonight's events have been most enlightening." Ré's voice had Habelle flinching, his rumble heard in her mind, an invasive lashing of wildfire. "Where to even begin."

Her panic surged as she felt the father of the High Gods' attention—searing and inescapable—settle on her son before drifting to Ms. Heiro, beside him.

The pair knelt next to Habelle.

Even when the gods fell from the heavens, Zolya had refused to leave Ms. Heiro's side.

A flare of anger pierced Habelle's chest then—sharp, thorned.

She knew Ms. Heiro wasn't entirely to blame for the disaster unraveling around them. But fear had a cruel way of twisting logic, of searching for somewhere—someone—to anchor the ache.

Right now, that someone was Ms. Heiro.

If she hadn't come to the palace, this never would have happened.

Yes, but why *did she come?* The familiar silken tenor of Naru filled her mind. *Because she was forced to, her family stolen.*

Habelle furtively glanced to the goddess of artistry, unease a coiling of smoke in her chest. She didn't know if the other gods could hear what was spoken, if Ré could, but it forced her to swallow her spite. Not only because the goddess was right but also because she didn't want to make the situation worse than it was.

"The strife in this realm has festered longer than any of you have drawn breath," Ré continued, his blazing form pulsing with each word. "But this must end. My daughter, Zenca, has made that clear to me."

The goddess of destiny's voice filled the hall then, a scratching layering of millions of voices. "If you stay this path, your end awaits. No being will be spared."

Icy fear shot through Habelle's veins.

"So, you see," Ré said with a theatrical sigh, "while I've cared little of the squabbles here, I care greatly for your prayers. If you destroy yourselves, who will be left to revere us? Who will receive our benevolence? The dirt? The clouds?" He tsked. "A tiresome fate, to rebuild what we've already made."

Habelle forced her expression to remain still as disappointment coiled tight inside. To hear the father of the gods simplify their existence to mere oblation—even as his reason to save them—was more insult than salvation.

Within her heart, her faith wavered.

A fissuring.

Though—still—another part of her refused to believe what had been spoken. Knowing, hoping, praying—not all the gods reduced them so.

"I hereby declare," Ré went on, "that all beings of this realm—high or low made—hold the right to life and liberty. For the sake of peace, you will see it done. Or you will answer to my wrath."

And there it was.

The decree that half their world had died to earn—including many of the guests tonight—now spoken into law with celestial ease.

It sickened her, even as a weary wave of relief washed through her that the bloodshed might finally cease.

Here sat the gods—the very ones who had sown this division, who had let it fester for centuries. Hatred and fear and the creed of Volari supremacy, all that had shaped their world. Had shackled Habelle to her family's will, bound her to her husband's ambition, and stolen her freedom over her own desires—and her son's.

Now it was meant to be undone with a handful of divine words.

She would have laughed at the irony if she didn't think such insolence would see her eviscerated where she knelt.

"And what of our chosen child and the one he loves?" Nocémi's gaze fell to Zolya and Ms. Heiro. "They are engaged in what has never been."

Habelle's attention refocused as her panic struck so violently it almost tore a scream from her.

Please, Almighty Gods, spare them. Spare him. *Please, please, please, spare my son.*

If any of the gods heard her plea, they didn't make it known.

"Yes . . ." Ré hummed, thoughtfully. "A most unconventional match. In both blood and rank. Zenca, daughter of mine, what future do you see?"

"This tale is not solely written by the heavens, Father," her unsettling voice cascaded. "Soil also takes root here. The decision of their unity is not ours alone to make."

"As I feared," Ré groaned, wearily. "While it pains me to speak it, my judgment cannot be cast this day."

Habelle—like the room—didn't dare breathe as he turned his full attention onto the cowering, awaiting crowd, a stretching of suppressive heat.

"We must consult my sister."

42

The cart jolted, jarring Tanwen against Zolya, his arms seeming to instinctively tighten around her.

They sat curled together on the hard bench of a wagon that—if the bars on the windows and heavy lock on the door were any indication—was meant to transport criminals.

Not the most promising of vessels.

She didn't know where they were going, only that it was toward their judgment.

Fear dug deeper into her panic, her two now-constant companions, as her gaze slid to the view outside their window.

A barren winter landscape stretched endlessly.

They were on Cādra, she knew that much. Perhaps close to the Bandon Lands, judging by the sparse scenery and occasional scattering of boulders.

How they got here, however, could hardly be described.

After Ré decreed that he needed to speak with his sister, Maryth, the throne room had vanished—space folding, time stuttering—to spit them into a new reality.

One blink and she and Zolya were here. Her disorientation had faded quickly, but her nausea remained.

Her worries were a constant and overwhelming tsunami.

What fate were she and Zolya being carted off to? What judgment could possibly decide whether a king could love a Mütra commoner? And beyond their fate, what had happened to her friends? Huw and Brynn and the rest of her Rebellion party from Galia. What was being done with the bodies of those who fell during the battle in the palace?

At her last pondering, visions of Kidar Terz stained her mind. Lifeless, lying in spilled crimson.

She eyed Zolya, beside her.

He hadn't spoken since accepting that no amount of his powers could break them out of this wagon. It appeared a godly contraption meant specifically to keep them in.

Now he sat stiff and silent, wings drooped, face drawn—his gaze fixed unseeing on the floor.

His grief was a looming presence in the small space—thick, inescapable.

The weight of which crushed down on Tanwen, guilt gnawing in her gut.

He'd taken Kidar Terz's life to save hers.

While she harbored no love for the commander, she understood what his death meant to Zolya.

What it cost to be the one to have driven the sword.

Zolya had killed his oldest friend.

To protect her.

A regret she feared he would come to never forgive her for.

"Zol," she started, nerves fluttering. "I'm sorry."

The sound of her voice, hoarse and broken, seemed to bring him back to where they sat.

His blue gaze met hers, a frown pinching his brow.

"Don't," he replied gruffly.

She blinked, confused.

"Do not take blame for this," he said. "There is *nothing* to be sorry for."

Tanwen's unease still twisted in her chest. "But . . . Osko—"

"—decided his fate the moment he hurt you." His tone was cold and final, shadows gathering in his expression.

Tanwen held in a shiver, sensing his magic lacing the air in a similar brooding storm.

"Still . . ." she forced out, "I understand that he was your friend."

Hard swallow to his throat. "He was, yes."

The tone in which he emphasized *was*—as if referring to an Osko who lived in his distant memory.

Zolya turned to her then, gripping her hands, gaze piercing. "Listen," he started, voice low, gravelly, imploring. "I will *never* regret saving your life. I'm only sorry to have ever been forced into such a position to do so. Osko was—not always like who he . . . became. There was a time, for the both of us, that the stakes of our differing beliefs were not so fundamental, not so divisive. A time when there were no secrets filling our silences. But such are the lives of children," he reasoned, a nostalgic tone pressing heavy on his words. "I will always carry the weight of taking his life, but the man I mourn left a long time ago."

Tanwen squeezed his hands, the ache in her chest unraveling.

He grieved his childhood friend, not the commander of his army.

She understood this now, though it didn't make any of it less tragic.

"I will help you honor that memory," she offered.

Despite what Kidar Terz had done to her, done to her family, she would do this for Zolya—she would practice the forgiveness she asked of the world.

His gaze clung to hers, a cascading of emotion filling their blue depths—shock, disbelief, awe. "You are too good for me." His voice was gruff. "None of us deserve you."

"Careful." A wisp of a smile played on her lips. "Your praise might go to my head."

He pulled her into a kiss, one that surprised her, muscles tensing, but too soon she relaxed into him. Heat flared beneath her skin, her pulse rushing as his hands skimmed up her waist, pressing her tighter to his chest.

His mouth was warm and inviting and—desperate.

She could sense his panic, then his fear, sharp and trembling, in the way he clung to her. As if this could be his last time doing so.

"Zolya," she whispered, pulling back just enough to meet his eyes, to draw air into the tight space between them. "Breathe."

He did. Barely.

"I'm terrified," he confessed, the words cutting through her, so raw, so unguarded.

Devastating.

"So am I." It felt both relieving and foreshadowing to admit to it. "Though not of dying," she added after another beat.

He frowned down at her.

"Not that I think that's what awaits us . . . Well, it's certainly a possibility, of course. And Maryth's Eternal River comes for us all eventually. But—"

"Tanwen." He cupped her cheek, settling her nervous prattle. "Breathe."

She did.

"Better?" he asked.

"A bit," she replied—her rapid heartbeats slightly slowing.

"Now, what are you trying to say?"

She took another slow inhale. "I'm afraid everything we've worked for might be lost depending on what the gods decide. And my soul will never rest if . . . if everything achieved in our peace agreements is torn down because of us."

"It won't be," he assured.

"How can you know that?"

"Because our agreements came to pass with more than your and my will. The treaties signed are not contingent on whether our union is accepted by the divine. They are not even contingent on myself remaining king. I made sure of that."

"You did?"

He arched a brow at her. "Did you not read them before signing?"

"Of course I did."

He eyed her skeptically.

"They were each *very* long," she finally admitted. "I read the important bits."

He huffed his mirth. "Well, an important bit you seem to have missed was that only our two opposing councils can amend or change the treaties, not by will of a single royal ruler."

Her mouth hung agape. "Why did you not tell me?"

"We hardly had a moment to confer privately," he argued. "Plus, that was what the review period was meant for, when the Rebellion and Royal councils looked over the treaties. I assumed you would have seen it then."

She shook her head, her disbelief mixing with her wonder at the man before her. For a blissful moment the weight and worries of their future slipped away. He had done it. He had secured a promise to their people. To his people. Her love for him almost became too much to bear. "You are a great king, Zolya."

He merely shrugged, clearly uncomfortable with her praise. "I understood that we both had fears with what might happen if our relationship was ever exposed. And once my mother found out, I couldn't take any chances. Nothing's ever certain, but I wanted to make sure our treaties would hold—no matter what happens to me."

Anxiety twisted anew once more.

"What happens to *us*," she corrected.

Their gazes held, Zolya's silence piercing through her chest.

"*What happens to us*," she repeated, almost desperately. "We are in this together."

"Yes," he said as he pulled her back into him. "We are."

Despite his reassurance, dread gripped Tanwen's lungs as she angled her horns away from his face, pressing her cheek to his chest. She didn't like the look he carried, the shadow of decisions not voiced.

To push away her worries, she forced herself to memorize the rhythm of his heart—steady, strong, alive.

As she nuzzled farther into him, he curled farther around her. His arms and wings enfolded her in warmth, shielding her from the cold that seeped through the wagon's open windows.

For a while, only the creak of wheels over hardened ground and the rattle of the cart filled the silence.

"If Ré demands peace," Tanwen murmured after a while, "then whatever judgment he and Maryth give . . . it must serve that peace."

"One would think," said Zolya, his fingers gliding soothingly up and down her arm.

"That must benefit us, right?"

A long pause. "In my decades of experience interacting with immortals, their expectations often exceed logic."

"What does that mean?"

"No matter our outcome, they will still demand peace in Cādra. At least for a time."

Tanwen frowned, shifting up to look at him. "You do not think peace will last? What of the treaty—?"

"The treaty is as ironclad as it gets. But I also believe that gods and mortals, when too long in their comforts, will always cause strife for the sake of something to entertain."

She blinked at him. "You have grown jaded in your old age."

Seemingly despite himself, he smiled, laying a gentle kiss to her forehead. "Which is why I need you and your sunny disposition."

She huffed her incredulousness. "I can be just as brooding as you."

"Exceedingly so," he agreed. "But it is your nature to heal, my wildflower. Not long will you allow melancholy to fester. Unless, of course, it serves in you getting your way."

She pinched his side, and he flinched, catching her hand with a rumbling laugh.

The sound seemed to instantly sober them both.

Something so light didn't belong here, in this bleak, uncertain space. It only sharpened the contrast, casting their grim reality in starker relief.

"Tanwen," he said softly. "I don't know what's to come . . . but I wanted to say, thank you."

Pain welled in her chest, not liking the finality in his tone. "For what?"

"I never thought finding love was something I'd ever be allowed." His brows drew in. "So much of being royal is being bound by duty and sacrifice—bound by obligation. But you . . . you broke through that. Knowing you, finding you, and having you love me in return—" His voice wavered, and he swallowed. "It is the greatest gift of my life."

"Please." Her throat tightened with the sob she refused to let free. "Don't make this a goodbye."

He squeezed her hands. "I only want you to know how grateful I am. Before you, my world was gray. Orderly. Dutiful. Then you crashed into it and shattered everything I thought I knew. You showed me how vivid everything could be. How different and right. Thank you for that."

Tanwen's vision blurred, eyes brimming with unshed tears. "Thank *you* for being stronger than the men before you. For being brave enough to stand against your own kind to help others."

"It is not bravery," Zolya said gently. "It's responsibility. A duty you know too well, meddyg Heiro. We have a responsibility to help those hurting."

"Yes." She nodded. "And it only proves what I've always believed—that no matter the divide in bloodlines, or class, or gender, there is always common ground. Love can take root even in the cracks of what society has tried to keep separate. We're living proof of that, Zolya. So are my parents, and all others like them. Whether we survive to see it or not . . . I believe there *is* hope for this world."

A faint smile curved his lips. "And there it is again—your radiant optimism."

She nudged him.

He responded by drawing her back in, his arms tightening, wings folding around them once more—wrapping them in a shield of safety and seclusion.

A brief moment of escape from their awaiting fate.

“Wherever we are headed,” he murmured. “Know this—whether in this lifetime or swimming the Eternal River, I will never leave your side, my wildflower.”

43

Tanwen hit the ground hard.

Their wagon had barely come to a stop when the doors flew open and an unseen force shoved them out.

She gasped, her nails digging into cold dirt, knees burning from the impact.

Zolya was beside her in an instant, helping her to her feet, his stance already angled protectively in front of her.

Somewhere behind them, the cart rattled away, wooden wheels echoing through the unnatural stillness.

But all thoughts of their transport shriveled in Tanwen's mind as she took in their surroundings.

They stood within a massive coliseum—an architectural marvel that could not have existed in their mortal world before now. Forged by divine hands, it was a blend of pristine marble and radiant gold. Towering columns, thicker and grander than anything at the royal palace, reached toward a sky streaked with shimmering light. That light poured down across every surface, harsh and greedy.

She might have stood there forever, marveling, if not for the figures she saw seated in the stands.

Blood drained from her.

Tier after tier of familiar faces watched them. Huw. Loji. Brynn. Azla's ashen expression beside her mother. Their entire Drygul refugee camp, as well as those freed from Both, and countless others who had fought alongside the Rebellion. Confusion and unease marked every expression.

But nothing gutted her more than the sight of her parents.

Gabreel and Aisling stared down at her, their faces carved with helplessness and heartbreak. The exact expression her mother had worn the day she had watched her son burn on his pyre.

Dread tightened around Tanwen's chest.

Panic prickled up her spine.

Grief swelled in her throat.

She had failed them. She was in danger—something she had promised she wouldn't be in, their last living child—and she couldn't bear to look at them any longer.

Her gaze flicked toward the queen dowager within another tier. Her steely expression gave nothing away—though the bruises under her eyes did: sleepless worry. Past the Royal Council and the rows upon rows of Volari citizens and courtiers, servants and other Süra, who filled the rest of the vast arena. They sat shoulder to shoulder, brought together for this impossible reckoning.

They watched in silence—waiting, as exposed and suspended as Tanwen and Zolya must seem in the center of it all.

"As always, Brother," came a voice steeped in shadow and time—a voice that sent ice slicing through Tanwen's veins and momentarily stopped her heart. "Your decor lacks any semblance of life."

Ré gave an indignant huff. "A bold critique from the Queen of Death."

A spike of fear locked Tanwen's limbs as her gaze rose to the highest mezzanine. It jutted forward into the heart of the coliseum, a shimmering of divine power, visibly split down the middle.

To the left lounged the Low Gods, cloaked in earthy tones—deep browns, mossy greens, and rusted oranges: the palette of Cādra. To the right, the High Gods radiated celestial brilliance, clad in gold, silver, and glass that glittered like bottled starlight.

But it was the two figures at the center who drew every soul's attention.

Ré and Maryth.

Brother and sister.

Mother and father of the gods.

Together, for the first time since . . . Well, Tanwen had no idea since when. Only that it was before Cādra was Cādra.

Maryth was more smoke than flesh—her black silks swirling like stolen breath. Her features were sharp and skeletal, her skin leached of all color. Her eyes were bottomless voids, like the deepest bends of the Eternal River. And upon her head rested an intricate white crown, unmistakably wrought of bone, even from a distance.

Beside her, Ré blazed with golden radiance, his presence all heat and blinding brilliance.

Their energies clashed, pressing against each other with mutual offense—and a hunger to consume.

Darkness craving to devour light.

Light threatening to burn away the dark.

A conflict as old as time itself.

"My dominion over the dead is exactly why I know when a place feels lifeless," Maryth said, her voice slipping into Tanwen's mind as if whispering at her ear. "No one understands life better than the one who claims it."

In an instant, the coliseum changed. The blinding glow was softened, now interwoven with an onyx sheen. Flowers bloomed from the mezzanines. Ivy crept up columns. What had once been stark and imposing now held a touch of warmth—a grounded beauty. Still awe inspiring, but alive.

"A millennium apart and still you can't help but impose your will," Ré muttered, clearly annoyed by the transformation.

"Oh, was it *my* will that led you to steal my wings and cast me from our home?"

Ré gave a dry chuckle. "That took you longer than I expected to bring up. What impressive restraint you've shown, Sister."

She met his comment with a deep, throaty laugh of her own—nothing in the sound joyous. "Restraint," she scoffed. "Spoken by the god who can't keep his touch off anyone but his wife?"

Ripples of mirth spread through ranks of the Low Gods just as the air seemed to fracture, thick and charged. Ré's heat flared as a faint tremor passed through the arena.

"How dare you—" Ré boomed, but the outburst was cut short as the very wife in question lay a hand on his shoulder.

Her touch—a small eclipse in motion, Nocémi's indigo starlight spilling over Ré's sun, night soothing day.

For a heartbeat, the father of the High Gods sat stunned by the contact, his light-bound gaze pinned to Nocémi. Tanwen couldn't be sure, but she thought she sensed a pulse of centuries-deep longing seep from him.

"Enough pageantry." Maryth's voice sliced cleanly through the moment. "You have brought us here to judge, Brother. Let us then judge."

Zolya threaded his fingers through Tanwen's.

Only then did she realize she had been holding her breath.

As she met his gaze, she exhaled.

He gave a small, steady nod. *Together.*

Yes, she thought. *Together.*

Still—a wave of nausea churned in her gut. A surge of panic and fear and regret.

Regret that they weren't given enough time—her and him. That she might not get to say everything she wished to say, learn everything she wished to learn and experience with Zolya.

"You may do the honors." Ré inclined his head toward his sister.

Maryth's attention landed like a weight—ancient, immense.

Tanwen's knees weakened, but Zolya's tightening grip kept her standing.

"The dilemma is simple," Maryth declared. "The issue before us is not about race or rank. The concern is that Mütra walk the line between our two pantheons. Born of both soil and sky. Both brother and sister. To whom, then, do you belong?" She paused. "To whom do you pray? The conflict of your kind was never about your right to exist. It has been about to whom are you loyal?"

Tanwen swallowed hard as time seemed to slow.

"This is what must be decided," said Maryth. "And in doing so, we shall determine the fate of your union."

The ground shook then.

Tanwen stumbled, her other hand reaching to grasp Zolya's arm.

A roar split the air as a fissure cracked open beneath them.

Zolya cried out as they were torn from each other's sides.

He tried leaping into the air toward her, but chains of smoke encircled his wings and arms. He fell with a heavy *oof*.

"Zolya!" Tanwen lurched forward as he struggled against his constraints, teeth bared, his magic crackling around him like a windstorm.

Nothing freed him.

She took another step, but the ground shifted once more before a violent quake split them farther apart. They were each lifted onto separate raised columns.

"*Tanwen*," he bellowed, eyes frantic.

But before she could respond, another sound of distress drew her attention.

With her pulse in her throat, she whipped around.

Her parents.

They stood on the other side of her, across the coliseum, together on their own pedestal, arms clutching one another, fear clear in their wide eyes as they looked down.

Tanwen followed their gazes, to where water now slid metallic around the base of their columns.

No—not water.

Tanwen's breath caught, her pulse stopping.

The Eternal River churned below.

Its dark depth winked silver where souls swirled along the surface, whispering, writhing, wailing.

Then the rumble came again.

Her parents' platform began to descend.

"No!" she screamed, reaching out.

"*Tanwen*," yelled Zolya.

She spun to find him lowering as well.

"No! Please, no!" She slid to the edge of her platform, bits of dirt falling over the ledge. The air was being choked from her, her heartbeats too quick.

"Make your choice, Tanwen Heiro." Maryth's voice rang out across the arena, cold and absolute. "Your Süra family, or your Volari king. Choose who you wish to save. Not only to prove your faith to one of us—but to show who it is you truly love."

44

Tanwen stood alone at the heart of the coliseum.

Her body trembled beneath the weight of the goddess's decree.

On either side of her, two stone columns loomed like altars—each bearing what she loved most in this world.

On one: her mother and father, clutching each other.

On the other: Zolya, eyes never leaving hers.

All three, slowly descending—sinking toward the Eternal River.

Above them, the gods watched. Her friends watched. Galia and Cādra watched.

Tanwen's breaths came out in panicked, ragged gasps as her gaze briefly met Azla's.

She mirrored her agony, reflected her anger as she struggled to fly.

Like her brother, Azla seemed grounded, forced to remain seated.

In fact, the entire crowd seemed paralyzed.

Compelled to be still, a docile group meant only to bear witness, not think, not act.

True terror stole through Tanwen then, seized her heart.

No one would help her. No one *could* help her.

"It's clever, don't you think?" mused Ré. "Choose which life for which side. One pantheon to serve."

Tanwen's panic morphed into rage, hearing how simple these immortals thought their lives. How binary.

To them, such a decision was a quick line drawn in celestial sand.

But to Tanwen, it was destruction.

It was a dismantling.

"These are not *sides*," she bellowed, her voice surprisingly steady despite her terror. "They are my world. My whole heart! I cannot choose what part of myself to save. I cannot be the one to choose who my kind serves!"

"Why not?" Ré challenged, voice thundering. "Have you not risen to be one that leads them?"

"Yes, but faith is not so easily won," she argued. "And *never* through force."

The pantheon of gods appeared perplexed at her words. Ré and Maryth glanced at one another with shared puzzled expressions.

The coliseum vibrated once more, her parents and Zolya's columns sinking lower.

"*Please*," Tanwen begged, desperation clawing her chest. "My father is Volari, and yet you have placed him with Süra. Does that not prove that those of two faiths can live as one?"

"Your father made his decision to become one of *my* subjects," said Maryth. "He abandoned my brother and his children when he was torn of his wings. As I was torn of mine. So too must you choose."

"But why can't we serve both pantheons?"

A stunned silence followed. Even the murmuring of the other gods stilled.

Until a deep, rolling laugh filled the coliseum. "You mortals never cease to amuse," said Ré. "I would consider your words blasphemous if not for your mortal desperation."

"I do not speak to be amusing," she argued. "If Mütra are made from both high and low, why then can we not pray to both?"

"Foolish girl," hissed Maryth. "You'd have *me* share worship with my brother. My betrayer—he who keeps my wings on display in his palace to this very day?"

"It would not be sharing," Tanwen said quickly, swallowing the nerves barreling up her throat. "It would be multiplying those loyal to you. What if you could have more than merely Süra as subjects? More than even the added Mütra? If you combined your great houses, all of Cādra and Galia could fill your temples and offer you prayers. Every mortal being. If you truly desire unity in our realm, then let it begin with *you*."

Ré narrowed his eyes. Maryth tilted her head—a thoughtful beat.

Tanwen knew, of course, the idea she was proposing *was* mad, dangerous—heretical, even. But wasn't that the point of all of this?

If the gods expected peace among mortals, they needed to embody it themselves.

Race might divide, might stoke prejudice, but it was differences in faith—in which god held higher power—that often ignited war. And yet, at the core of the conflict, it was always devotion that had led them there. Devotion and love. Could they not find commonality in that? After all, the two pantheons still made up their world, still bestowed their powers high and low. And the two who ruled each were *siblings*, for gods' sake—despite their millennia-old feud.

"The mortal has your child Ridi whispering in her ear," accused Ré to Maryth.

"She does not," countered the god of mischief from where he lounged nearby. "Though I do approve of such a suggestion. It sounds positively delightful." His grin was far too sharp to offer comfort.

"Never a positive endorsement, coming from you, Cousin," Izato, the High God of revelry, quipped. His tone shifted as he addressed Ré. "Which is why it pains me to agree with him, Father. There is promise in what the mortal suggests—for all of us." He turned to the other High Gods then—to his brothers and sisters. "Imagine the celebrations held in our honor across Cādra." His voice grew almost hungry before his gaze slid to Ilustra. "The lust to be indulged." Then to Naru. "The artistry they could exalt in your name." Finally, he looked to the brooding Orzel. "And you, dear brother—you'd at last have patrons near the very waters you rule."

The mezzanine of gods slipped into a buzz of discussion then—some for and some against the idea she had put forth.

Tanwen stood rigid, impatient—her attention half on the chaos above her, half on those she loved still slowly sinking on either side.

Please, do hurry! She wished to scream.

"Could such a thing be possible, Sister?" Ré's deep voice interrupted the chatter, fiery gaze holding Maryth.

"I do take all souls in the end," she replied, thoughtfully.

"As I light all their days when they live," he mused.

Tanwen didn't dare blink, breathe, as a spark of hope kindled. It was thin, but it was there, like a slice of sunlight slipping through a crack in a shuttered window.

"And there was a time," began Ré, "when we sat as one."

"Yes," said Maryth, her voice turning sharp once more. "But *you* changed that, remember, Brother? An atonement would be in order, from *you*," she clarified. "For me to entertain such a unity."

A pause. A beat. A collection of tension.

Tanwen would have prayed to the gods then, prayed for their mercy, their reason, at the very least for Ré to *finally* apologize to his sister—but they appeared too busy currently brooding. Too prideful to bridge the chasm they had created.

Silence stretched between Ré and Maryth, a wordless exchange that spanned eons, though only seconds passed.

"*Perhaps* such an act is in our future," said Ré, attention turning back to Tanwen, "but for today—we still require a decision. Which of us shall your kind serve?"

Her hope was stamped out, Tanwen's heart shattering again.

Despair swallowed her whole as she looked to the balcony of immortals, took in their riveted gazes pinned on her.

She realized then—this was their sport. They had come here not necessarily for a solution but for a spectacle. And she and her parents and Zolya were to be this century's entertainment.

She wanted to curse them. Wanted to scream, to spit, to let loose all the grief and rage roiling inside her.

But what would that buy her? How would that spare the ones she loved?

Her gaze shifted to her parents.

Sadness cloaked their expressions—but so did a quiet acceptance, as if they already knew what she would choose. As if they had once stood in her place and made the same impossible choice. To leave their past behind, their families, so they might love.

Her chest felt cleaved open, a sob trapped in her throat.

She looked to Zolya next.

He stood stoically within his binds, lips parted as if ready to say her name.

And all the while, the three of them sank. Closer to the river. Closer to their end.

Lower.

Lower.

Tanwen broke.

"I can't . . . I can't . . ." she whispered as tears carved tracks down her cheeks.

But before the gods could press her further, Zolya's voice filled the arena.

"Your Benevolences." He addressed them from his sinking perch. "You speak of sides and choices and atonements, but don't you see, you've already chosen, already forgiven. For you have allowed the creation of Mütra. A people born of sky and soil, shaped by two opposing pantheons, magic inherited by both low and high. The fate of your houses has already come, sealed by you." He nodded toward Tanwen, his tone firm with conviction. "*She* does not need to choose a side, not when her blood is the bridge. *She* is what binds what you have broken."

"Zolya," Tanwen whispered, soul aching.

But if he heard her, he didn't show it. His gaze never left the gods.

"*She* is your miracle," he told them. "*Your* legacy. Her kind *are* the future of Cādra and the unity of your two pantheons. Let them help shape that future—our world's future—our collected devotion to you. Unbound by sides. For I will never be the man, or the king, who stands in the way of that."

He turned to Tanwen.

Reverence softened his features. His gaze held no fear—only peace.

"I love you," he said, the words a promise. "In every realm. In every life."

Zolya then jumped.

Tanwen screamed.

The Eternal River swallowed him whole, leaving behind nothing but a silent ripple.

45

There was no light in the Eternal River.

Zolya drifted aimlessly through a void absent of color, shape, and time.

The sensation was not unpleasant—it held a weightlessness. An unmooring. A blessed slip of quiet reprieve from life's agonies.

Then came the cold.

It slithered into his nostrils like a snake, poured down his throat like a crashing wave, and curled around his heart like thirsty tentacles. Ice froze his veins, turned his blood to crystal. His breath, though he had none, burned as the river infiltrated his lungs, pulling him apart and remaking him with every ripple.

Sound struck next.

Zolya's own gargling scream of pain layered with millions of others—sobs of longing, gasps of grief, fits of laughter, sighs of relief—all reverberating too close, too invasive. The emotions battered him, relentless.

Last came touch.

It started soft, gentle, before never-ending. Slick and ephemeral forms brushed against his side, his cheek, his neck, his arms, his wings.

Souls.

Everywhere.

Panic surged in his stilled heart as he urged his body to move, to twist away.

But he was a limp, drowned blade of grass, floating through millions of other blades of grass, succumbed to the current of death.

And then—

He was torn away.

The void collapsed as the river relinquished him.

Zolya fell forward onto a smooth, chilled surface as he expelled slick obsidian onto an onyx floor. His chest was on fire as he heaved, desperate to release the river's grip as his senses reeled. Hearing his own gasps was both jarring and a flood of relief.

Air. He was once again breathing air.

His wings pressed heavy and wet at his back. He didn't have to try to know they were now useless, flightless. But with that knowing a panic surged, a reckless haste to flee from his body—search for the one he knew, the one he had control over. As well as find what he had just sacrificed—Tanwen and ever seeing her again.

Grief hit him so violently it threatened to drown him all over again.

"Welcome to my home," came a voice like beetles skittering over ice.

Zolya glanced up.

From the dark void, she came into focus like smoke curling from a newly kindled flame. Gradual. Purposeful. Until form took hold of the formless.

Maryth, goddess of death, mother of the Low Gods, sat enthroned.

Her seat was a monument to mortality itself—an intricate sculpture wrought from black-dipped bone, each curve depicting a stage of life, from cradle to corpse. She reclined in her twirling shadows, her eyes now silver shimmers, frost on a blade.

"You surprised us," she said, voice neither kind nor cruel. "A feat few mortals manage."

Zolya pushed himself from all fours, drawing himself into a kneel. "Is this my judgment?"

All souls faced her, eventually. Maryth, arbiter of endings, decider of which of the three currents would claim them—one of suffering, one of recompense, or one of peace.

"In a way." Her gaze bore down on him, vast and unrelenting, the weight of his fragile existence a mere twinkle in her glowing eyes. A speck of life suspended between choice and consequence.

Zolya held still—the phantom sensation of a pulse pounding in his veins.

"Explain your decision, mortal," she demanded. "You gave it all up. Not only your love but also your crown."

"What use is a crown if it oppresses rather than empowers?" he asked.

Maryth tilted her head, assessing. "You are a peculiar king."

"I am only a man," he corrected, "who understood his life was not worth saving at the cost of what Tanwen would have lost."

"Ah, but you see . . ." She slipped from her throne, approaching like a snake weaving through water to circle him. It took all Zolya's strength to not cower at her nearness, not to shrink at the graze of her lethal power. "Your choice revealed more than devotion to your Mütra," she whispered, her voice a caress of cold at his ear. "It revealed your allegiance to Cādra and to your people. You broke the cycle, King. You offered yourself—not just for love, but for the seed of something new."

Zolya held no answer. To disagree felt perilous. To agree, presumptuous.

So he remained still.

Silent.

As he always had in the presence of powers far greater than himself.

Maryth circled him once more. "We heard reason in your defiance," she said. "We heard wisdom, in your words as well as your lover's." She slid to loom in front of him then, a pouring mist of shadow. "With the birth of Mütra, our decision had been rendered, otherwise they would not have come to be. Despite my brother's and my quarrels, Mütra *are* the tether between us. The proof that our bond still lives despite our history. Proof that unity can indeed exist in your realm."

Hope stirred beneath Zolya's grief. "And what of yours?" he dared to ask. "Is there then room for unity in your great houses?"

Silence stretched—as vast and still as the throne room. "My brother wronged me greatly," she eventually answered, voice as chilled as the floor on which he knelt. "An act I had promised to see avenged. The death of your father was part of that plan. While it came to pass, mollifying me slightly, no gaining of a mortal soul will ever replace the lost might of my wings."

Zolya had no reply to that, his emotions in an uncomfortable choke hold at the mention of his father and his eventual demise—all part of schemes and revenge plots between two immortals.

"*But*," Maryth continued, tone turning thoughtful. "If those as fragile as mortals can prove so resilient in mending ways, then certainly so, too, can gods."

He blinked, at first not registering her words.

Until . . .

Precarious relief swept through him like his first breath after drowning.

Could he be understanding her properly?

Gods, he hoped so. For this—*this* was why he had given everything.

Why he had jumped.

Even if he was not to live to see a new Cādra rise, Tanwen would.

And that was enough.

Would be enough for him to eventually find peace.

"Your benevolence forever astounds, Goddess." Zolya bowed low. "To allow reconciliation between your house and your brother's—"

Maryth gave a short, knowing harrumph. "Our past is hardly healed. I will never forget what he did to me—nor will I let him forget. That history will always be ours to carry. But I have come to understand something in my exile from the heavens. Had he not cast me down, I would not have borne my children. I would not have forged a kingdom of my own. And in my long reign over the dead, I have judged more souls than there are stars, and I have come to know an undeniable truth about your mortal kind."

She paused, and Zolya waited, reverent.

"Love is your greatest weakness as much as it is your greatest strength. Again and again, I have seen it. Despite what brought them to me, all those who have knelt as you kneel cling to one thing in the end. Love. Love of a person, a place, a cause. A final memory that holds them together as I judge. That is where my brother and I differ. He rules from on high, untouched by the lives he governs. But I see. I see *you*. I taste the shape of your longing. I feel the weight of your grief. I cradle your pain. My children began to glimpse what might be gained from the mending of our divide—now I too see what I will claim. *Love*," she hummed as if tasting something sweet. The sound was an eerily cold melody that slid across his cheek. "Devotion not merely from the dead, but now from all living."

Her smile was like skin splitting to reveal a gleaming rib cage.

Zolya held in a shiver.

"As for you, Zolya Ajno Diusé, king of the nineteenth Royal Volari House, I hope that you prove me correct."

Zolya's confusion must have been plain on his face, for the goddess of death's grin grew.

"To be the first Volari king to erect my temple up in your clouds, as well as my children's." Her eyes sparked, triumphant. "You've shown what kingly devotion can look like. The power of your unwavering faith. You have proven yourself to me. Only those who need no crown are worthy of its weight. I look forward to your prayers, King."

"I . . . don't understand?"

A flicker of amusement played across her cold features. "Most forget that while I rule death"—she leaned in, her voice a silken whisper—"I also command time. Do not forget what I require when you return."

From the swirling folds of her cloak, a single finger emerged—reaching.

She touched his brow.

A kiss of ice.

Their world shattered.

Zolya was flung from the onyx throne room.

Reality bent and spun as he crashed through water and light. He was thrown through memories of his childhood; of his sister as a babe; of his young mother, smiling down at him; of Osko as a boy; of his father's heavy hand; then through moments yet to happen, visions too beautiful and hopeful to comprehend. Then he was wrapped in grief so deep he thought it would crush him—Tanwen's horror-stricken face as he jumped.

Her curdling scream invaded his senses. Raw, broken, aching.

Zolya's eyes snapped open.

Sky filled his vision, gray clouds parting high above to allow a sliver of blue. A ray of sunshine.

Someone was fisting his shirt, sobbing over his body.

Tanwen.

His heart thumped.

Then thumped again.

A soothing lungful of air.

Her sobs tore through his deep breaths, tore through him, as she trembled, crumpled over him.

Zolya blinked.

Tanwen.

She was here.

He could see her.

Hear her.

Feel the warmth of her palm against his chest.

It was like lifting an anvil, but Zolya managed to raise one of his hands, closing his fingers around hers.

Tanwen froze.

Gasped.

Her tear-stricken gaze found his. Grew wide with disbelief.

"Zolya?" His name spoken in a hoarse whisper.

"Wildflower," he croaked in return.

Stunned quiet engulfed them before her lips crashed down on his. Both their tears mixed, warmth sliding across cheeks.

And Zolya knew.

He was alive.

46

Tanwen couldn't stop shaking.

Zolya was here, breathing, in her arms, his wet tunic twisted in her fingers—but it seemed like a trick.

Another godly cruelty.

A test to force her faith.

While her tears had slowed, her grief hadn't.

She had seen him jump.

Had witnessed the river claim him.

Her heart had been torn from her chest as she leaped after him.

She hadn't known what would happen if she ever actually reached Zolya.

She only understood that she must.

For this was not how it was meant to be.

Not how they were meant to end—with his sacrifice.

With her traversing the rest of her days like a specter—haunted by his absence, all because of her inaction.

But before she could touch water, the arena's floor snapped back into place.

The river vanished, the dark swirling waters gone.

Her pedestal disappeared.

The crumbled ground had re-formed in a blink, her parents suddenly at her side.

Her mother's arms had wrapped around her in a crushing embrace, before her father's.

They had fallen to their knees in a large heave of sobs.

It was once again the day they had brought Thol's body to Drygul. Their family's collective wave of pain, but this time it was laced in a layer of relief. In whispers of her name from her parents' lips. The sound like a prayer, an aching of gratitude.

For a breath, Tanwen allowed herself this reassurance. Her parents were with her. Her parents were alive. Until she once again remembered *why* they lived.

Because Zolya did not.

She had torn free of them then, her rage and sorrow ready to form damning curses aimed at the watching gods.

Until—from the corner of her eye—

Zolya.

His body splayed alone on a wet patch of dirt a mere few paces away.

His white wings were spread, his legs and arms sprawled, his face turned away from her. The entirety of him soaked through.

Her gasp had gotten caught in her throat as she had run.

And now he was sitting up, clinging to her as she clung to him.

His breaths came one after another.

And still . . .

He felt deathly cold, a body thawing from ice.

"Zolya," she whispered again, the word barely holding together beneath her disbelief, her fear. Her hands trembled as they roamed over his shoulders, then framed his face, as if needing to confirm he was real, solid, alive. "Is it really you? Are you here? Are you—are you okay?"

"I . . . yes. I think I am," he said, voice rough. His brow was furrowed—dazed and still processing—but the relief in his eyes mirrored her own.

"What happened?" she asked.

Before he could reply, a sudden wash of golden light spilled across the arena floor, pulling both their gazes upward.

Tanwen had nearly forgotten they were not alone.

Ré stepped to the balcony, along with his sister, sun pressing against shadow. "Well, well," he mused, "we had forgotten just how entertaining mortals can be. Your actions were a reminder of why we created this realm."

"You have also reminded us," intoned Maryth, her eyes fixed on where Tanwen and Zolya remained clutching. "Of the power of mortal devotion, toward each other as well as toward us, your creators. There is much still to gain from this world and to learn from. Love may weaken your kind, but today yours proved its power to endure—to transform centuries of belief."

A soft scoff echoed in the air. "I've only been saying this for *eons*," came the lilting voice of Ilustra, goddess of love and lust. She lounged in her divine beauty, lips pursed in an elegant pout. "If my counsel had been sought, we would not have been languishing in such melodrama for so long." She flipped a gleaming strand of hair over her shoulder.

Ré coughed—a sound laced with a hint of reproach—as he returned the arena's attention to himself. "After much deliberation, my sister and I are of the same mind," he continued as if his daughter hadn't interrupted. "The arguments put forth as well as the devotion displayed here is worthy of recognition. On this day, may the tomes of history be written: We bless this union and all future unions alike. No longer shall bloodlines and birthrights define boundaries. And with this ruling comes one other—if mortals can find unity in their differences, so too can we. The sundered houses of the High and Low will be bridged—joined in the chorus of every living prayer."

A shocked hush fell over the crowd, thick as velvet.

Tanwen's breath caught.

Her heart nearly soared from her chest.

She faced Zolya, met his stunned expression, his hands tightening around hers.

Then—he smiled.

That breathtaking smile that had undone her from the beginning.

It shattered what remained of her restraint.

She let out a sobbed laugh, half delirious, happiness rising in her throat like dawn breaking through storm.

They could be together.

Her love—*their* love—had been accepted.

And with it the two pantheons would be joined.

By gods! What miracle is this? she wondered in a daze.

"My wildflower," Zolya murmured, bringing her closer. "We did it. We really did it."

A deep ache began to unspool inside her, a pain she had carried far too long. A lifetime spent hiding, of shouldering the shame of her existence, of lying about who she was, what she was. Twenty-three years of turmoil and frustration leaked out of her with each breath. The months she and Zolya had held their love in secret, in fear, the same as her parents had.

Every stolen moment, every quiet suffering so that they could remain together, and Thol's death—it had not been in vain.

Now, at last, they could stand in the light. As could all those like them. And all the souls who had been banished to Both. They were accepted, allowed to live and pray freely.

Tanwen's chest swelled with joy so complete it almost hurt. Tears brimmed in her eyes. For the first time, she felt it, could see it, truly—their future.

A shaky laugh escaped her again as she answered Zolya not with words, but with action.

She curled her fingers into his tunic and brought his mouth to hers.

Heat bloomed, a racing of liquid flame through her veins.

His answering grip around her waist was possessive.

She hardly noticed his chill now as it pressed against her, her body too enflamed in need.

A need that was now allowed.

Too quickly he was drawing back, however, his dark gaze capturing hers.

"Soon," he whispered, promised. "When we're alone."

Despite him gently settling her at his side, the humming between them remained. An impatient, feverish longing.

"No!" A shout echoed from a lower tier, turning heads and disturbing the still-shocked crowd. "This cannot be your ruling!" A Volari nobleman stood, features twisted in disgust as he faced the gods. "The low *cannot* gain favors from the High. It is blasphemous! And our king *cannot* desecrate our throne by taking a Mütra as consort. It is mockery to our centuries of being! To our pure bloodline. It is filth—"

A bolt of flames lanced downward from the sky.

It smote the man, turning him from flesh to ash in less than a blink.

A small trail of smoke and charred wood was all that was left of where he stood.

Gasps tore from nearby onlookers, many scurrying away from the struck spot in terror.

"A soul for your river, Sister," said Ré simply. "To replace the one you returned."

"Thank you, Brother," Maryth replied, touched.

Tanwen met Zolya's gaze, a cautious look shared.

The siblings' reconciliation clearly had begun. As had the seriousness of their ruling.

Zolya threaded his fingers back into hers. "Shall we go home?" he asked.

Tanwen smiled, though her joy momentarily faltered.

Home.

She looked up to the packed coliseum.

Some of the gods had already vanished, retreating to wherever it was they went. The rest were drifting away. Around them, the arena had softened—the crowd beginning to talk, to move, the weight of what had happened here today already spreading in feverish, eager murmurs.

Her parents stood waiting nearby, and when she met her mother's eyes, Aisling gave her a small, reassuring nod as her smile grew wide.

The gesture set loose a lacing of tension along Tanwen's shoulders.

She turned back to Zolya. "Whose home?" she asked.

His grin dazzled as he lifted a hand to her cheek, gentle and certain. "Ours," he said. "The one we will build together."

PART VIII

After

47

With more than two centuries of life behind her, Habelle had come to believe there was little left in the world that could surprise her.

In the past year, however, she had been proven wrong more times than she cared to count.

And today was no exception.

"I take your silence as a compliment," said Callia.

The pair stood atop a central dais, surrounded by not twelve but twenty-four altar houses—half for the High Gods, half for the Low. The construction wasn't finished, but its ambition was clear in every elegant detail: frescoes taking shape in delicate outlines across sweeping columns, mosaic tiles carefully pressed into winding pathways, their patterns catching the sunlight like scattered gems.

Habelle eyed where Ré's temple stretched tall beside Maryth's. The central meeting of the two pantheons.

Even though this construction was blessed by the gods, it still left Habelle—a traditionally devout woman—feeling rather off balance. The siblings' rivalry had been older than time. It still astonished her, even a year later, that this was now their world.

"It'll draw many to visit our city," Callia continued as they strolled slowly along the outer ring. Her amber wings glowed under the morning light, the scar carved down her cheek as striking as her pale features. "To be the first city on Cādra to honor the full pantheon in one sanctuary. And with such grandeur . . ." She swept her arm wide, gesturing to the sun-soaked facades. "It won't be as spectacular as what is being built on Galia, of course. But it will certainly rival any other temples found on the continent, not to mention a great source of revenue for our economy."

"Yes," Habelle replied dryly. "A script you've repeated through the entirety of my tour."

Callia glanced sideways at her, grinning. "Do I detect a hint of jealousy?"

She scoffed, incredulous. "You'd like that."

"Yes," Callia admitted with a laugh. "I would. But you must admit, Sister—New Spira is coming along splendidly, is it not?"

The compliment sat heavy on Habelle's tongue—but she had to concede. "It is, indeed."

New Spira, or "new hope," had made remarkable strides in just a handful of months since last she visited.

Built on a wide stretch of land granted to both citizens of Both and Mütra refugees, the city rose west of the town of Fuelt, nestled in the Bandon Lands. Two rivers flanked its borders, supplying ample resources, and a new vibrant forest—gifted by Bosyg—now wove its way between growing buildings, markets, and multiple town squares. It was truly a marvel.

A triumph in how much could prosper in such a short amount of time.

But then again, much had felt that way since the gods' decree a year ago.

Peace indeed had taken root.

Though dissent lingered in quiet corners—mostly elders who had grown too calcified in their ways to embrace change—those voices had grown faint. The old order's grip was loosening, especially with prosperity blooming across the land in recent months.

And ever since word spread like wildfire of the man struck down by Ré, one truth had become undeniable: The gods were watching.

Now more than ever before.

As Habelle and Callia moved on from the temple grounds, Habelle's royal guards shadowing their steps, she took a moment to embrace the swirl of life around them.

Mütra and former Both prisoners walked freely among Süra and Volari, no longer separated by fear or forbidden by law. The streets here felt lighter. Open. Whole.

All who passed the sisters offered respectful bows.

While Habelle was still queen dowager, Callia's role had shifted. In place of her crown, a simple gold brooch was pinned to the breast of her green gown—eight slender lines converging at its center, the mark of New Spira's council leadership. Eight elected officials who vowed to uphold New Spira's founding oath: to be a safe harbor for all, championing innovation and acceptance.

Habelle smiled to herself, marveling at how far her younger sister had come. From the girl who once delighted in tormenting palace staff, who refused to lace her own slippers, to a fearsome warrior queen of island prisoners . . . to this woman.

This woman who greeted citizens with warm, measured words. Who smiled easily and spoke with grace—a polished politician in every sense.

Clearly, it wasn't merely places that could change, but people too.

Herself included.

So much of Habelle's life had been bound to the will of others—her parents, her husband, even her gods. Yet through it all, she had endured: patient, steadfast in her duties, clinging to the faith that one day her devotion to her son, and her own quiet ambition, would be rewarded.

Now here she stood, basking in that boon—free to journey from Galia across the continent, free to live a life she once doubted she'd ever be granted.

The thought brought a sting of tears to her eyes, gratitude welling—though not to the gods, but to herself, for her tireless endurance.

Change could come, even to a woman more than two centuries old.

Yet change was never absolute—wealth and status still carved their hierarchies. Classes endured, as they always had. But at least no longer were they divided by blood or race.

Even the infamous Galia Recruitment had been revised: no longer a life sentence, but a term-bound civil service with the right to terminate and reenlist at will.

Because of the peace treaty, trade now flowed more fairly. The mines of Both were producing as promised. Orzel's previously violent waters had calmed—miraculously, some said—allowing ships to travel between the continent and the island's coasts, passing the rare minerals to the continent and up to Galia without the old blood tax of lost lives.

Habelle took a deep breath, the weight of it all settling inside her.

The world was not one she recognized. It was reforming, but for the first time in centuries, it was for the better.

Réol would have hated every corner of it. To see what had become of their world, of his kingdom, his spirit would be howling in rage within the Eternal River.

It made Habelle's smile widen.

She couldn't think of a more fitting end to her husband's legacy.

"The last I saw you grin like that"—Callia eyed her cautiously—"you were removing a title from a lord at court."

"Yes, well"—Habelle nodded politely to another bowing citizen as she passed them by—"if memory serves, he was accosting his staff."

"Still . . . what has you looking so pleased?"

"Can I not enjoy the successes of my younger sister?" questioned Habelle. "You have done well here, Callia."

Callia's expression twisted. "All right, now you're really scaring me."

She rolled her eyes. "Are my compliments really so hard to come by?"

"For me? Yes."

"Well then," she said, drawing to a stop in the middle of the stone lane. The scent of lavender from nearby planters drifted on the breeze. "Let's amend that." She turned to face her sister fully. "Take my hands."

Callia frowned. "Why?"

"Take my hands," she repeated, more insistently.

Callia eyed her skeptically but reached forward anyway.

"My dear, Callia," Habelle began. "My favorite sister—"

"I'm your only sister," Callia deadpanned.

"—seeing everything you've accomplished here, I am so very proud of you."

Callia stared, her mouth parting slightly, stunned. "I . . . Thank you."

Habelle gave her hands a final squeeze. "Now enjoy that, because as you pointed out, it may not happen again for another decade."

Callia huffed a laugh, pulling away. "You almost had me there."

"I meant it," she said, tone softening, honest now. "Truly. I'm proud of you. I hope you are proud of yourself as well. What you've survived, come back from, and now built . . . It's a marvel."

"All right . . ." Callia blinked rapidly, as if to force away growing tears. "Enough standing around. Let's go find our children."

Arm in arm they continued down the lane, eventually finding the winding path to the open-air gymnasium.

Built on a large terrace overlooking the north river, its columns circled a space bustling with movement, grunts, and laughter. A mixed crowd—Mütra, Süra, Volari, even a few satyrs and centaurs—sparred or practiced drills in the training yard. It was a public space used for anyone wishing to learn the art of self-defense, regardless of gender.

They found Zolya and Azla at the heart of the arena, holding the attention of a large group of students. In fact, the group was more than large; it was overflowing.

But so was it always when Zolya paid a visit.

Everyone wanted to be near the king who had helped free so many of them. Plus, from the flushed faces of more than a few—which had nothing to do with the heat—they clearly didn't mind the view.

"No, not quite like that," Azla said as she stepped in to adjust a young woman's stance. "You want to loosen the knee—not break it. Unless that's the goal, of course."

A ripple of laughter spread through the group.

"Here—" She moved the girl's foot into a better position.

After Azla had expressed interest in learning combat, proving to be an eager, focused pupil, Zolya had poured everything he knew into her education. And given that he was practically born with a blade in hand, that was considerable. In just a few months, she'd gone from his pupil to one of the gymnasium's most respected instructors.

Watching them together, Habelle felt a warmth spread in her chest.

She could tell the strength of their bond had grown as they worked in tandem to demonstrate a disarming technique.

A king and an exiled princess sharing laughs and advice.

Though it was easy to forget both were of royal bloodlines in their common training uniforms.

Here, they were simply two people offering their strength, their skill, and their time to those who wished to learn.

"You could always use your magic as well," called out Callia from where she and Habelle observed under the shade of an awning.

The yard quieted as heads turned, before quick bows, the students noting the councilwoman and queen dowager's arrival.

"That is true," said Azla. "But not everyone here has magic to rely on, remember?"

"Of course I remember," replied Callia with an easy grin, walking forward. "It was a quick test for you, my child."

"And here I thought I was the instructor." Azla raised a wry brow.

"A mother cannot help but want to teach, even when out of turn."

Azla gave a soft laugh as she embraced Callia. "What brings you both here?" she asked.

"We merely wished to see you," said Callia. "I finished showing Habelle the new improvements."

"And what did you think of them, Aunt?" Azla called over to where Habelle had remained beneath the awning.

"*Improvement* is certainly an apt word choice," she replied.

Azla seemed to bite back a grin as she shared a look with her mother.

"We'll take a short break," Zolya said to their group.

The crowd dispersed, fetching their waters, seemingly more than pleased to find a reprieve in the shade of trees.

Azla and Callia made their way toward Habelle, Zolya joining them as he dusted chalk from his hands.

"I did not realize the time." Zolya squinted to where the sun had risen to sit high in the sky. "I told Tanwen I'd meet her for midday meal."

"Go," said Azla. "I can finish up here."

But it was Habelle Zolya seemed to wait on for a reply.

It both pleased her but in the same instance made her stomach twist with guilt. She loved an obedient son but didn't exactly want to be one of *those* mothers.

"Yes, go." She shooed. "A lady should never be kept waiting."

Zolya's responding grin was radiant. He leaned in to give her a chaste kiss on the cheek. "We'll see you all for dinner at our place tonight?" He eyed their group.

"Unless my dear Azla is wishing to cook the meal again," said Callia, "of course. We wouldn't miss it."

"It wasn't *that* bad," countered Azla with a frown.

"It really was," both Zolya and Callia said at once.

Azla punched Zolya in the arm.

"Hey!" he laughed, rubbing the spot. "Your mother agreed."

"Yes, but I can't punch my mother, now can I?"

"There's always a first for everything." He grinned.

"*Not* for that," countered Callia, fixing him with a stern glare.

He merely laughed harder, retreating into the open stretch of the arena. "Until tonight," he said—and with a snap of his wings, he launched into the air, three royal guards rising after him, their previously inconspicuous presence suddenly revealed.

Habelle watched her son climb higher and higher until he disappeared into the blue.

A tight ache settled in her chest.

She was still adjusting to everything, but most of all to *them*.

Tanwen had earned her place, Habelle would admit that. She was sharp, resourceful, cunning, and, most importantly, fiercely loyal.

She reminded Habelle a bit of herself.

Still, it was a shift.

A new presence in the relationship she and her son had shared for so long.

A new dynamic to learn.

But she would learn it.

She knew it was because of Tanwen that her son smiled more now, laughed more easily.

There was a lightness to him that hadn't been there before.

And with it, her own heart had lifted too.

Nothing brought Habelle more peace than seeing her son truly happy.

In a world where love was rarer than mined ambrü, what he and Tanwen had found and fought for—it was nothing short of remarkable.

They had challenged not only the world, but also the gods, for their right to stand side by side.

And they'd won.

Habelle's throat tightened. She was proud of her son. Proud of the leader he had become and the partner he had chosen to be by his side.

Gods—she blinked rapidly, pushing away the sudden sting in her eyes. She was becoming sentimental in her old age.

She cleared her throat, turning back toward her sister and niece.

"Well"—she lifted a brow at Azla—"are you going to stand here all day, or are you going to show me how to bring a man to his knees?"

Azla's gaze gleamed with her grin as she ushered her forward. "Step this way, Aunt."

48

"You know," Tanwen grunted, hefting a heavy box of vials from the cart to the back door. "When you said you'd help me, I assumed you meant it."

"I *am* helping," argued Huw, fanning himself as he leaned against the wall. "I'm supervising."

Tanwen huffed. "You can supervise *while* lifting boxes."

"But I just got my manicure," Huw pouted.

"Loji doesn't even have hands, and she's managing."

They both turned to look at the large wolf, who was dutifully nudging the boxes Tanwen had left by the door onto a wheeled cart, then dragging it inside with quiet determination.

"Not all of us are creatures made for manual labor."

Tanwen wiped sweat from her brow. "Dare I even ask what you *are* made for?"

Huw's gaze lit up as someone caught his attention at the end of the alley. "Pleasure," he answered as his grin widened.

Tanwen followed his line of sight—and laughed.

A dark-haired satyr strode toward them with an easy confidence.

"Hi," Ramul greeted, leaning in to kiss Huw.

A kiss that went on a bit longer than was appropriate.

Tanwen cleared her throat.

Ramul pulled back, a flush blooming across his brown cheeks. "Sorry."

"I'm not," Huw said, still admiring him hungrily.

They'd been together six months now. A personal record for Huw, and one Tanwen quietly hoped would hold. Ramul was a professor at one of New Spira's academic halls, and—perhaps most miraculously—he was a positive influence on Huw.

"Do you need help?" offered Ramul, already stepping forward.

Case in point.

"Yes—" said Tanwen.

"*No*," Huw cut in quickly.

Ramul glanced between them, confused.

"We were just finishing up," Huw said breezily, linking his arm through Ramul's.

"We were?" Tanwen arched a brow.

"Yes. I was certainly done here ages ago. Let's get food—I'm wasting away."

"What of the rest of these?" Tanwen gestured to the pile of boxes still left on the cart.

"Let's be honest, little fawn—you were always going to finish them yourself."

"Sorry!" Ramul called, looking sheepish as Huw tugged him down the lane.

"Remember, we have dinner tonight!" Tanwen shouted after them.

Huw gave a *yeah, yeah* wave before he was gone.

She let out an annoyed exhale, eyeing the remaining boxes.

She had told her mother she'd help with the incoming meddyg supplies—but she hadn't expected *this* many.

She glanced at the back door, briefly debating whether to go find more help, but she knew the truth: Everyone was stretched thin these days, busy preparing for the grand opening of the Thrynpion—a new structure devoted to healing.

For once, the sick wouldn't have to wait for a meddyg to find them. They could come here—to a space blessed by Thryn, Low Goddess of nurture and healing—and receive care directly.

Aisling had been named one of the leading meddygs, with Tanwen offering whatever hours she could spare.

"Need a hand?" came a deep voice behind her.

Her heart leaped as she spun to find Zolya.

His plain tunic and pants did nothing to dim his impressiveness. His wide shoulders stretched the material as his wings hung in a relaxed sweep at his back, the white plumage catching the trickling daylight like silk. And his smile—dazzling, crooked, familiar—aimed entirely at her.

"I have my guards as well." He gestured to the men who loomed at the far end of the alley.

"Oh, gods, yes," she breathed.

Zolya laughed as he and his men stepped in to help. Between the group of them, the remaining boxes were sorted and stacked in record time.

"I should have asked you to help instead of Huw," said Tanwen, taking a long drink from her canteen. She offered it to Zolya, who took it.

"Ready?" he asked after he placed it down on the empty cart.

She glanced around, satisfied. "Ready."

They strolled down the lane toward the front of the building—only to be jolted as the ground rumbled beneath them, a deep, echoing boom ringing out. Tanwen stumbled slightly before Zolya steadied her.

"Well," she muttered, "we finished just in time."

Overhead, a massive cyclops carefully lifted a cut stone slab into place atop the rising structure. The ground shuddered again under its weight.

The cyclopes had been instrumental in New Spira's rapid expansion—not just because of their height and brute strength, but also because of their surprising architectural ingenuity. Tanwen's father had been ecstatic when he discovered this particular trait.

In fact, there was her father now, down at the base of the construction site.

She waved to him as they caught eyes, before his attention got pulled quickly back to his schematics.

Tanwen smiled to herself, her chest filling with warmth.

Her parents were flourishing here.

No longer in hiding—no more disguises, fake names, or dark forests. Aisling and Gabreel Heiro had found space for their talents to prosper—and with that, their relationship had blessedly begun to mend.

Their roots, like hers, had finally found fertile ground.

"All right, up you go," said Zolya.

Tanwen let out a surprised yip as he swept her into his arms without warning.

"What are you doing?" she demanded, hands gripping his shoulders.

"Taking you home," he replied simply.

And then—with a powerful beat of his wings—they were in the air.

Tanwen clung to him, her arms looped around his neck, her cheek pressed to his chest. The warmth of him soaked through her skin, and though they soared high above the city, she felt nothing but safe.

Below, New Spira shimmered in the morning light, alive. But up here, it was quiet—just the sound of wind and wings and Zolya's steady heartbeat, thudding strong and sure beneath her ear.

Angling north of the city, he headed toward a large tree that stood alone by the river's edge. They landed lightly on an upper platform of their tree den. Zolya didn't set her down as he descended stairs, the canopy of leaves rustling gently around them.

As he strode toward their front door, the usher by the seam opened it quickly, allowing Zolya to carry her over the threshold.

"Don't follow us in," he called back to his guards.

Still in his arms, Tanwen cocked a brow. "I thought we were meant to have midday meal."

"We are," he said, crossing into their large bedroom and laying her on their cool sheets. "After I've had you first."

Her breath caught as he pulled his tunic over his head in a single sweep and dropped it to the floor. The afternoon sun poured in through the tall balcony windows behind him, outlining the hard lines of his body in molten gold. His wings shimmered at his back.

Tanwen's skin heated, then flushed full flame as he slipped off her shirt, unlaced the ties of her boots, and moved on to her pants with careful fingers.

"I'd have thought training would have left you famished," she managed to say, voice wavering as his lips brushed the hollow of her throat.

Zolya's mouth curved into a grin against her skin. "Training sharpens my appetite," he murmured. "But only you satisfy it."

Any reply of hers was robbed as his skillful hands slipped to where she was already wet and ready. He hummed his approval in the same moment she gasped, pleasure melting through her.

Zolya took her mouth then, his tongue brushing gently against hers as he settled between her thighs. He teased her with his hard length, and she squirmed, impatient.

A gruff laugh rumbled from him. "Still thinking of midday meal?"

"More like how I'll get you back if you deny me—*ah*," she groaned, her words stolen as he pressed inside with a possessive thrust.

"I'd never *dream* of denying you, my wildflower," he murmured, beginning a rolling rhythm with his hips.

"*Gods, yes*," she sighed, sliding her hands from his shoulders to grip his arse, reveling in the taut strength of his muscles and movement.

The rest of their afternoon was consumed with all the ways they could consume each other. Their cries carried on the tepid breeze slipping through their open bedroom windows, tangling with the warmth of their bodies. Until at last, only silence remained—save for their mingled breaths, steady and sated.

◆ ◆ ◆

Tanwen popped a grape in her mouth, savoring the sweet flavor across her tongue as she leaned against Zolya's bare shoulder from the foot of their bed.

He had procured them a plate of food from the kitchen, no doubt causing a stir by strolling about in only his loose trousers. But then again, perhaps their staff was growing accustomed to their ways here—and to the sounds that often drifted from their bedroom.

Tanwen's cheeks warmed at the thought.

New Spira allowed them certain liberties the palace never could. And both of them seemed eager to embrace every one.

Here, their titles slipped away like water off stone. She was not merely the king's consort, and he not merely king. They were Tanwen and Zolya—a man and a woman wishing to help build the new world growing on Cādra.

Galia was also changing, but there were certain traditions that would always remain. The rigid decorum of rank, the ever-watchful eyes, the Galia court . . .

She and Zolya could leave all of it when they came here.

And in its place: a deep breath, muscles relaxing—especially for Zolya.

The shift in him had been subtle at first, a slow loosening. He smiled and laughed easier now, without restraint or worry.

He carried himself with a lightness she'd only ever hoped to give him.

When she'd first suggested their new residence be modeled after a traditional Süra den, Zolya's eyes had lit up.

Of course, there needed to be modifications—higher ceilings, open balconies, wider halls, and larger windows, not to mention generous landing platforms—but with the help of her father's brilliance and Zolya's resources, they had made it work.

And now, nestled at the edge of town, the gentle rush of the north river nearby, they had their own place.

Their home.

A slow, steady warmth spread through Tanwen's chest as she looked out the large open balcony doors.

Home.

Not a cold, opulent room in the palace, stuffed with too many servants to count, or a hollowed-out campsite, nor a world held together by fear and rebellion.

This place was theirs—built, chosen, and worn in by them.

A place all their own that held peace and, for the first time in Tanwen's life, safety.

She let out a contented sigh, nuzzling closer to Zolya.

He placed a hand around her, cocooning her in his warmth.

"We'll need to get dressed soon," she murmured, though she made no move to rise. "Our guests will be arriving."

Her parents were coming, along with Huw and his boyfriend; Azla; her mother, Callia; and the queen dowager. It had become a tradition when they were all in town—one they clung to like a tether between old wounds and new beginnings.

Soon, their table would be surrounded by family and friends—voices of different generations and races weaving together in a familiar, chaotic melody of conversation, teasing, and laughter. The kind of noise that filled a house with life.

"They can wait," said Zolya, placing a gentle kiss to her head. "This is my favorite time of day in our home."

There it was again—that breathtaking squeeze of happiness around her heart.

Our home.

"Mine too," Tanwen replied softly.

She reached for his other hand, threading their fingers together as they sat side by side, gazing out at the untamed sprawl of land stretching before them.

The sun was dipping low, casting the world in a wash of vibrant orange, molten gold, and gentle violet. The day was ending, setting with a contented sigh, before a new one would rise again tomorrow—bright and welcoming.

Tanwen and Zolya sat looking ahead.

Out at their future.

One that stretched further than the horizon.

ACKNOWLEDGMENTS

Well, here we are—at the end of another tale that has consumed my heart and mind for so long. Finishing a book, especially a series, always leaves me with a storm of emotions: relief that, *phew, I did it*; disbelief that, *wait, did I really do it?*; and finally, unhinged delight that, *yes, wow, I really did it!*

While this book may close, Zolya and Tanwen's story—and that of their companions—will continue to live in my imagination forever. I hope it will in yours as well. As I mentioned in *Scorched Skies*' acknowledgments, I set out to write this duology not only inspired by the myth of Icarus but also as a way to challenge the constraints our society places on so many of us daily. I wanted it to be an escape, a battle cry, a safe place to explore grief, loss, and love—but most of all, a place for hope. Because one way or another, love will always triumph over hate.

So, thank you. Thank you for traveling with me all the way to *The End*.

This job is a wild one, filled with highs and lows and massive emotional swings. But I am always, always grateful—and honored—that I get to do it. And you, my dearest reader, are the reason I can.

Of course, there are others who make these stories possible. At the forefront is my husband, Christopher, who forever champions my work and graciously shoulders the mental and physical load of caring for our family while I'm on a deadline. My son, who delights and inspires me daily with his boundless imagination. My parents, sisters, and friends, who check in throughout the process and celebrate each milestone alongside me.

To my editors, Lindsey Faber and Lauren Plude—the wisest of them all—thank you for your invaluable skills in shaping romance and weaving emotion that aches from the page. To the entire Montlake team, thank you for your support. To my agent extraordinaries, Aimee Ashcraft and Kimberly Brower, who have been with me since day one of my career—thank you for believing in me and my stories. You've helped make so many of my dreams come true.

I cannot wait to see what we'll create together next!

ABOUT THE AUTHOR

Photo © 2022 Jacob Glazer

E. J. Mellow is an award-winning and bestselling author of magical mayhem. Her work has been translated into multiple languages and has appeared on best-of lists such as BuzzFeed and Gizmodo, reaching number one on multiple Amazon charts and receiving medals from eLit Book Awards and Next Generation Indie Book Awards. Readers have praised her "lyrical, vibrant, and imaginative" writing for sweeping them into "stunning worlds." Mellow is also the cofounder of She Is Booked, a literary-themed fundraising organization that supports women's charities.